As the daughter of an officer in the Royal Air Force, Sandra Wilson has travelled and lived in various parts of Europe. She now lives in Gloucestershire with her family, where all her spare time is spent writing.

HIDE AND SEEK

Annabel Gresham is worried about her financial future. The codicil to her grandfather's will and her own father's recently altered will have been stolen. Without them her half-brother, Roderick, will inherit the family fortune leaving Annie penniless. It seems that Roderick's best friend took the documents and hid them in a London bawdy house. Although determined to find them, Annie becomes distracted by the charming Richard Tregerran she encounters at every turn. Aware of his bad reputation Annie also suspects that he has despicable morals, but he could prove invaluable in this high-stakes game of hide and seek . . .

Books by Sandra Wilson
Published by The House of Ulverscroft:

THE CHALBOURNE SAPPHIRES
THE ABSENT WIFE
RAKEHELL'S WIDOW

SANDRA WILSON

HIDE AND SEEK

Complete and Unabridged

ULVERSCROFT
Leicester

First published in Great Britain in 2008 by
Robert Hale Limited, London

First Large Print Edition
published 2009
by arrangement with
Robert Hale Limited, London

British Library CIP Data

Wilson, Sandra, 1944 –
 Hide and seek
 1. Inheritance and succession- -Fiction. 2. Great Britain- -
History- -George III, 1760 – 1820- -Fiction. 3. Love
stories. 4. Large type books.
 I. Title II. Health, Sandra.
 823.9′14–dc22

 ISBN 978–1–84782–749–4

Published by
F. A. Thorpe (Publishing)
Anstey, Leicestershire

Set by Words & Graphics Ltd.
Anstey, Leicestershire
Printed and bound in Great Britain by
T. J. International Ltd., Padstow, Cornwall

This book is printed on acid-free paper

1

'Mr Gresham, are you quite sure you wish to draw up a new will at this late hour?' Holding a candle, the young lawyer leaned shortsightedly over the bed.

It was nearly twelve on a stiflingly hot night toward the end of June, and the Perton House peacocks were still calling on the moonlit lawns. The notes of a stagecoach key-bugle drifted from the Cheltenham turnpike about a quarter of a mile away.

To Mr Sebastian Gresham, the elderly hypochondriac propped in the bed, the thick lenses of the lawyer's spectacles made him appear like a worried owl. 'Yes, of *course* I'm sure!' he cried, incensed by such an impertinent question. 'Why else do you imagine I wish to see you? To request for some moonshine to be left on the doorstep at dawn? Or discuss the stratagems of Mr Pitt? Sir, I may die at any moment, and so must make certain that my daughter, Annabel, is properly provided for!'

As far as Annabel was concerned, her father seemed far from death's awful door; in fact, she thought he had made a miraculous *recovery* in the last few hours! Admittedly, when he had taken to his bed at noon, he had still been greatly upset by the business of Widow Frankley and her marauding goats, but there had been no suggestion of a new will or the imminent hereafter. She watched him pull the bed coverlet up to his chin and tug his tasseled nightcap further onto his balding head, even though on such a night she had insisted upon throwing open the windows. Knowing him only too well, she decided he was up to something. But what, that was the question.

Meanwhile, the lawyer was so apprehensive about preparing such an important document in haste that his hand shook, making the candle flicker and smoke. He was a plain young man, long-faced and pale, with lank brown hair he had tied back by a black ribbon. His name was Jeremiah Pilkington, and he wore ordinary clothes of nondescript color. 'Yes, I quite understand your wishes, sir, but in the absence of the codicil, I fear this original will of your father's still stands.' He held up the offending document, which had been brought from the little strong cupboard in the library for him to examine.

'Do you take me for a nincompoop? I know only too well the implications of the codicil being missing!'

'Then with all due respect, sir, I don't see the purpose of drawing up a new will.'

'Oh, you don't, eh? Then you will just have to humor me, will you not!' Mr Gresham was at his most acid.

'But — '

'But? *But?* Is your hearing defective, sir?' Mr Gresham glowered from the bank of snowy pillows, his thin face pinched with disapproval. A rangy sixty-five-year-old, he was still very active in spite of his conviction that his health was precariously balanced. His eyes were a piercing, rather watery blue, and he had beetling gray brows that met above a prominent nose. In spite of his admittedly intimidating appearance he was generally of a warm and kindly nature; certainly he was much loved by Annabel and his stepson, Toby.

Mr Pilkington felt foolish, but nevertheless held his ground. 'Er, no, of course my hearing is not defective, sir, it's just that a new will cannot change the situation.'

'You would be surprised, sir, you would be surprised.'

Mr Pilkington refrained from responding to this, for he would indeed be surprised! More than that, he'd be astounded. He cleared his throat. 'But Sir Humphrey usually acts for you, Mr Gresham, and if I do so instead, I might be perceived to have, er, poached on his preserve.'

'Poached? Damn me, sir, I'm not a gamecock!'

'No, sir, but . . . ' The lawyer's voice trailed away uncomfortably. He was accustomed to handling the business of farmers and the coaching trade, not the clients and close friends of no less a legal personage than Sir Humphrey Smythe-Castle, one of the foremost of the profession in the realm, who had an address in exclusive North Audley Street, Mayfair.

'It may have escaped your notice that Sir Humphrey is in London, whereas I am rather inconsiderately dying here in the country. Things must be altered immediately, so you will have to draw up the new will in his absence. I'm hanged if I'm going to have that villainous son of mine deny his half sister so much as a roof over her head. My stepson will convey the new document to Sir Humphrey tonight.'

'Eh?' Thirty-one-year-old Toby quickly took his hands out of his pockets and straightened from one of the sturdy carved oak posts of the enormous bed.

Mr Gresham wagged a very stern parental finger. 'And once you are there, sir, you are *not* to visit any dens of disorder or vice!'

Toby was offended. 'I became embroiled in one scrape, that's all, sir.'

'Hm. See that it remains just one, for as I recall it was somewhat costly to my purse. Now, go and get ready, because I want you to set off the moment this numskull has penned the necessary clauses.'

'Do I really have to go tonight?'

'Yes, sirrah, you most certainly do! It is the very least you can do for your sister!' cried Mr Gresham.

Annabel could see that her father was becoming quite overwrought, so she waved Toby from the room, then imposed her calming influence by taking the jug of blackcurrant cordial from the new maid, who hovered with interest near the door. Pouring a little cordial into a cup, Annabel sat on the edge of the bed after first moving aside the heavy tome her father had been reading. It was a complete volume of the works of William Shakespeare, her father's favorite silver bookmark placed neatly between its pages.

'Please don't distress yourself, Father. Drink a little of this; you know how good it is.' As she held the cup gently to his lips, she knew that Mr Pilkington was correct to point out the absurdity of a new will, because without the missing codicil it was impossible to overturn her grandfather's original testament. She could not even begin to guess why her father was doing this. The codicil had been missing for two months now, and it suited her elder half brother, Roderick, offspring of her father's first marriage, to deny that the vital appendix had ever existed. Of *course* it suited him. Perton House itself was not the prize, for it was a relatively modest estate, but its contents were of enormous value. Grandfather Gresham had assembled a matchless collection of medieval paintings, the sale of which would bring in a huge fortune.

Mr Gresham sipped the cordial, then smiled fondly at her. 'Ah, Annabel, my dear, what would I do without you?'

'I'm sure you would do very well,' she replied, returning the glass to the maid, a petite brunette named Molly, who looked French but was very English, and who had set her rather knowing cap at Toby in the month since she had been in the house. Other maids before her had done the same, for he was a very handsome fellow with blond curls, blue eyes, and a boyish smile. His common sense was debatable at times, but his charm was more than sufficient to coax pretty birds from the trees.

Molly Simmonds came from London,

where she had seen the position advertised in an edition of the Cheltenham newspaper she found on a bench in St James's Park. She was as knowing and artful as they came, altogether too pert and worldly for quiet Perton House, and at twenty-two she had probably already forgotten far more than twenty-nine-year-old Annabel Gresham would ever know! It could not be said that she was a good maid, for she could not be relied upon, but she was a very talented coiffeuse, which was very important indeed if one possessed hair as obstinate and downright impossible as Annabel Gresham's!

Mr Gresham fixed the lawyer with another glare. 'Right, Mr Pilkington, have you pen and paper?'

'I . . . I do, sir.' The harassed man took the candle to the corner table and fumbled with his portable escritoire, which lay open in readiness. When he had everything assembled, he flicked his coat-tails back, and poised his new quill above a pristine sheet of paper. Mr Gresham began to dictate.

Annabel made herself comfortable on the window seat. The enormous bed dominated the room behind her, and the light from the candle created looming shadows all around. It was a plainly furnished chamber, still decorated in the cream and gold Annabel and

Toby's late mother had chosen ten years before. The house itself dated from the time of Queen Anne, and was set in formal water gardens that were always a joy to behold, whatever the season. It was acknowledged to be one of the prettiest properties in Gloucestershire, but its renown came from the collection of medieval paintings assembled by Annabel's grandfather.

The cool of night, scented with roses, crept in through the open casement, and the peacocks called again. She studied her reflection in the glass, and wished she was small and dainty with dark hair and dark eyes, which attributes were all the rage. Why, even Molly Simmonds was all of those things! But not Annabel Gresham. Oh, no. *She* was tall and willowy with unmanageable honey-colored hair, and even features that were deemed pleasant but definitely not beautiful. She did have good eyes, she supposed, but they were gray instead of the admired dark brown. Even her clothes were not particularly *à la mode*, but that was entirely her own fault. The gown she wore tonight was of unfashionable blue-and-white checked seersucker. It had the required high waist, short sleeves, and flowing skirt and train for the summer of 1800, yet would not have done for Mayfair. Clinging white muslin was the thing now, but she simply did not care for such a pallid material, deeming it fit only for the French or wrapping around cheeses. Toby would say that blue-and-white seersucker was splendid, but then he was good-natured enough to praise everything she wore.

She sighed to herself as her father continued his dictation, for she knew how very worried he was about her future. It was pointless to wish things were different, for she was the offspring of his second wife, who had come to him as a young widow with Toby barely toddling. Toby had expectations through his paternal family, and so was set up for the future, but Annabel's situation was very different. By the terms of Grandfather Gresham's will, made some years after the death of her father's first wife, absolutely everything would eventually go to the then only grandchild, Roderick. However, the unexpected advent of a second Mrs Sebastian Gresham, with the possibility of more grandchildren, caused Grandfather Gresham, then ailing, to amend his will. But instead of drawing up a completely new document, he merely added a codicil. It was this that had now gone astray. Without it, Annabel was at Roderick's mercy.

Sebastian Gresham thought his firstborn was a heartless profligate, calculating, cold, and lacking in all moral ethics. A thoroughly bad lot, in fact. This opinion had been freely and often expressed, a fact to which Roderick had not taken kindly. He had therefore fallen out so seriously with his father that he now despised everyone at Perton House, including his half sister. Two years before, at the age of forty, Roderick had been elevated to the ranks of the peerage, as Lord Mavor, a gift from a grateful Prince Regent. A great deal of land and wealth had come with this new elevation, and when the codicil disappeared, Mr Gresham hoped that Roderick would at least be lenient toward Annabel, with whom he should not have had any quarrel. But Roderick was unable to stay away from the hazard and faro tables, where he was not in the least successful, with the result that he had already depleted his new fortune.

More funds were required to maintain his expensive ways, so he was not only seeking a gullible heiress to become Lady Mavor and save his unpleasant bacon in the meantime, but his greedy eyes were turned upon the future acquisition of Perton House and its priceless paintings. Thus, even though he knew of the codicil's existence, it more than pleased him to say he didn't. He implied that his father was being untruthful, and said that when the time came he would resort to law if necessary to eject Annabel. As soon as the property was his, lock, stock, and barrel, he would sell everything to feed the hungry gaming tables of St James's.

2

Annabel sighed again, for today had been strange from the outset. It had begun with her father drawing back the curtains at this very window and espying the Widow Frankley's rapacious goats devouring everything in the formal flower beds directly below. The gardeners had driven off the cloven-hoofed robbers, but as it was not the first time such an intrusion had occurred, Mr Gresham decided to confront the troublesome relict.

The weather had been warm and fine, and he had been in unexpectedly good spirits as he set off on horseback later in the morning. As a rule he was too mindful of his health to go anywhere unless in a closed carriage, but on this occasion, with his mood so excellent and only a balmy zephyr to stir the summer leaves, he elected to ride his old hunter, an animal as elderly and rickety as he.

The Widow Frankley was a formidable matron possessed of a monstrous temper, who set about him with a besom the moment he unwisely ventured to her cottage door. The devastation of his pride and dignity was continued by her assortment of scrawny, dagger-clawed cats, and made complete by the goats, which butted him here, there, and everywhere before he at last managed to scramble, bruised and shaken, onto his horse.

As he fled home to Perton House in disarray, Mother Nature was contrary enough to deposit a violent thunderstorm directly over his head, together with a cloudburst that soon had him dripping and shivering. He arrived in a state of collapse, and immediately took to his bed — or rather his deathbed, as he informed Annabel and Toby. There he had remained for the rest of the day, reading Shakespeare and looking generally sorry for himself. Then suddenly, just as she and Toby came upstairs to go to their own beds, he had rung his bell and demanded that a local lawyer be sent for without delay. Nothing else would do. He was absolutely set upon it, and seemed in such an overexcited state that she had soon given in and sent someone to Cheltenham.

Annabel wasn't concerned that he really was on his deathbed. After all, during the past year he had twice proved himself hypochondriac enough to be sure he was *en route* for St Peter and the heavenly gates. On both occasions he had made a swift recovery and promptly taken himself off for a month of

Weymouth's bracing sea air. She therefore had no reason to think this occasion was going to be any different, except that there was a rather worrying air of controlled anticipation about him now, as if he knew something no one else did, something very important indeed.

Mr Pilkington finished taking down the dictation, and Mr Gresham tried to pull himself up on the pillows. 'Give me a hand, sir!' he commanded, and the lawyer scrambled to obey. Annabel's father then beckoned to her. 'My dear, there is something I wish you to do for me.'

'What is it, Father?' she asked as she returned to the bedside.

'Please open Shakespeare at the marked page.'

She was taken aback. 'You . . . you wish me to read to you?'

'At a time like this? Whatever for? No, I simply wish you to open the book.'

Annabel could feel him watching her, his expression bordering on the gleeful. She soon realized why, for as she opened the heavy volume, there, folded neatly and in perfect condition, was the missing codicil, complete with the imprint of her grandfather's signet ring in emerald green sealing wax. Molly gasped and almost dropped the jug of cordial, and Mr Pilkington stared at the piece of paper as if he expected it to spontaneously combust.

Annabel was bewildered. 'Where did you find it?' she breathed, hardly able to believe her future was safe again after all.

'Right where you took it from, my dear. I was reading *Henry IV, Part I*, the duel scene between Prince Hal and Harry Hotspur, when I turned the page and there it was. I could not believe it myself, but then I recalled that this very volume was open on my library desk when last I examined the will. I was called urgently away and put — as I thought — everything back in the strong cupboard. Instead of which, the codicil must have slipped onto the book, which I promptly closed and did not read again until today. Oh, praise be to the Widow Frankley and her foul-smelling goats!'

'So the codicil was only mislaid?' Annabel felt a little guilty, for she had begun to wonder if Roderick had gone so far as to steal it in order to ensure getting his hands on everything.

'Yes, my dear. Oh, to be a fly on my dear firstborn's wall when he hears! I despair that such a scoundrel has my blood in his veins! Well, he shall not turn you out of house and home now, Annabel, for I have thought very carefully about the working of my own will, as Mr Pilkington will realize if he examines it without his blinkers. The document drawn up tonight, combined with the codicil, will ensure that you have the house, its contents, and its income during your lifetime, and then your children during theirs, and so on. The fine new Lord Mavor won't be able to sell Perton House, but instead will be obliged to pay for its upkeep! That is what I was studying when the codicil was lost. I have always known that Roderick was not to be trusted, so I have been putting my mind to legal phrases for some considerable time now. My labors were rewarded by the discovery of a neat little loophole, which tonight I have slipped through and then plugged behind me. There is nothing dear Roderick can do about it, and serves the scoundrel right. Oh, it is splendid, is it not? Now do you see why I am so anxious that Toby shall take all to London without delay? I should have heeded Sir Humphrey's advice years ago and lodged all my legal documents with him, instead of which I arrogantly believed them safe here. This whole business has been a very salutary lesson, and I will not fail you again, my dear.' Mr Gresham regarded the lawyer coolly. 'So, Mr Pilkington, I am *not* a doddering old fool whose brain has curdled!'

The lawyer colored, for his thoughts had indeed been along those unflattering lines.

Mr Gresham continued. 'My father's signet ring was buried with him, and I have been careful not to disturb the seal on the codicil, so Roderick cannot claim I have forged it. Now then, Mr Pilkington, I shall sign the new will, with you and Molly as impartial witnesses.' A thought struck him, and he addressed the maid. 'Molly, you can write, can you not?'

'Yes, Mr Gresham.'

'Good. Well, get on with it, Pilkington, get on with it. I wish this to be over and done with so that I may eventually go to my Maker in peace and contentment.'

'Yes, sir.' Mr Pilkington hastily signed and then beckoned to Molly, who hesitated rather oddly before penning her name. Annabel thought she seemed reluctant, as if she did not want to be a witness.

Mr Gresham then sank back on the pillows and closed his eyes. 'If the end should come now, I will not have you on my conscience, Annabel.'

Annabel took his hand quickly. 'You are not to be rowed over the Styx just yet, sir.'

'You think not?'

'I know not.'

He regarded her. 'Forgive my subterfuge

17

today, my dear, but I could not help a little teasing.'

She smiled. 'I will forgive you only if you promise not to take to your deathbed again this year.'

'Oh, very well, if you insist.'

'I do.'

He considered for a moment. 'However, although I admit to have played to the gods a little today, I still think I would benefit from another visit to Weymouth. I shall leave early the day after tomorrow.' He looked at Molly. 'Bring me some more of that cordial, girl. Then get me some of that cold roast beef I had last night. With plenty of bread and pickles.'

'Yes, Mr Gresham.' Molly refilled the cup and then hurried away.

★   ★   ★

Toby was ready to leave for London at just before dawn. A mist hovered above the Perton House water gardens as he and Annabel came out to where a groom waited with a good horse. To the east a paler light heralded the new day, and the peacocks were already strutting the lawns like ghosts, uttering their loud cries.

Toby turned up his collar and adjusted the

18

angle of his top hat on his blond curls. 'Well, if I ride with my tail on fire, I fancy I will be in town by noon.'

'You will take care on the road, won't you?'

'Which are you more concerned about, Annie? Me, or the documents I am to deliver?' he asked a little wickedly as he checked that his portmanteau was securely fixed upon the saddle.

'Both, of course,' she replied.

'Ah, ever the diplomat.'

'And please continue to take care in London,' she said then.

'You know I will.'

Her smile was wry. 'Do I? The last time you went there Father had to cross several palms with silver in order to save you from appearing before the Bow Street magistrates.'

'None of that was my fault. I simply happened to be in that cockpit when the trouble started. Annie, I swear it was the fault of two rival groups of Bond Street Loungers, and I was caught between them.'

'You shouldn't have been at a cockfight in the first place. You know how Father disapproves of them, and of bearbaiting, prize-fighting, and anything else of that low ilk.'

'I'll have you know that a great many gentlemen of *ton* attend such events, but I nevertheless promise to avoid them this time.'

'Good.' She smiled. 'And no bad company, either,' she added.

'What do you mean by that?' he protested. 'I don't know any *bad* company!'

'Some of your friends from Oxford are very dubious indeed, and appear to consider propriety the eighth and most deadly sin. They are all Rodericks to a man.'

'I say, that's a bit strong, isn't it? Scoundrels they may be, but never bad enough to call Rodericks,' he replied with a teasing grin. 'All right, Annie, you have my solemn word, torn from my lips under duress, that I will shun all doubtful company.'

'If you have your fingers crossed behind your back, Toby Vernon, I will never forgive you!' she warned. 'There is one thing more — '

He groaned. 'What now? Am I not permitted a glass of wine with my dinner? Or a rasher over two for my breakfast?'

'This is to do with your return here. Toby, I want you to promise you'll stay away from Molly.'

'Molly?'

'Don't ape the innocent, sir, for you and I both know she has her sights on you.'

'I don't think she has. Her problem is that she cannot help making sheep's eyes at the opposite sex. Anyway, what *she* does is of no importance, it's what *I* do that is. You know I never dally with our maids, even though I have more than ample opportunity. I keep such, er, activities well and truly away from home.'

'Yes, but . . . ' She glanced away, for she didn't really know why she was so perturbed by Molly Simmonds.

He regarded her curiously in the dawn light. 'What is it, Annie?'

'There's something about her.'

'Something? Such as, for instance?'

'To begin with, she's far too knowing.'

Toby pursed his lips. 'Well, I can't deny *that!*'

Annabel pulled her shawl a little more around her shoulder. 'She didn't want to witness the new will.'

'Why ever not?'

'I don't know, but it's a fact. Oh, she makes me shiver, and I intend to be rid of her at the earliest opportunity. I shall give her a good testimonial, but I cannot keep her on here. I just don't trust her.'

'Oh, come on, Annie, what has she ever done to warrant all this? Just because she isn't an innocent? That's hardly fair, for I think she is a good maid. She certainly does wonders with your hair.'

'Meaning that without her I look like an ill-made haystack?'

'I didn't say that.'

'No, but you thought it, and you're probably right. My hair and pins are anathema to each other.' Annabel sighed. 'Oh, I'm probably making something of nothing about Molly, but all the same, when you return, I would feel happier if you actively discouraged her.'

'You are, but if that is what you want.'

'It is.'

'Actually, she has just given me something to deliver to her aunt.' He held up a letter that was neatly tied and knotted with some thin white ribbons.

'I didn't know she had an aunt in London. Indeed I was under the impression that she had no family left,' Annabel said, examining the address. *Mrs Smith, 3a Pav'd Alley, St James's, London.*

'Nor did I. Apparently this Mrs Smith has a small haberdashery.'

Annabel noticed the figure fourteen in the top right-hand corner. 'What's this, do you think?'

'I have no idea. I hadn't even noticed it,' Toby replied.

'I think it rather presumptuous of Molly to ask you to take her letters. You are hardly an errand boy.' Annabel just couldn't help being critical where Molly Simmonds was concerned.

Toby grinned. 'Why not? Father seems to think I am. Oh, come on, Annie, it's hardly that much of an inconvenience to take the wretched letter. After all, I shall be at the Dog and Duck, which isn't far from Pav'd Alley.'

Annabel glanced at the portmanteau. 'I see you intend to stay for a few days.'

'Yes, but I will send word back here the very moment my errand is done at Sir Humphrey's. I think I may as well do some shopping while I'm in town. A fellow has to look his best, you know. I'll bring you something fashionable, I promise. Something clinging and all transparent white muslin, just as you have been secretly sighing for.'

'I most certainly have not been sighing for such a thing! I loathe white muslin, and you know it. But I *would* like a dress length of the very best apple green taffeta,' she said hopefully.

'Then you shall have it.' He bent forward to kiss her cheek. 'I'm glad this pesky codicil has turned up again, Annie, for this house and everything in it *should* be yours. But you do know, don't you, that I would have taken care of you?'

'Yes, I know, Toby.' A mere parting peck on

the cheek did not suffice, for she loved him a great deal, so she flung her arms around his neck and hugged him tightly. 'Have a safe journey, Toby, for you are the best brother any sister could ever have.'

'Best half brother,' he corrected.

'Well, if you are going to be pedantic, the sooner you set off, the better,' she chided.

He grinned. 'À bientôt, Annie,' he said, and took the reins from the groom to mount the waiting horse. A second later, he had ridden away down the drive.

3

Toby's promised message from London reached Perton House the following evening. It arrived just as Annabel had given up attempting to read to her father. The chosen work was *Paradise Regained*, which seemed singularly appropriate for prevailing circumstances, but Mr Gresham had fallen asleep after barely ten minutes.

There was a tap at the door, and Molly came in. She looked cautiously at Annabel's father, then spoke in a whisper in order not to awaken him. 'Begging your pardon, Miss Annabel, but a message has been brought from Master Toby.'

'Oh, good.' Annabel set the book aside and rose from the bedside. She wore a pale gray lawn gown embroidered with pink rosebuds, and Molly had earlier pinned her hair up very daintily beneath a lacy day bonnet from which pink ribbons fluttered loose.

Molly continued to whisper. 'The man who brought it says it's very important and for you alone to read, miss. He is waiting in the hall.'

A finger of apprehension began to pass slowly down Annabel's spine. Something was wrong. She slipped quietly from the room, with Molly following.

Toby's courier was a ruddy-faced little man with a decided smell of horse about him. From his well-worn leather breeches to his shabby brown coat and bright red neckerchief, he was a groom if ever Annabel had seen one. Probably from the Dog and Duck, she thought, as she reached the foot of the staircase and crossed the black-and-white-tiled floor to where he waited nervously by the central table, turning his low-crowned hat in his bony hands.

'You have something for me, sir?' she said as she halted before him with a flourish of her gray lawn train.

'If you're Miss Gresham of Perton House, then yes, I have something for you,' he replied, fishing inside his coat for a sealed letter. 'I'm to await your reply,' he added as he handed it to her.

Annabel hesitated before opening it, for she hardly dared to think what news it might contain. Please don't let it be that the codicil was lost again! Taking a deep breath, she broke the seal and began to read.

Dog and Duck, Piccadilly. Midday.

Annie, I know of no easy way to confess that as a result of not keeping my promise to you, I have been robbed of my money and the documents. The fault is entirely mine, for I fell in with an old acquaintance from Oxford, by the name of Boskingham (we all called him Bosky, because that's what he was most of the time). Anyway, he has become the most of a thief I ever knew.

I will tell you all when you arrive, for you MUST come. The suite I am in here can easily accommodate us both without any impropriety. I cannot do anything as I am laid up in my bed, having been set upon by some muscular louts outside a notorious (and fashionable!) King's Place seraglio, and would have been left for dead had not a Good Samaritan rescued me.

Please come, I beg of you, for I am at my wits' end with worry. It should not be difficult for you to leave Perton House if Father is going to Weymouth. If you need an excuse, tell him you are overcome with a desire to join me for some capital shopping. Whatever you do, don't let him realize what has happened.

I await you with all impatience.

Your loving half brother, Toby.

PS. Please tell Molly that her missive at least was successfully delivered.

Annabel stared at the letter in unutterable dismay. Oh, how could Toby have been so *stupid!* She turned to the messenger. 'Do you know anything about this?'

'Me? No, miss. All I know is that I have been paid handsomely to come here today. I don't even know who wrote the letter, because Mrs Ferguson just — '

'Mrs Who?'

'Ferguson, miss. She's the licensee of the Dog and Duck.'

'Really? I thought Mr Parsons was — '

'Oh, he gave up the lease last year, miss. It's Mrs Ferguson now.'

'I see. Do go on.'

'Well, she just came out into the yard and offered a good reward for anyone willing to ride posthaste to Gloucestershire. I fancied the countryside, so I accepted.'

Molly was lurking nearby as usual. 'Is something wrong, Miss Annabel? Has something happened to Master Toby?'

Quickly refolding the letter, Annabel turned irritably. 'Everything is quite all right, Molly.'

'But — '

'Are you questioning me, Molly?'

The girl recoiled a little. 'No, Miss Annabel, of course not.'

'I will satisfy your curiosity. Mr Vernon merely urges me to join him in London for some shopping. He says he has managed to secure an excellent suite of rooms at the inn in Piccadilly, and declares that the fashionable shops are filled to overflowing with all that would please me.' As she spoke, Annabel wondered greatly why her brother had gone to the expense of taking a suite. Surely a single room would have been sufficient for the few days he had expected to stay.

'Did he take my letter to my aunt, Miss Annabel?' asked Molly, something in her dark eyes telling Annabel she did not believe the story about shopping, but then it was hardly surprising, for such an invitation would not require a special messenger, or placing into Annabel's hands alone. There was no need to keep a mere shopping expedition secret from Mr Gresham, especially when that gentleman was off to Weymouth in the morning.

'Oh, yes, he says he has.'

'Thank you, Miss Annabel, I'm truly grateful.'

So you should be, thought Annabel as she turned to the waiting messenger. 'Now then, Mr er . . . ?'

'Corbett, miss.'

'Mr Corbett. There is no need for me to write a reply, for I am sure you can tell my brother that I will join him at about noon tomorrow.'

He nodded. 'Very well, Miss Gresham.'

'I am also sure you and your horse are in need of some refreshment before setting off again.'

'You are most gracious, Miss Gresham.'

'Not at all. Molly, please conduct Mr Corbett to the kitchens and instruct the cook to provide him with something to eat and drink. And then go out to the stables and inform them to attend to his mount.'

The maid bobbed one of her pretty curtsies, and led the man away toward the door to the kitchens, which lay off the rear of the hall, behind the staircase.

Annabel remained alone in the hall. What on earth was Toby expecting her to do? *She* could hardly go to the sorts of places to which he referred in the letter! Oh, if he were here right now, so help her she would throttle him! She closed her eyes, trying to compose herself. She would go to London, but doubted very much if the new will or grandfather's codicil would ever be seen again. Sooner or later her father would have to be told that this time the codicil really was gone beyond all redemption, and that even if it and the new will were still in existence, which was doubtful, they might be anywhere in the largest city in the world!

★ ★ ★

Mr Gresham set off for Weymouth after a very early breakfast the following morning. He was in excellent spirits as his traveling carriage drew away from the house. He had been delighted to learn that Annabel was joining Toby in London, and urged her to spend well as she did not do nearly enough to pamper herself. After informing her that he had enjoyed a trifling success in stocks and shares, enough to purchase her a frock or three, he patted her hand and told her she was a jewel among daughters. Then away he drove.

Annabel felt dreadful as she waved him off, for she had been guilty of telling him the very great fib that Toby had successfully delivered the document to Sir Humphrey Smythe-Castle. This was because the letter seemed to hint that the documents were recoverable, and she could not bring herself to tell her father the truth. Now she regretted her words, but it was too late — the deed was done.

The post chaise she had ordered from the Plough in Cheltenham arrived half an hour later, and her portmanteau was carried out. She had already changed for traveling, and emerged from the house in a three-quarter-length sky blue pelisse over a gown of cafe au lait silk. Her honey-colored hair was swept up beneath a straw gypsy hat tied beneath her chin with sky blue ribbons, and she carried a reticule and pagoda parasol. As she entered the waiting chaise, she thought rather wryly that her appearance would pass muster for the capital, although hardly warrant a fanfare of trumpets!

The postboy urged the horses down the drive, and she lowered the glass to gaze back at the house, retention of which was again in jeopardy. She saw that a curtain had been pulled aside at her bedroom window, and someone was looking out. It was Molly, and even at that distance it was possible to see the smile on the maid's lips.

4

The journey to London took longer than Annabel had anticipated, and it was late afternoon when the post chaise at last approached Hyde Park Corner. She had been obliged to keep the window firmly raised for the latter part of the journey because the closer to London the more dust was raised by the increasing traffic. As a consequence she was now hot and uncomfortable. But still presentable enough for the Dog and Duck, she thought.

A thin skein of clouds obscured the June sun, and a breeze fluttered the foliage in the park where the daily parade of high fashion was on display. She would not normally have been able to see because of the high brick boundary wall, but part of the wall was being rebuilt, and for several seconds she had a clear view of the famous carriage road just inside, and beyond that the riders in Rotten Row.

What an especially colorful show the carriage road provided, she thought, leaning forward quickly to observe the ladies and gentlemen in open vehicles, determinedly braving the dust. There were barouches, landaus, traps, curricles, and phaetons, some of the latter even driven by ladies who performed the task with such style and verve that they turned all heads, especially those of the gentlemen. In Rotten Row itself, where only riding was permitted, there were dashing blades on prancing horses, and army officers and hussars on thoroughbreds. Ladies were well represented, too, all of them stylish equestriennes in modish, tight-waisted riding habits.

Annabel was just about to sit back again for the final few hundred yards to the Dog and Duck, which stood on the south side of Piccadilly just beyond Green Park, when a foppish gentleman driving a curricle overtook the chaise at breakneck speed. He was tooling along with complete disregard for others on the highway, cracking his whip in order to fling his lathered team forward even faster. From his windswept appearance and the dusty, travel-stained state of the curricle, Annabel guessed he had driven a long way, and she could not help wondering what could be so urgent that he would risk life and limb. A veiled woman sat beside him, and there was luggage strapped to the back of the vehicle.

It was then that Annabel realized she had already seen the vehicle once that day, for it had a long scratch on its emerald green lacquer, probably the result of driving so close to an obstacle that it touched, a failing known as featheredging. She had happened to notice the very same color and scratch on a curricle driving in the opposite direction barely a mile from Perton House, which had skimmed past the chaise with only an inch or so to spare, earning much rainbow-hued abuse from her infuriated postboy.

The gentleman had been alone on that occasion, and she had seen that he was about Toby's age, rouged, with a patch at the corner of his mouth. He hadn't been wearing a hat, so she had also seen that he had very neatly curled golden curls that must have taken an age to comb. A dandy if ever there was one, he had worn an enormous yellow silk neckcloth, vermilion coat, black pantaloons, and overdecorated Hessian boots. Now, however, his curls were concealed beneath a tall hat that was tugged over his brow, and the rest of his gaudy attire covered by a caped coat that must have been insufferably hot. There was even a muffler that so enveloped his face that all distinguishing features were impossible to see. He clearly did not wish to be identified, but Annabel did not doubt that it was the same man because he now proceeded to featheredge the chaise for a second time, and again received the furious damnation of the postboy.

The featheredging occurred because there were works on a sewer taking place down the middle of Piccadilly, resulting in extra congestion that almost choked the way completely. The dandy was forced to swerve so close to the chaise that the postboy had to haul his horses to a complete halt in order to avoid a collision. Such shocking language was hurled after the fleeing curricle that Annabel lowered the glass to lean out.

As she did, the gentleman's female companion turned to look back. The woman was small and neat in an obviously new but not particularly good quality buttermilk spencer and pale pink gown, and her flounced veil was draped over her hat like a little tablecloth. As she continued to gaze back, Annabel began to realize that there was something familiar about her, even though she definitely had not been with the gentleman earlier in the day. It was the angle of her body as she turned, and the tilt of her head. Annabel had seen both somewhere before, and recently at that. But who was she? Who were they both?

The curricle disappeared into the throng of traffic, threading its way through the congestion with an ease that marked the dandified gentleman as a skilled exponent of the ribbons, in spite of his even greater talent for leaving mayhem in his wake. Annabel drew back into the chaise, raised the glass again, and dismissed the curricle and its occupants from her mind because she had more important things to consider.

Two years had passed since she was last in London, and she had forgotten how very noisy and bustling a place it was. The work on the sewer was causing all manner of problems in Piccadilly, which was always one of the busiest thoroughfares. Countless stagecoaches came and went from the inns and West End ticket offices that proliferated along its entire length. Apart from the Dog and Duck, there were the Spread Eagle, White Horse Cellars, Gloucester Coffee Shop, Yorkshire Stingo, Blue Ball, and the offices of the Bull and Mouth, Belle Sauvage, and Swan with two Necks. Others found a place there as well, to say nothing of the fine tally of excellent shops that could not help but flourish so close to the exclusive streets and squares of Mayfair.

Vehicles of every description inched along the cobbles, as well as animals that were being driven to or from market, and the pavements jostled with people who all — to Annabel's country eyes, at least — seemed in an inordinate hurry to be somewhere else. At last she saw the sign of the Dog and Duck, a remarkably rural hound with a mallard in its jaws, but even before her chaise had finally maneuvered through the narrow archway into the yard, Annabel was longing for the peace and quiet of Perton House. There was another entrance to the yard from adjacent Arlington Street, for the inn occupied a corner site, and she was tempted to instruct the postboy to drive straight through then back to Gloucestershire! But distraught half brothers, missing codicils, and her own future security did not permit such a craven retreat.

Ostlers and grooms hastened to attend the newly arrived vehicle, then the door was opened and she stepped down. Her nostrils were immediately assailed by the smell of stables, cooking cabbage, and fresh-baked bread; and her ears by the whinnying of a fractious cart horse and the shrill singing of a maid in the kitchens. Two stagecoaches were about to depart, for Reading and Salisbury respectively, and a private carriage had just arrived ahead of her. There were two gigs with patiently waiting ponies, a scarlet high-flyer phaeton drawn by a team of six, and a brewer's wagon to which were harnessed four enormous Shire horses, including the irritable one with too much to say for itself.

Something else with too much to say for itself was a group of the so-called Bond Street Loungers, such as those Toby claimed were responsible for his difficulties at the cockpit. The Loungers were bored young gentlemen of means who delighted in being as affected, noisy, disruptive, and selfish as possible. This group was strolling arrogantly through the yard rather than around the corner on the pavement, and anyone unfortunate enough to be in the way was elbowed rudely aside. They spoke in an exaggerated drawl that was virtually impossible to understand, and uttered suggestive comments about young women who caught their attention, Annabel included. To her relief they soon passed beneath the archway to Piccadilly, and she was able to inspect her new surroundings in more detail.

The two street frontages contained the main body of the inn, while the other sides comprised the stables, coachhouses, and servants' quarters, with a narrow alley that led through into a flourishing vegetable garden at the back. An altercation was in progress between two hawkers of meat pies, each one insisting that the yard was his sole preserve, and a newspaper seller bawled headlines. It seemed there was fresh agitation for a proper police force instead of the traditional watch, and word had arrived of a French victory over the Austrians at a place called Marengo.

A stagecoach ticket office stood in the corner by the archway into Arlington Street, and the bell rang for departure time. Bugles promptly blared out deafeningly in the confined space, and Annabel pressed hastily back against the chaise as the two stage-coaches swept past within inches of her. Even after they had gone, it still seemed there was pandemonium all around as she picked her way over none-too-clean cobbles toward the door into the inn, above which was painted the name of the new licensee, Hester Ferguson.

The innkeeper proved to be a genial widow in her forties, with a twinkling smile and soft Scottish accent. She was a little embonpoint now, but had clearly once been quite a beauty; indeed her brown eyes were still extraordinarily attractive. She wore a navy blue taffeta gown with the customary innkeeper's nosegay — in this case honey-suckle and pansies — pinned to the bodice. A bunch of keys hung from her belt like those of a housekeeper, her thick brown hair was swept up beneath a very fancy mobcap, and her starched white apron crackled as she moved. The moment Annabel gave her name, the woman responded with a beaming smile.

'Ah, yes, my dear, you are Mr Vernon's sister, I believe. If you will come this way, I will take you to his rooms.'

Following the woman upstairs, Annabel wondered again about the need for Toby to have taken a suite when a single room would have sufficed. The rooms in question were on the first floor overlooking Piccadilly, and were clearly the finest the inn had to offer. Before leaving the brother and sister alone Mrs Ferguson kindly insisted upon sending up a tray of tea for Annabel's refreshment after such a long, hot journey.

Toby languished dolefully on his bed, but brightened a little when Annabel entered. He was very bruised from his drubbing at the hands of the 'muscular louts' from the King's Place seraglio, and the first thing he said to her was that he feared one of his front teeth was now loose.

Annabel placed her reticule and parasol on the table, then teased off her gloves. 'I know your tooth is infinitely more important than anything else, but nevertheless I am glad to report that I had a relatively good journey,' she replied dryly.

He flushed. 'Forgive me. Er, have you been on the road for long?'

'Long enough,' She faced him. 'Have the

documents been returned?' It was a faint hope.

'No.'

'I see. Well, I'm so relieved that at least Molly's letter was handed over safe and sound.'

Toby winced at the sarcasm. 'I'm sorry, Annie,' he said.

'So you should be.' With a sigh she sat on the chair by the bed and glanced around the room. It was clean and well furnished, with a dressing-table, two chairs, and a blue-canopied bed. An open door showed the parlor through which she had just come, with its chintz-covered armchairs, writing desk, and a dining-table by the fine window over the street. Through another door of the parlor was a large dressing-room with wardrobes and a washstand, and through another a second bedroom, smaller than Toby's, with a colorful tapestry counterpane on the bed. A grand suite indeed, she thought.

Toby hauled himself up onto an elbow. 'If I could undo my actions, I would, believe me . . . '

'If I could undo your actions, I would as well,' she replied. 'All right, tell me exactly what happened, although what I can do about it all I fail to see. We might as well resign ourselves to the inevitable.'

5

Toby was about to commence his tale of woe when there came a knock at the parlor door. 'Yes?' he called.

A waiter's voice replied. 'Your tea, sir. With Mrs Ferguson's compliments.'

'Excellent. Please bring it in.'

The man, an elderly fellow with a long white apron and red waistcoat, carried the heavy tray to the table in the parlor, then waited expectantly for a tip. Annabel got up again to take him a coin from her reticule, and when he had gone she took off her hat and began to pour from the satisfyingly large, well-filled blue pottery teapot. 'My, my, half brother of mine, you are treated very handsomely in this place,' she called into the bedroom.

'Yes, well, it's all paid for, before you start wondering if I have the wherewithal to settle.' Toby got up from the bed and hobbled painfully to join her, then they sat opposite each other at the table.

'Satisfy my curiosity, Toby. Why on earth have you taken rooms like this? Wouldn't one have done?'

'Yes, and one was what I originally took, but after my mishap I found it so difficult to get about, it was thought better if I have this suite instead. It's as well, for you are now able to stay here.'

'I suppose so. Anyway, you were about to tell me what happened.' The noise of the street drifted through the closed window, and Annabel gazed across at the corner of Dover Street opposite as Toby told his story.

'Well, it commenced casually enough. I had just begun to make myself comfortable in my original room, when there was a knock at the door. It was Bosky Boskingham. You can imagine my surprise, for I did not see how he could have known I was here, but he explained that he had been walking along Piccadilly when he saw me arriving. He had a little brief business to conduct, then he had called upon me. It was good to chat about old times and share several bottles of good hock — '

'*Several* bottles?'

'Well, you know how it is.'

'No, I don't.'

He cleared his throat. 'I, er, suppose you don't. Anyway, where was I? Oh, yes, we had some hock and jawed about the old days at Oxford. He had come from Jamaica, and I presumed he returned there afterward, but it seems he never left England again. He doesn't look much of a womanizer, but by all the saints that is exactly what he is! And he sometimes likes to lead by the other foot, too, if you know what — ' He broke off hurriedly, for Boskingham's varied amorous appetites were not the sort of thing to speak of in front of a lady.

Annabel was impatient. 'I am not interested in his private life, Toby, just in how he came to make off with the documents.'

'Well, he told me all sorts of amusing stories about this and that, but studiously omitted to mention that he and your brother Roderick were cronies until a recent falling-out. By the way, Roderick is very much a fixture at the nunnery I mentioned in my letter, although I didn't see him the night I was there.'

'Nunnery?'

'Seraglio.'

'Oh, you mean the iniquitous den of vice.'

He colored a little. 'Call it what you wish. Anyway, Bosky didn't mention Roderick once, and after we'd lounged here for several hours, he said he would take me all over town, introduce me to many capital fellows, and see that I had a generally good time. I thought it an excellent notion, and did not believe a delay of a single day before handing the codicil and new will to Sir Humphrey would make that much difference.'

'Oh, Toby . . . '

'I know, it was selfish and irresponsible, but I did it nevertheless. Please don't look at me like that, for I feel dreadful enough already. If I had only gone to Sir Humphrey first, and then spent a riotous time with Bosky, all would have been well.'

'Except that no doubt he would still have stolen your money.'

'Well, there's that, of course, but at least the wretched papers would have been safe.'

'What happened next?'

'He took me all over town as promised, and was such an excellent guide and host that I had a high old time. It was a marvellous day, crammed full of interest, and then we returned here to dine. The food is very good indeed, by the way, and Mrs Ferguson stocks some of the most choice wine you'll find at any establishment in London. Bosky and I had another bottle or two . . . ' Toby paused, waiting for another derogatory comment, but she remained silent, 'It, er, was then that he suggested touring St James's for a night of excitement as well.' Toby cleared his throat again, this time with considerable embarrassment.

Annabel eyed him. 'At this point the house of ill repute comes into it, I presume?'

46

'Look, Annie, we didn't go there for the reason you think!'

'No?'

'No! Most of them are gaming dens as well, you know.'

'Yes, of course,' she murmured.

'It's the truth!' Toby got up indignantly, then had to sit down again with a wince of pain. He drew a long breath. 'I'm not trying to humbug you, Annie. Well, not about myself, anyway. Bosky certainly likes the ladies — indeed he has very expensive tastes in that direction. That was the cause of the trouble. There was a new attraction at La Wyatt's, a lissom little filly with black curls, and — '

'At La Who's?' Annabel interrupted.

'La Wyatt, Juno Wyatt. The abbess. Surely you've heard of her? *Everyone* has heard of Juno Wyatt!'

'Strange as it may seem, I am not well up on the names of madams and procuresses.'

'Er, no, I suppose you wouldn't be. Well, she is the most famous demimondaine in London. Duels have been fought over her charms. She is in her early forties, I suppose, but looks ten years younger, and she keeps a very select seraglio in King's Place, St James's. All the best nunneries are in King's Place,' Toby added.

'I see.'

'When we first went to Juno's, her black footman, Claudius, seemed uncertain about letting us in because Bosky was in rather too high spirits, but then Juno herself came, saw Bosky, and told the fellow to admit us.'

'How very riveting, Toby, but you were telling me what happened when Mr Boskingham saw the, er, pretty little filly.'

Toby drew a long breath. 'Well, it is Juno's rule, and the rule of some of the other abbesses, that all the nuns wear masks or dominos, but even so I could tell that this new one was particularly attractive, and because she was, er, new, Juno set a very hefty price upon her. Bosky said — '

Annabel broke in again. 'What, exactly does 'er, new' mean? Either she was new or she wasn't.'

Toby colored. 'New isn't exactly the right word. Oh, be sensible, Annabel, what do you think it means? She was untouched, pristine, pure . . .'

'A virgin?' she supplied.

'Yes.' He shifted uncomfortably. 'Anyway, Bosky said Juno wasn't asking a price but a damned ransom! Ransom or not, the whole thing soon turned into an auction.'

'How very distasteful.' Annabel was shocked.

'It was, actually,' Toby agreed, remembering. 'By the end it came down to Bosky and

Sir Richard Tregerran, but then the price exceeded Bosky's purse so he asked if he could dip into mine.'

Annabel regarded him. 'Did you oblige?'

'No. Truth to tell I'd had enough. I had overindulged in wine throughout the day. I'd lost at the card tables, I'd been fending off persistent, er . . . '

'Bawds? Trollops? Doxies?' Annabel refused to grace them with loftier names, for nuns they were *not*!

'Yes. And I was upset about the auction, so I told Bosky I wanted to leave. I desired him to do the same, because by then it was clear to me that Richard was going to get the prize, and — '

'Richard? You are on first name terms with this . . . this person?' As far as Annabel was concerned, Sir Richard Tregerran could not be a gentleman.

'Eh? Yes, I'm on first name terms with him. All will become clear. Anyway, Bosky did not take kindly to my opinion or my refusal to help, and became most insulting. At that point I bloodied his nose.'

Annabel blinked. 'You *struck* him?'

'I most certainly did. No one calls me a namby-pamby milksop damsel and gets away with it.'

Annabel could not help smiling. 'I can

quite understand that, especially as you are none of those things.'

'Precisely. Anyway, there was a bit of a set-to, during which I know he managed to relieve me of my property because the little nun saw him do it and subsequently told Richard. Then Juno had me ejected, and before I knew it her ruffians were dealing me the customary punishment for all trouble-makers.'

'And then simply left you in the street?' Annabel was appalled.

'In a corner of King's Place. I passed out, and when I came around again later, I staggered out into Pall Mall to get a growler from one of the ranks, when I — '

'To get a what?'

'A growler. It's the name they now give to hackney coaches. Anyway, I found one all right, for it ran me down. It was going at a surprising lick for such a ramshackle old drag, and the coachman didn't even know he'd touched me. I fell unconscious in the middle of the street, and if it hadn't been for Richard, I would probably have been fatally struck by the next vehicle that passed.'

'This Sir Richard Tregerran is your Good Samaritan?' Annabel did not approve of Sir Richard, or indeed of any man who could take part in an auction such as Toby described.

'Yes. He brought me safely back here, summoned a doctor to attend my injuries, and paid Mrs Ferguson very handsomely to accommodate me in this suite until I am fully recovered.'

'A Good Samaritan indeed.' Maybe this person had one or two redeeming features.

'He is capital fellow, one of the very best.'

'That I doubt very much.'

Toby went on. 'Annie, if it weren't for Richard, I would have believed the documents long gone. He was the one who told me about Bosky being friendly with Roderick. Bosky has apparently skipped the country with all manner of duns at his fancy heels. But Richard *did* learn from his landlady that the documents are safely hidden.'

Annabel sat up hopefully. 'They are? Where?'

'That's the trouble. It seems Bosky was trying to leave without paying his rent, so the landlady cornered him with her son, who, I am informed, is built like Goliath. Bosky was able to convince them that he had no money, and managed to get himself off the hook by telling them what he could remember about the documents, which he said could be sold to your father or Roderick for much more than his outstanding rent.'

Annabel awaited more information. 'Well,

is that all he said?'

'No. He said he had been to several St James's temples that night, and became so inebriated that eventually he was taken up to a bedroom to sleep it off. He recalled waking up still in a stupor at about dawn, and for some reason thinking he was about to be robbed, although why *he*, of all stout fellows, would think that I really can't imagine! Anyway, he saw a set of candlesticks on a mantel, the sort that unscrew, so he hid the papers in one of them. Then he lurched back to the bed and fell asleep again. Not long after that he was carried out of the house, put in a growler, and sent back to his lodgings. He didn't know where he had been, and only remembered about the candlesticks when he'd sobered up.'

Annabel was staring at him. 'He could not remember where he had been? Tell me you are teasing me, Toby.'

'I wish I were! It's the honest truth, Annie. At this moment the documents are within a few hundred yards of this inn, but exactly where is a mystery.'

6

Annabel got up to go to the fireplace, where a bowl of bright marigolds stood in the hearth. She looked back at Toby as a belated thought occurred to her. 'You don't think this whole thing was a trick, do you?'

'Trick? What do you mean?'

'Well, if Mr Boskingham is Roderick's friend, maybe his purpose all along was to steal the codicil. Roderick has squandered his fortune, so he wants to be sure of inheriting Perton House in order to acquire Grandfather Gresham's collection of medieval paintings.'

Toby stared at her, then shook his head. 'No, I'm sure Bosky isn't Roderick's creature anymore. Besides, I didn't tell him I had the codicil, which is the only way he could have found out because the roll of documents remained in my coat throughout.'

'Maybe, but it still seems a very unsettling coincidence that he and Roderick are — were — so close.'

Toby thought about it. 'Well, I can't say categorically that you're wrong, for it all fits very neatly, but they are enemies now, and I still fail to see how Bosky — or anyone else for that matter — would have been aware of what I was carrying.'

'Everyone in Father's bedroom knew about it,' she pointed out.

'Pilkington himself? I hardly think so — he was almost afraid of his own shadow. As for thinking it could be Molly — '

'I may be biased, but I am afraid I can well believe *she* would be implicated,' Annabel said immediately. She recalled how the maid had lingered in the room that night, how she had dropped the cordial when the codicil was produced, how she had hesitated about signing the new will, and how she had watched from the window as her mistress departed.

Toby rolled his eyes. 'Oh, not that again! Molly Simmonds is only a maid.'

'Hmm.'

'Annie, can't you forget everything else and just think about the missing papers? The codicil secures your future, so we have to get it back. Nor can we allow the new will to fall into the wrong hands, because it gives away how Father intends to trump Roderick once and for all. I can't for the life of me think what to do right now, but I'm sure that if we put our heads together — '

Annabel rounded upon him. 'What do you suggest? That I march boldly into every bawdy house in St James's and dismantle all candlesticks until I find the right one? Oh, yes, I can imagine the madams putting up with such a game of hide-and-seek! No doubt I would be promptly auctioned off as well!'

'You would make a terrible nymph, Annie, because you have a horrid sharp tongue at times,' Toby replied, guilt making him churlish, but then he smiled a little. 'I suppose it is a game of hide-and-seek, isn't it.'

'Except that this is not a game, at least, it isn't as far as I'm concerned.'

'It isn't for me either, Annie. Truly it isn't.' Something occurred to him. 'Actually, there is a clue. Well, of sorts, anyway.'

'A clue?'

'Bosky recalled that the candlestick was one of a set of four of clearly Indian origin, for each was supported on a beast of that region, an elephant, a tiger, a monkey, and a crocodile. He thought he used the elephant, but he wasn't sure.'

'I am surprised he recalled such details about the candlesticks, but not where they were! Surely such an unusual set should be easy enough to trace? *Someone* must know them. Can't your dear Sir Richard find out? After all, he clearly haunts these establishments.'

'He doesn't know. Don't you think I've

asked him? He has made inquiries of friends as well, but no one knows anything about such a set of candlesticks. And please do not keep criticizing him, because he has been putting himself out considerably on my behalf. He even paid over and above Bosky's outstanding rent to persuade the landlady to tell him what she knew.'

'Isn't he peculiarly lavish with his money, considering you and he hardly know each other?'

'He's a gentleman through and through, Annie, a true Good Samaritan.'

'Hmm.'

Nothing was said for a moment or two, but the silence was very resounding indeed, then Annabel turned back to the marigolds, which were as orange-gold as the sun. 'Oh, I don't want to talk about it anymore for the moment. I vow my head is ringing with it all.'

'Have another cup of tea,' Toby suggested, and began to pour one.

'Tea, the universal cure-all,' she murmured.

'So it is rumored,' he replied.

Suddenly, Annabel found herself thinking about the two dangerous brushes her chaise had shared with the curricle on the way from Perton House. 'Toby, do you know a gentleman who drives an emerald green curricle?'

'Several, why?'

'I'm curious about one I noticed during the journey.'

'During the journey? Annie, there must be a fair number of green curricles in England.'

'I do realize that,' she replied drily, 'but I passed this man about a mile out of Perton House when he was going the other way, then I saw him again just after Hyde Park Corner, when he overtook me.'

'Really? How very odd.'

'Whoever he is, he drives like something fleeing from Bedlam.'

'That just about describes every fellow I know,' Toby pointed out. 'What does he look like?'

'Very much a dandy, with rouge, a patch at the corner of his mouth, and such serried golden curls that he either wears a wig or spends an hour or more before his mirror before sallying forth.'

Toby stared at her, then shook his head. 'No, it can't be . . . '

'Can't be who?'

'Well, you have just described Bosky to the last letter.'

'Really? Well, I suppose it cannot be him if he has left the country.'

'No, I suppose not.' Toby's brow furrowed as he considered various other gentlemen of his acquaintance, then he shook his head. 'Well, I know gentlemen with very blond hair and gentlemen with green curricles, but Bosky is the only one with both.'

Annabel resumed her seat at the table and toyed with her cup and saucer. 'To be honest, there was something very odd about the man and his lady friend.'

'There was a lady?'

Annabel nodded. 'Yes. She was with him here in London, but not before, so I suppose he could have gone to get her. Anyway, she was veiled, so I couldn't see her face. Her clothes were new, but not up to very much, that is for sure. He had a muffler and had his hat pulled as low as possible over his face.'

'Then how do you know about his rouge, patch, and hair?'

'Because when I first saw him he wasn't hiding his identity. He probably felt safe from detection in Gloucestershire.' She paused. 'Toby, you don't think it *was* Mr Boskingham, do you?'

'Richard seemed pretty certain he'd left the country. The landlady mentioned Rotherhithe and a ship bound for Madeira.'

Annabel raised an eyebrow. 'Which might be true, or might be a clever trick. After all, if *I* wanted to disappear, I would make certain any pursuit was sent in the very opposite direction.'

'Well, anything is possible I suppose, but somehow I think your man in the curricle is just a fluke. Bosky is well out to sea now, I hope in the most stormy Bay of Biscay for over a century.'

Annabel's thoughts remained on the curricle. 'Actually, the woman was familiar to me,' she said.

'Eh? But she was veiled.'

'I know, nevertheless . . . '

Toby jingled a teaspoon with his finger. 'If I thought Bosky really was still in London, I'd find him and wring the whereabouts of the candlesticks out of him!'

'If only that could be,' she replied with immense feeling. *Where were they?* Suddenly, her words of earlier slipped back into her mind. *What do you suggest? That I march boldly into every bawdy house in St James's and dismantle all candlesticks until I find the right one?* It was an impossible idea, a shocking one even, but it was beginning to take root. She would not need to march boldly anywhere, just slip slyly in. All she needed was a mask or domino, a little courage, and the good fortune to elude discovery . . .

Toby looked curiously at her. 'Have you

thought of something?'

'No, except . . . '

'Yes?'

'Well, I suppose I should at least take a tour of St James's and see where these establishments are. I don't know what it will achieve, but at least I'll be doing *something*. I'll go in the morning. In the meantime you must write me a list of all the likely places your Mr Boskingham may have gone.'

'Annie, I won't have you walking around St James's on your own, even in the morning. The only women found there on their own are from the demimonde.'

'Well, since you are indisposed, I have no choice but to go out alone. If I simply stay here with you, there was hardly any point in my leaving Gloucestershire!'

'I, er, thought I would ask Richard if he would escort you,' Toby ventured.

'Certainly not!' she declared hotly. 'Toby, I am grateful to Sir Richard for looking after you, but I despise him for that business of the auction. If I ever have to meet him, I do not think I shall be able to be civil, so you may count upon it that he is the last man in London I wish to have as my escort!'

Toby had seldom seen her so opposed to anything. 'Well, if that's how you really feel . . . '

'It most certainly is.'

At that moment there sounded the discreet tap of a cane on the door. Toby put out a reassuring hand. 'I think that's Richard's knock,' he whispered, then called out. 'Is that you, Richard?'

'The same,' came the reply.

Annabel's lips parted, and without further ado she hastened into the bedroom that was to be hers and closed the door.

Toby gazed after her in confusion, then rose awkwardly to his feet and called out to Richard again, 'Come in, come in.'

Annabel leaned back against the door. She felt a little foolish to have cut and run like this, but she really did not feel like facing Sir Richard Tregerran, auction-bidder extraordinary. It would not do for her to give him a piece of her mind, and that was precisely what might happen if she came face-to-face with him now. She would have liked to see him, nevertheless, for she had a picture in her mind of a Casanova fellow with an olive skin, full sensuous lips, and libertine eyes.

She moved from the door, intending to lie on the bed until he had gone, but then something made her glance back. The door had an empty keyhole, and she could see the light in the parlor beyond. The temptation was too much, and almost before she knew it, she was on her knees with an eye pressed to the hole.

Her view of the other room was surprisingly good, and she saw immediately that Sir Richard Tregerran was not at all as she had imagined. There was nothing about him that suggested the Venetian profligate, for he seemed only too coolly and fashionably English, with a handsome, slightly tanned face that was fine-boned and aristocratic. He wore his dark hair in the tousled *à la Titus* style, and his eyes were a surprisingly noticeable green, with long lashes and a thoughtful aspect. She reckoned him to be in his late thirties. His figure was tall and strong, with broad shoulders and slender hips that could only enhance fashionable clothes. The cut and quality of his coat was perfection, from its superb charcoal cloth and tailoring, to its deep but tasteful cuffs of fine gray-and-black stripes. His old-rose marcella waistcoat and olive green silk neckcloth were masterly touches of color, and his fine white kerseymere breeches were so close-fitting that very little of his lower anatomy was left to conjecture, or so it seemed from the view through the keyhole. The ebony cane with which he had tapped at the door now lay on the table with his upturned hat, into which he was in the process of placing his gray kid gloves. If there was a gentleman in the land who was more elegant and well turned out, she would be very surprised indeed, although she disapproved of him more than ever when she saw that he wore a wedding ring.

7

If Annabel thought herself undetected by Sir Richard Tregerran, she was mistaken, for he had already glanced at the blue-ribboned gypsy hat she had left on the increasingly cluttered table. Now his curious attention moved on to the two cups and saucers, before coming to rest on the only other closed door apart from the one through which he had entered. Either Toby was entertaining an inamorata, or his sister had arrived. It must be the former, he decided, for Miss Gresham would have no reason to hide.

Toby had followed his new friend's glances, and colored a little. 'It's good of you to call again.'

'Not at all.' Richard's voice was soft and well spoken.

'Shall we sit down?'

'By all means.' Richard chose the chair Annabel had occupied a moment earlier, and lounged back with his long legs stretched out. He rested an arm over the back of the chair. 'How goes it today?' he inquired, looking at the gypsy hat again.

'Oh, aches and pains still, but I fancy I am

a little better. Is there any news?'

'About your missing documents? I fear not.'

Toby sat forward. 'A curious thing, Richard, but someone who exactly fits Bosky's description has been seen here in town this very day.'

'But the maggot has left the country.'

'And there is no doubt about that?'

Richard gave a slight laugh. 'Well, I didn't actually wave him farewell from the quay, but all the signs are that he's gone into exile.'

'That's what I thought. I wish I knew who this other fellow was, though.'

'Probably some newcomer from a distant shire.'

Toby grinned. 'Like me, you mean?'

'I fear so, my bumpkin friend.'

Toby's thoughts returned to the mysterious gentleman. 'Do you know anyone who might be mistaken for Bosky, even to the emerald green curricle?'

'I fear I don't.' He changed the subject. 'Actually, Toby, I came here today for two reasons. First to see how you are, and to invite you and Miss Gresham to dine with me at Tregerran Lodge tomorrow night. Provided you feel sufficiently recovered, of course. In any case, I will be sure to send my carriage, so that my coachman can assist you.'

'That's most handsome of you, Richard. Yes, I accept on Annie's behalf.'

Richard smiled. 'Excellent. I'll send the carriage at half past eight for nine. Now, however, I must toddle off. If I learn anything, rest assured I'll let you know without delay. In the meantime, *pax vobiscum*.' He rose, gave the keyhole another glance, then departed.

Annabel immediately came out of the other room. 'Oh, Toby, how *could* you!'

'How could I what?'

'Accept the dinner invitation when you could so easily have declined! I haven't brought a suitable gown with me, just something I can wear at an inn like this, and I don't want to meet him anyway!'

Toby was flung on the defensive. 'How am I supposed to think of everything? Why don't you simply buy another gown.'

'And stitch it together by tomorrow night?'

With typical male cowardice, Toby wished to leave such a contentious female topic alone. 'There's no point in arguing after the event.'

'That is so easy for you to say. Tomorrow night *I* will be like a parson's wife from the back of beyond, while Lady Tregerran will no doubt be dazzling enough for a royal drawing-room!'

'Lady Tregerran?'

'Sir Richard's wife.'

Toby looked blankly at her. 'There isn't a Lady Tregerran. Whatever made you think there was?'

'The fact that he wears a wedding ring.' Annabel was a little taken aback.

'So you weren't just eavesdropping — you were spying through the keyhole, too!'

'And if I was?' she replied defiantly — knowing that telltale color was again creeping into her cheeks.

'Oh, no reason, I just find it amusing to think of you stooping to such a measure. As it happens, Richard's wife — her name was Elizabeth, I believe — died about three years ago, and as he adored her to distraction, he has yet to overcome his grief. So please do not accuse him of being an unfaithful husband as well.'

'So it is grief that makes him frequent bawdy houses and bid at disgraceful auctions for female favors? Quite understandable, of course,' she replied acidly. 'Well, no matter what you say, Toby, I simply cannot approve of him, and I certainly do not wish to dine at Tregerran Lodge. I shall have to sink beneath a headache, or some such indisposition.'

'I don't know what you're fussing about. Richard's a good fellow, I tell you. Be sensible now. I'll warrant you brought that washy blue silk with you.'

'It isn't washy blue, it's aquamarine, and yes, I have brought it with me, but it's hardly suitable for Mayfair.'

'You look lovely in it, and Richard doesn't live in Mayfair. Tregerran Lodge is about two miles north of London in Marylebone Park.'

Annabel's eyes flashed. 'Oh, the country, you mean? Just the thing for a bumpkin's sister!' With that she flounced back into her room and slammed the door. Once inside, she put her hands to her hot cheeks, for it was embarrassment that prompted her display of anger. She had made a fool of herself by fleeing from the parlor, for her presence must have been only too obvious to Sir Richard, what with the hat *and* her cup and saucer. Tears stung her eyes suddenly, for it had been a long day, and this was the last straw.

Toby tapped at the door. 'Annie?'

'Yes?' The word was choked.

He opened the door and hobbled in concernedly. 'Please don't cry, Annie. I didn't mean to upset you,' he said gently, and pressed a clean handkerchief into her hand. 'Tell you what, I'll have Mrs Ferguson serve us a meal up here, then you can have a good rest. It will all seem better in the morning, I promise.'

'Yes, I'm sure so, too.' But she thought everything would be exactly the same as now.

★   ★   ★

It was early evening, the Dog and Duck's food had proved as excellent as its wine, and Annabel felt a little restored after eating. The dinner consisted of three courses, a little vegetable soup, then chicken, salad, and new potatoes, followed by rhubarb tart and cream. With it she and Toby shared a bottle of hock that was agreeably cold from the inn's cellar.

It was strange to sit at a window that faced over Piccadilly instead of the quiet grounds at Perton House, but Annabel had to admit that the view was very interesting, for there was so much to see. She knew that whenever she ate these particular dishes in future, she would think of this moment. Especially rhubarb tart, for it was as the waiter set this before her that she glanced out and saw the woman from the curricle again.

For a second Annabel thought it was imagination, but then she sat forward attentively. Was it likely there were two women wearing identical 'tablecloth' veils, buttermilk spencers, and pale pink gowns? 'Oh, Toby! Over there, inspecting that print shop window. It's her. I know it is!'

'It's who?' Toby glanced out, but there was more than one woman by the print shop, because it was a very popular place to go.

'Buttermilk and pink, with a veil. Oh, she's going around the corner into Dover Street! She's gone!' Annabel turned urgently to him. 'Did you see her?'

'Well, a glimpse before she disappeared.'

'Did she look familiar?'

Toby sighed. 'Oh, for heaven's sake, Annie, how could I tell? She was concealed like a sultan's concubine!'

'I know she was, but even so . . .' Annabel glanced out again. 'She was the same woman, I'd take a vow upon it. The same shape, build, manner . . .'

'You observed all *that* in a second or so?' Toby's tone was dry in the extreme.

'Oh, you're probably right.' Annabel decided it was best to agree with him, for truth to tell she couldn't be *sure* of anything. Buttermilk and pink were hardly uncommon colors, and veils were as prevalent as parasols for the protection of sensitive complexions from the summer sun.

The waiter cleared his throat. 'Er, will there be anything more, sir?'

Toby glanced at Annabel. 'Annie?'

'No, thank you. It was very good indeed.' She smiled at the man. 'Please convey my

70

compliments to the kitchens, and tell them that their efforts were much appreciated.'

'Thank you, madam. Thank *you*, sir,' the waiter added as Toby pressed a coin into his ready hand.

As the door closed, Toby pulled a face. 'One needs as much in tips at these places as to pay one's bill,' he grumbled, then rose painfully to his feet. 'Oh, I've been sitting on this hard chair for too long. My bruises are better than they were this morning, but they're still playing the very devil. I think I'll lie down again.' He studied her. 'You should go to bed as well. I know it's early, but my advice of earlier still stands. You're having a wretched time of it because of me, and you need some sleep.'

'All right. I'll just sit here a little while, then I'll retire. You go ahead.'

He came around the table and bent to kiss her on the cheek. 'You'll never know how sorry I am about all this, Annie,' he said.

'I do know, Toby,' she said, putting her hand over his and squeezing gently.

She remained at the table as he made his way to his room, then she heard the bed squeak slightly as he lay down. The moments passed, and gradually his breathing became slow and deep as he fell asleep. She glanced outside, and suddenly saw the woman come out of the print shop, having clearly changed her mind about something and come back. Instead of returning up Dover Street the way she had gone before, the woman stood at the edge of the pavement, waiting for a moment to cross Piccadilly toward the Dog and Duck. At last there was a break in the constant traffic, and she hastened across, stepping over a makeshift wooden bridge that spanned the sewer works. Then she disappeared into Arlington Street.

In a moment Annabel was on her feet and tying on her hat. She meant to follow the woman who had so aroused her curiosity.

8

The summer evening was warm and very pleasant as Annabel set off after the woman. Arlington Street was lined with fine town houses, including a rather startling gothic residence called Pomfret Castle, which was complete with battlements and front lodges. The street stretched a short distance south from Piccadilly, ending in a cul-de-sac, and there was only one other egress, Bennet Street to the east.

At first there seemed no sign of the figure in buttermilk and pink, but then just a glimpse by the Blue Posts Tavern as the woman entered Bennet Street. Annabel caught up her skirts and hurried toward the corner, but the moment she turned it she saw that Bennet Street was very short indeed, leading almost directly into busy St James's Street, into which the woman had already vanished. Here lay superior hotels, coffee shops, bagnios, and emporiums of every description, to say nothing of many of the most exclusive gentlemen's clubs in London, including White's, Boodle's, and Brooks's, the last of which abutted Bennet Street. There was almost as much traffic as in Piccadilly, although not nearly so much noise. It was as if even wheels and hoofs were in awe of such exalted surroundings.

To Annabel's relief, she saw the woman walking down the crowded far pavement in the direction of St James's Palace, the turreted Tudor façade of which closed the vista at the southern end of the street. Annabel followed the woman on the nearside pavement, and soon noticed the entrances of various courts and alleys. She was to discover that these secretive places harbored the light ladies she regarded as expensive doxies, but who were the toast of London's masculine society, which called them 'fashionable impures.' The favors of these ladies were not purchased cheaply.

King's Place and the premises run by Juno Wyatt must be somewhere near here, she thought, as the figure opposite paused to look in a pastry cook's window. The shop was open, as were all the businesses in the street, for there was much custom to be had on sunny summer evenings. The woman had raised her veil in order to inspect the delicious display, but try as Annabel would, she could not make out her face in the broken reflection afforded by the small panes. One thing was certain, however, Annabel was now more certain than ever that she knew the woman from somewhere. If only she could remember where!

Veil lowered again, the woman walked on. Annabel anticipated Pall Mall as her quarry's destination, because it joined St James's Street by the palace, but instead she turned east again, into the narrow confines of Pav'd Alley, where Molly Simmonds's aunt kept a haberdashery. Annabel crossed the street to peep cautiously around the corner. The alley was open to the sky, but far too narrow for a carriage to pass through, and it contained shops of various kinds, including Mrs Smith's haberdashery. It was very busy, with people passing between St James's Street and King Street at the other end, but there was no sign at all of her quarry.

Suddenly, Annabel was addressed by a sneering voice she knew and had come to loathe, even though it was some years since last she had heard it. 'Well, if it isn't my little half sister come to town. What a happy coincidence.' She turned in dismay to see Roderick standing immediately behind her.

Lord Mavor was tall and pale, with the same heavy eyebrows and prominent nose of his father, but there the resemblance ended, for he was unpleasant through and through. His eyes were such a light blue they seemed almost without color, and their coldness suited his character. Wealth had clearly given him a taste for costly clothes, for the cut and cloth of his burnt orange coat and fawn breeches would have done justice to the Prince of Wales himself, as would the enormous topaz that graced the knot of his cravat. His thick light brown hair was carefully disheveled, and he sported side-whiskers that made his thin face appear almost hollow-cheeked. He did not accord Annabel the courtesy of removing his tall hat, or indeed of even inclining his head. Such graceless omissions were as much a mark of the man as his callous intentions regarding the fate of Perton House and its priceless contents.

He gave one of his thin, humorless smiles. 'How unfortunate that this very evening I am to drive down to Brighton, and so cannot escort you hither and thither over town.'

She recovered a little from her shock. 'How are you, Roderick?' she inquired, deciding that she at least would introduce a modicum of civility into the proceedings.

'I am in excellent spirits, thank you.'

'Good. Well, please don't let me detain you from Brighton.'

'It is a long-standing invitation to the Marine Pavilion, but a few minutes' delay in agreeable chitchat with you will not ruin my chances of royal favor.'

'Royal favor? How high you fly these days, Roderick. Now, if you will excuse me — ' She made to enter Pav'd Alley, but he hurried in front of her and put his cane to the wall to block her way.

'Not so fast, sweetness.'

She recoiled. 'Roderick, I don't think you and I have anything to say to each other, so please let me pass.'

'Why are you in town?' he demanded.

'Toby and I are on a shopping expedition,' she replied, meeting his gaze squarely and trusting she did not look as furtive as she felt.

'So Vernon is with you, eh? What is the fellow thinking of, allowing you to loiter on such a notorious corner as this? Indeed, what would dear Papa think if he knew?'

Notorious corner? Oh, how she hoped it wasn't; but as she glanced past him, she had a sneaking suspicion that it probably was, because there were two rather obvious women standing opposite, their charms more displayed than was even vaguely proper. 'I am hardly loitering.' She met his eyes again.

'No?'

'Certainly not, indeed I would no longer be here if it were not for your insistence.'

His lips twisted into what went for a smile.

'I am merely concerned for your welfare, sister mine.'

She raised her chin. 'That is one thing I know you are not, sir.'

'Ah, the thorny subject of Perton House crosses your mind, I perceive.'

'Why should you leap to that conclusion, Roderick? Does your conscience bother you?'

'I have no need of conscience, my dear. There is no codicil, therefore when dearest Pater meets his Maker the house will be mine to do with as I please.'

'You know full well there is a codicil!'

'Then produce it.' Again the smile played upon his lips. 'There, you see? You cannot.'

'How can you be so sure of that?' she demanded.

'Because I know dear Papa lost it two months ago. Oh, yes, news travels, my dear.'

So he didn't know about more recent events, she thought, which presumably meant he was at least innocent of involvement with Boskingham. However, innocent of that or not, he was still vile. 'I despise you,' she whispered, her words almost lost in the bustle of the crowded alley. She pressed back against the wall, debating whether or not to duck beneath his cane and try to make a determined dash for it.

'I'm glad to hear you say so, my dear, for it

eliminates any obligation I might conceivably come to feel where you are concerned.' He drew the tip of a finger slowly along the brim of her hat. 'Just don't do anything foolish, Sis, for I don't wish to become truly annoyed with you. Bear in mind that I am not a man to cross.'

'Let me pass,' she demanded, feeling suddenly afraid of him.

'When I am good and ready,' he replied.

'If you don't let me pass right now, I shall scream,' she warned.

'And draw attention to your maidenly self on a corner like this? I think not.' He was supremely sure of himself, but a moment later his face changed as she gave the loudest, most piercing scream she could muster. It echoed shrilly in the confined alley, and was followed by a hush as everyone turned to see if murder was being done.

Roderick's eyes became icy. 'I warned you not to annoy me further,' he breathed.

'Let me go!' She tried to get away from him, but he grabbed her arm so tightly that his fingers pinched her quite painfully.

Suddenly, she was rescued, for a gentleman's hand clamped authoritatively on Roderick's shoulder.

'What monstrous trick are you up to now, Mavor?' asked Sir Richard Tregerran.

There was an eager stir among the onlookers, who thought they were about to witness what followers of the fancy would probably term a bang-up scrap. Annabel was mortified, for although she was relieved to be rescued, she wished her St George were anyone but Sir Richard Tregerran. She could only think of bowing her head to conceal her face, although why she bothered she didn't really know, for Roderick was bound to identify her at any moment. Her foolish whim to follow the veiled woman was about to cost her reputation very dear indeed.

Still holding her arm, Roderick spoke to Richard. 'Damn you, Tregerran! Keep your nose out of my business!'

'Now, now, that isn't very gracious. If I happen upon you accosting an innocent young lady in the street, you surely do not imagine I will pass by on the other side, do you?'

'This is no concern of yours, so I warn you — '

Roderick's voice broke off on a gasp of pain as Richard's fingers tightened like a vise. 'I have never liked you, Mavor,' he said softly, 'and now I like you even less. Unhand the lady immediately, or I will break your shoulder like a twig.'

Evidently this was not an idle threat, or so

Roderick feared, for although he gave Richard a look of pure venom, he complied immediately.

Annabel's first instinct was to escape while she had the opportunity, but Richard's next words froze her to the spot. 'Now I have you in my grasp, Mavor, perhaps you would be so good as tell me where Boskingham is?'

'Eh?' The change of subject caught Roderick off guard, for Annabel could see he had been expecting another question entirely.

'You heard me. Where is Boskingham?'

9

Roderick met Richard's gaze. 'Believe me, Tregerran, if I knew dear Bosky's whereabouts, I would put him six feet under.'

'What's this? A schoolboy tiff?' Richard replied.

'Put it this way, he has nailed his colors to his own mast instead of mine, so it wasn't because of the duns that he fled his lodgings. For all that, I doubt very much if he has left the country as he would have everyone think!'

Annabel's lips parted. Did this mean that the man in the curricle could indeed be the odious Mr Boskingham after all? she pondered.

Richard searched his face. 'I'm greatly intrigued, Mavor. Do tell.'

Roderick had begun to recover a little from his shock, for a scornful smirk appeared on his unlovable visage. 'Come now, Tregerran, where are your priorities? Aren't you going to ask me about a certain lady?'

For a moment Richard didn't respond, and as Annabel glanced at him, she saw that his lips had stiffened until they were almost white, and his green eyes had assumed a dangerous new light. 'So you are behind it — I thought as much,' he breathed.

'I'm not behind anything, Tregerran, I merely know that she is no longer beneath your roof.'

Who were they talking about? Annabel wondered. The nun at the auction?

'As a protector you don't amount to much, do you?' Roderick sneered.

It was the wrong thing to say, for Richard suddenly seized him by the throat and rammed him against the wall. Annabel flinched, and there were gasps from the watching crowd as Roderick squirmed and spluttered, his eyes suddenly wide and alarmed, for courage was not one of his qualities. Richard's eyes were like flint. 'Where is she, damn you? Where?'

Roderick managed a choked reply. 'Harm one hair of my head, and my friends know what to do! It will be final, I promise!'

Richard's loathing was almost tangible, but the threat to the unnamed third party was only too clear, so he slowly released him. Roderick immediately seized the initiative and swung viciously at him with his cane. Richard managed to duck in the nick of time, but Roderick had already taken to his heels and was off up St James's Street as if every Bow Street Runner in London were after him.

Annabel was too startled by the swiftness of events to do anything but remain where she was. Her wits told her to run off as well; her legs were not in agreement.

Richard had quickly removed his hat and was already addressing her attentively. 'Are you all right, Miss, er . . . ?' he inquired as the onlookers began to disperse to go about their previous business.

Keeping her head lowered, she nodded. 'Yes. Thank you.' She employed a hoarse tone in the hope of conveying a considerable indisposition of the throat, for she did not dare to use her ordinary voice in case he recognized it later. Maybe he recognized her hat now! After all, it was not all that long since he had seen it lying on the table in Toby's room. She had seldom felt more vulnerable and guilty than she did at this moment, but did not know what to do except stand there, praying she somehow managed to remain anonymous in every way. However, this was made ten times more difficult than it might otherwise have been because she so wanted to look at him properly. Now that he had played such a gallant St George, she was quite confused because it did not equate at all with her opinion of him! She wanted to look into his eyes, to see if she could see the real Sir Richard Tregerran in their steady green depths.

He hadn't as yet recognized the hat, and remained solely concerned for her welfare. 'Are you quite sure? Forgive me for doubting your sincerity on the point, but before you screamed and I intervened, I could not help observing how very disagreeable Lord Mavor's manner was toward you.'

'It was a misunderstanding. He, er, mistook my reason for being here,' she replied in her newly acquired croak. Oh, heavens, she thought, she sounded like a frog in distress!

He concealed a smile. 'Oh, I do not doubt that he was in error, for you are clearly a lady.'

'Thank you, sir.' She wished he would suddenly remember something urgent he had to attend to elsewhere.

'With all due respect, Miss, er, I do not think it wise of you to come here alone.'

'I . . . I realize that now, sir.'

He smiled, wishing his secretive incognita would raise her head so that he could see her face, but she permitted him only a splendid view of the brim of her hat. Interest stirred unstoppably through him. He would have dearly liked to learn exactly who she was, but knew she had no intention of telling him. Her anxiety on the point touched him, and he could no more have pressed her than he could have flown, but neither could he quite leave her alone. She intrigued him, attracted him even, and he wanted to make her stay awhile, even though he knew she wished to escape. 'Perhaps it would be better if I escorted you safely wherever it is you are going?' he suggested.

'No! I . . . I mean, no thank you, sir. There really is no need.'

'A gentleman should not permit a lady to proceed alone, especially a lady who has just suffered a disagreeable experience.'

He was right, of course, but his continued company was most certainly *not* what she desired. Well, it was, but right now she was in no position to follow her heart, which was leading her astray anyway. Maybe he *had* rescued her from Roderick, and maybe he *was* being gallant and protective, but that must not blind her to the facts of the auction.

He pressed a little. 'Where are you going?'

There was nothing for it but to state her point as bluntly as possible. 'Sir, I do not wish to be escorted, nor do I wish to linger a moment more in conversation. I am very grateful for your assistance, but you may now consider your duty as a gentleman to be fully discharged where I am concerned.' It was no easy matter to say all this and maintain her hoarse voice, but somehow she managed. She also managed to keep her head lowered, again no easy matter when really she longed to look him in the eyes.

He was amused. It was a new experience to

find a young woman who wished he would go away, for he was more accustomed to the opposite being the case. As a consequence she began to intrigue him more than ever.

'Please go, sir,' she said then.

'Am I being given my *congé*?' he said incredulously.

'Yes, sir, you are!'

'Be that as it may, madam, I cannot leave you like this.'

'Then I will leave you,' she answered, and turned to walk into the alley, but he caught her arm.

'Don't be foolish. This area is *not* for the likes of you. At the very least allow me to put you in a hackney coach.'

'I wish to be allowed to proceed.'

'And I have just said I cannot permit you that hazardous luxury!' he replied, gently but firmly.

'I shall scream again,' she warned.

'Do so, by all means, but it will not alter the fact that I am merely attempting to protect you.'

She didn't want to scream, for if the constables came there would be a very real risk of her identity being revealed, so instead she tried to pull free again. His fingers immediately tightened determinedly on her sleeve, and to be certain he seized her other arm as well. She squirmed, but he held her even more. Their bodies brushed together once, then again. For a fleeting moment he glimpsed her face, her parted lips within inches of his. Temptation stirred. Suddenly, he wanted to kiss her, to taste those lips he was sure would be as honeyed as the color of the stray curl that brushed her cheek. But then she wrenched away, ran into the crowded alley, and was lost from view almost immediately.

He gazed after her, shaken to know that he had come very close indeed to forcing his advances upon her. That would have reduced him to Mavor's base level! He took a long, steadying breath. 'Forget her, Tregerran,' he instructed himself; but he knew he would not forget her, *could* not forget her.

Annabel had slipped into one of the shops instead of running through into King Street, which was why she passed out of his sight so quickly. The shop she chose happened to be Mrs Smith's haberdashery, although as she made her way to the darker recesses of the premises, she didn't notice or care which emporium it was. She needed a few minutes to collect her wits — and her senses. Her heart was pounding, and she felt almost weak from the force of emotion that tumbled through her. She wanted to feel nothing for

Sir Richard Tregerran; indeed she *needed* to feel nothing for him, but the very opposite was the case. For the space of a heartbeat she had thought he was going to kiss her. More than that, she had *wanted* him to kiss her! Common sense seemed suddenly to have deserted her completely, leaving behind the sort of wanton little fool who usually dismayed sensible Annabel Gresham of Perton House.

The shop was very quiet after the bustle of the alley, and smelled of violets, or so she thought. In an effort to regain her composure she made a pretense of examining the labels on the little dark oak drawers that stretched from floor to ceiling, the topmost requiring the assistance of a stool if one wished to open them. She kept an eye on the shopwindow, fearing to see Richard again. There was tomorrow night's dinner invitation to consider, for no matter what she had said about crying off, in her heart she knew she had no choice but to go.

She opened one of the drawers, and at last realized which shop she was in. Immediately, she turned to look at the assistant behind the dark oak counter, expecting to see a woman who might be Molly's aunt, Mrs Smith, but to her great shock she saw instead a very effeminate, wasp-waisted young man. He wore a vermilion coat and voluminous vermilion-and-white-striped neckcloth, but although he no doubt believed the two vermilions were identical, to her eyes there was a subtle difference that turned the mixture into a disagreeable clash. Most certainly he was not Mrs Smith, even though he was prinked and painted, and the scent of violets that pervaded the shop she now realized was emanating from his direction.

Annabel had never seen such a personage before, and found it very difficult not to stare, but she was mindful of her manners and made herself continue with the examination of the drawers. As haberdasheries went, this one was very well stocked indeed, although much of what it supplied was of as dubious a nature as the young man. It did not take a great leap of the imagination to guess that Mrs Smith catered for the demimonde. With hindsight, Annabel wished she had not chosen to cross this particular threshold, but the deed was done now, and to leave again would be to risk bumping into Richard. Common sense told her to return to the Dog and Duck immediately, but she was still desperately curious about the veiled woman. *Where had she gone? King Street? One of the shops?*

Annabel opened another drawer, and with

a start saw that it contained a selection of sequinned masks and little veiled dominoes. Surely this was fate! Again her words to Toby had returned. *What do you suggest? That I march boldly into every bawdy house in St James's and dismantle all candlesticks until I find the right one?* She also remembered what Toby himself had said. *Well, it is Juno's rule, and the rule of some of the other abbesses, that all the nuns wear masks or dominos.*

She sorted through the drawer for something that would go well with her aquamarine gown, and as luck would have it there was a domino that was almost an exact match. It comprised a dainty little eye-mask with a short gauze veil that would hide the lower half of the wearer's face. In a moment the item had been purchased from the effeminate young man, who eyed her as if she had trodden in something horrid. Annabel found him most perplexing, for he seemed neither one sex nor the other.

Pausing for a moment or so by the counter, she tried to fit her acquisition safely into her reticule, but it was a rather tight squeeze because a generous square of brown paper wrapping had been used. The assistant watched her as if she were a fumbling imbecile, and made no attempt at all to help. She was still thus employed when the shop door opened and a young lady in mauve lawn came in.

'Hello, Freddie,' she said to the assistant.

'Oh, it's you,' he replied in a bored tone.

She nodded. 'How observant you are. Are there any letters for me?'

He was displeased. 'Well, I'll look if I must.'

'I'm afraid you must, Freddie, for how else are we going to find out?' the young woman replied cheekily.

'What number are you?' he inquired, giving her the same wrinkle-nosed glance he had Annabel.

'Twenty, if you please.'

With a theatrical sigh he minced through a doorway at the back of the shop, and the young woman immediately turned to Annabel. 'Freddie is always so glad to see the fair sex, is he not? A warm welcome every time, and no mistake.'

Freddie returned. 'Here you are,' he said, and placed two letters on the counter. They were both addressed to Mrs Smith, and the number twenty was neatly marked in the corners, just as fourteen had been on Molly's letter.

'I was expecting three,' the young woman said.

'Expect what you like, ducks, but there are still only two!' he replied.

'Are you sure you searched properly?'

To Annabel's astonishment he stamped his foot. 'If I tell you there are only two, that is exactly what I mean!'

'All right, all right, don't get in a pet. I'll call again tomorrow.' The young woman pretended to blow him a loving kiss, then left.

Freddie pouted after her. 'Uppity mare,' he muttered, and began to examine his finger-nails again.

Annabel had retreated from the counter, but not from the shop because she was curious about the business of the numbered letters. It was almost as if the haberdashery was some kind of *poste restante*. That being so, Molly's missive to her aunt began to appear in a different light. Just how many nieces could this Mrs Smith possibly have?

'Can I help you?' Freddie demanded suddenly, eyeing her with disapproval as she stood in thought.

'I . . . I beg your pardon?'

He tutted. 'Can I be of any more assistance?'

'Er, no, thank you.' She made for the door. *Assistance?* He had barely brought himself to give her the time of day. This being so, she decided to dent his vanity a little. Returning to the counter, she leaned across to flick his neckcloth. 'A little advice, sir. The color on *this* item does not rest at all easily with the color of *this* item.' She flicked his lapel. 'To be truthful, the two are waging war in a most unsettling way, and I think you should change one or the other before you reduce someone to a bilious attack.'

Affront registered large upon his painted face as she swept triumphantly from the haberdashery. When she stepped out to the alley again, her intention was to return to the safety of the Dog and Duck without further scrape, but then fate took another hand in things. Who but her mysterious veiled woman should leave the florist's opposite, carrying an enormous bunch of pink roses known as Maiden's Blush. Annabel knew the name because there were several bushes at Perton House. The sanctuary of the Dog and Duck immediately ceased to matter as she followed the woman toward King Street, where stood Almack's, the most exclusive and superior assembly rooms in all England.

Annabel did not aspire to Almack's, of which she had anyway heard unfavorably from Sir Humphrey and Lady Smythe-Castle, and right now it could hardly be said that balls were uppermost in her mind! The woman walked along the southern pavement past Nerot's Hotel and the entrance to Angel Court, then vanished beneath an archway that separated Almack's from the Golden Lyon tavern.

The moment the woman disappeared from sight, Annabel caught up her skirts to hurry after her, and on reaching the archway, which apparently led through into a court of some sort, glanced up and saw the name King's Place! Taking a long breath, she peeped into the archway, then drew sharply back again because only a few yards away the woman was in conversation with none other than Sir Richard Tregerran!

Annabel knew the wisest course would be to hurry away immediately, but curiosity held her there. She simply *had* to observe them for a while, maybe even hear a little of their conversation if she listened carefully enough. Very tentatively indeed she peeped around the corner again. The woman had raised her veil, but her back was still toward King Street so that, infuriatingly, her face remained a mystery. However, she was clearly well acquainted with Richard, who was all gallantry and smiles as they chatted. Unfortunately, their voices did not carry far, so Annabel had no idea at all what was said, but after a minute or so she could tell that he was offering to escort the woman wherever she was going. He relieved her of the roses and her purchase from the Piccadilly print shop, then they strolled into King's Place, a former stableyard now containing residences that were among the most notorious addresses in all London. At one time the only access had been from King Street, but the building of the houses had resulted in a seven-feet-wide way being opened into Pall Mall.

Watched by Annabel, Richard and the woman walked toward a three-storey house that had balconies at the upper windows and a pedimented green door approached up four steps. He then returned the purchases, kissed his companion's hand very dashingly, and departed toward Pall Mall. The woman remained on the doorstep when he had gone, and Annabel watched her most attentively, for it was almost as if she were apprehensive about knocking. From the way she bowed her head for a moment, then raised it again, it was clear she had taken a deep breath to compose herself, for then she reached out to rap the brass knocker.

A liveried black footman answered almost immediately. Annabel presumed he must be Claudius, whom Toby had mentioned. She saw the startled look on his face as he saw who stood there. He glanced uneasily back inside, then shook his head at the woman, who pleaded with him. His quandary was great, but at last he gave in, and allowed the woman to enter. Then the door closed.

Annabel did not linger anymore, but decided the time had definitely come to return to the Dog and Duck.

10

Things did indeed seem slightly better in the morning, as Toby had said they would, but unanswered questions still crowded uncomfortably on all sides. At dinner that night Annabel intended to pump Richard about the veiled woman. She would do it subtly, of course, although exactly how was still in the realm of the unknown.

However, it was the whereabouts of the stolen documents that was uppermost in her mind. It was true that she had now walked through parts of St James's, and that she knew where to find King's Place, but that was *all* she knew. The Indian candlesticks might be in any number of bordellos, so she needed to see much more of the area. Why she felt this urge she really did not know, for she could hardly don the domino and invade every single one. Not that she was feeling quite as resolute about the domino plan this morning. Maybe it was the cold, sobering light of day.

Nevertheless, her conscience wouldn't allow her to sit back and do nothing at all, and since a navigation of St James's was the only inspiration she had at the moment, she intended to press ahead with it. But, oh, the whole thing was so difficult, she thought. Her experience on the corner of Pav'd Alley had proved Toby correct in forbidding her to walk alone in that particular part of town, so she decided to take a growler. But that still left the problem of where to look. The houses in King's Place all seemed eminently respectable, and yet she knew they weren't. So how would she know which address was to be properly noted? She would have to remind Toby about a list, and that would inevitably mean meeting with his opposition. Still, she would try. And she would be very careful indeed not to let slip that she had been out the previous evening.

She announced her intention concerning a growler as she and Toby took a very early breakfast. The morning sunshine of Piccadilly was bright and clear, and Toby had been enjoying his deviled kidneys until that moment. He put his knife and fork down with a clatter. 'A growler? You can't do that!'

'Why ever not?'

'Because I don't want you going anywhere alone, even in a hackney coach. It really isn't safe, you know.'

Guilt warmed her cheeks, as well as annoyance that he seemed intent upon blocking any suggestion, so she took refuge in attack. 'You are quite impossible, Toby Vernon. I don't notice *you* supplying any useful hints as to how to proceed!' She got up from her scrambled eggs before she gave in to the temptation to tip the plate over his infuriating head.

He watched as she began to pace up and down, the train of her peach cotton morning gown hissing over the floorboards. 'Annie, I just have your well-being at heart, that's all. Growlers may be safer than walking, but even so, I don't want my sister driving around St James's in one. Some of them are a little disreputable, you know.'

'Do you suggest I go to the expense of hiring another post chaise?' She was at her most acid.

'No, of course not.'

'Then what *do* you suggest? That we sit here like Nero and twiddle our thumbs while Rome burns?'

'Nero fiddled, not twiddled.'

She rounded on him. 'This isn't funny!'

'All right, all right . . . ' He tossed his napkin on to the table and eased himself up from his chair. His bruises had improved even more, but he had slept so awkwardly that he now had a stiff neck as well. Feeling sorry for himself, he hobbled to a comfortable armchair and sat down gingerly. 'Oh, do stop pacing like that, Annie, you're making me giddy.'

'Good.'

'Thank you for the sympathy.'

She halted. 'And you think you deserve sympathy?' she inquired in a tone that warned him to think very carefully indeed before answering.

'Annie, I know this disaster is all my fault, but I'd rather you didn't rub it in. Be fair now, if you were me, would you think your going alone in a growler was a good idea?'

'Yes.' But she hesitated.

'Ha!' he cried, pouncing upon the moment of thought. 'You see? You aren't so sure yourself. Look, if you will just wait another day, I'm sure I will be up to escorting you, then all will be well.'

'Another day? I cannot do with delays, Toby, I want to start now.' It was at this moment that the ultimate solution presented itself to her. 'I know, I will ask Mrs Ferguson to provide me with a maid.'

'A maid . . . ?' Toby pondered this, then shrugged. 'Well, if you must you must, I suppose. It would certainly satisfy propriety.'

'Good. I'll go down to speak to her right now — '

'I'd rather we asked her to come up here.'

Annabel turned. 'Why?'

'If you ask her downstairs, who knows who might overhear? I don't want the world and his wife to know you intend to tour the nunneries of St James's! It's a little questionable to say the least, and maid or not, your reputation might suffer if it got out.'

'Right now I care less than a fig about my reputation. It's my future that concerns me. Father can have another new will drawn up, but the codicil is irreplaceable. I have to recover it, otherwise I am going to be a burden to you. Or hadn't you thought of that?' Annabel eyed him.

'Of course I've thought about it, and you would never be a burden, Annie. I would be glad to have you beneath my roof.' Toby was indignant that she would think he'd ever view her in a such a light.

'Maybe, but you are bound to marry one day, and I doubt if your wife will wish to have a penniless half sister as a millstone around both your necks.' Annabel went to the door. 'Nevertheless, I think you are right about speaking to Mrs Ferguson up here, for the fewer people who know our business the better.' She was thinking of Richard as she said this, for his acquaintance with the veiled woman nagged a little at the back of her mind. Was he quite the Good Samaritan he purported to be? she wondered.

Mrs Ferguson came at Annabel's request. Today she wore bottle green linen, and the frills on her day bonnet bounced as she entered. 'Well, good morning to you, Mr Vernon, Miss Gresham. I trust all is in order?' she inquired in a tone as bright as the nosegay of marigolds pinned to her bodice.

'Oh, yes, indeed,' Toby replied immediately, struggling to rise from his armchair again.

The woman waved him to remain seated. 'Please do not disturb yourself, sir, for I know you are not well. Now then, Miss Gresham, you said you had a favor to ask?' She turned to Annabel.

Annabel, who was already seated, indicated another chair. 'Please join us, Mrs Ferguson.'

The innkeeper subsided gratefully onto the sofa, for she had been on her feet for several hours. 'How may I help, Miss Gresham?'

'I wonder if it would be possible to borrow one of your maids this morning?'

'Borrow? For what purpose, exactly?' The question was asked lightly, but the underlying note of curiosity bordered on suspicion.

Annabel had an innocent fabrication ready, but inexplicably and to her horror found herself blurting the truth. 'Because I must make a circuit of a number of houses of ill repute in St James's. I intend to take a

103

hackney coach for this, but my brother is still too bruised to escort me, and he does not wish me to be alone, even in a vehicle.'

Toby gaped at her, then groaned and leaned his head back resignedly. Mrs Ferguson blinked as if she had just heard a confession of high treason, but at length she recovered. 'And why, may I ask, is it necessary to go around to such places?'

Annabel continued to be frank. 'Because Toby was robbed of certain important documents in one of these places — the premises of Juno Wyatt, actually — and they were subsequently hidden in a candlestick, possibly in the same house, possibly in another. I need to retrieve those papers, one of which is particularly vital to me.'

Feeling under attack, Toby pulled himself hastily to his feet. 'Mrs Ferguson, before you think the worst of me, let me assure you that I went there to play faro!'

The innkeeper smiled. 'Oh, I am sure you did, sir.'

'I *did*, I tell you!' He stomped angrily into his bedroom and slammed the door behind him.

Mrs Ferguson smiled at Annabel. 'They all say that, of course.'

'Yes, I imagine they do.' Annabel returned the smile. 'Mrs Ferguson, I will tell you everything, so you will understand why the one document is of such consequence.' She described her family background and told the story of the codicil's theft and concealment in the unknown bawdy house. As it happened, she did not at this point actually describe the rather unusual candlesticks being sought. If she had, the answer to their whereabouts would have been revealed almost immediately. Nor did she mention her excursion alone the evening before, or her secret plans for the domino. The fewer people who knew about these things, the better! But she did speak of the curricle gentleman and his veiled companion, because of the former's strong likeness to Boskingham.

Mrs Ferguson listened intently, then drew a long breath. 'Well, my dear, you certainly have a task, do you not? Not least being the fact that Lord Mavor is your half brother.'

'You know him?'

'Oh, yes, I know him, and a very unamiable fellow he is, if you don't mind me saying.'

'Say away, for I am in hearty agreement,' Annabel replied.

'I confess I was a little dismayed when your brother received a visit from the equally unamiable Mr Boskingham, who is Lord Mavor's closest crony. Boskingham is not the sort of man I wish to have beneath my roof, because he is known for his, er, light fingers.'

'I wish Toby had known it,' Annabel said with feeling.

Mrs Ferguson smiled. 'To return to the matter of touring St James's in a hackney coach. My dear, maid or not, you cannot possibly enter the houses you refer to, so I cannot really see what purpose will be served by looking at them from the outside. You are exceedingly unlikely to see a bedroom candlestick from the street.'

Annabel smiled ruefully. 'I know, I'm just hoping a brilliant idea will occur to me, I suppose.'

Mrs Ferguson got up slowly, and for a moment Annabel thought she was going to turn down the request, but to her surprise the opposite was the case, although not regarding the maid. 'I will help you all I can, my dear, but a maid will not do.'

'Oh, but — '

'I will accompany you myself, Miss Gresham,' the woman interrupted gently.

'You?'

Mrs Ferguson smiled wryly. 'I was born and brought up an innkeeper's daughter, Miss Gresham, which is how I know the trade so well. As well as the Dog and Duck I will soon take over the Peach Tree in Marylebone, a popular country tavern and tea garden, which will be mine the moment the present lessee retires at the end of this summer. However, in between my childhood and the acquisition of the Dog and Duck, there were many years when I followed a very different vocation. The fact is that I know rather more about houses of, er, civility than you realize, because it was with the proceeds of just such an establishment that I acquired this hostelry. I fear I was an . . . abbess.'

Annabel was shaken. 'You ran a . . . a — ?'

'*Une maison de tolérance?* Yes, my dear, I did, and very respectable it was, too.'

'Respectable?' Annabel repeated incredulously.

Mrs Ferguson nodded. 'Oh, well you might eye me in that way, but it's the truth. Nothing devious or underhand went on beneath my roof it was all as honest as could be. I was known for my rather recherché summer *bals d'amour*, not for purchasing poor orphan girls barely into their teens, or forcing anyone to become one of my lovelies if she did not wish to.'

Annabel could not help wondering what went on at those *bals d'amour*. Perhaps it was better for a demure young lady not to know!

Mrs Ferguson went on. 'My girls were all willing and happy to be with me. I ran a good salon, and when anyone wished to leave my protection, she was allowed to go. For that very reason there were precious few who ever left me, and those who did were wont to come back from time to time as it pleased them.'

'And . . . and now you run the Dog and Duck?' Annabel began to wonder about the inn. 'Does my brother know you were . . . ?'

'He may if someone has informed him, but somehow I think he does not.' Mrs Ferguson chuckled again. 'Oh, my dear, I can read you like a book. There is nothing going on here. It is all that a good inn should be.'

'If you mean it's respectable, that's how you described your other, er, premises,' Annabel reminded her.

'Well, respectable when said of an inn means one thing, when said of an academy of love, it means something else entirely.'

'I hope so.'

The woman still chuckled. 'My dear Miss Gresham, you do not need to fear any stigma because you have stayed here. That much I can definitely promise you. Now then, knowing the shocking truth about me, do you wish to take up my offer? I shall quite understand if you do not, for your present and my past are rather like oil and water, but I come from that world and I have many contacts there still. I believe I can be of great assistance.'

'I gladly accept your kind offer, Mrs Ferguson, for I need to regain that codicil very much indeed. I could not bear to be thrown out of my home, or to impose myself upon Toby for a roof over my head. I wish to be as independent as I can.'

'And for that I respect you immensely, my dear. It is settled then. You and I will drive out later in my private chariot, and I will show you all the streets, alleys, and courts a lady should not know.'

'You are very kind, Mrs Ferguson.'

'And you are very spirited, Miss Gresham. Most young women in your situation would have resigned themselves to a future of dependency upon relatives, but you are fighting against such a fate. I vow that you would indeed have been a favorite if you had been one of my nuns.'

Annabel colored. 'Would I?'

'Oh, yes. You can take my word for it.' Mrs Ferguson got up. 'I have one or two things to attend to right now, but I can be ready in about an hour. Will that suit?'

'It will suit very well, but please do not put yourself out unduly, for I am quite able to wait.'

'I am glad to help you, Miss Gresham.'

'Thank you very much.'

'Thank me when we are successful in

locating the missing codicil, my dear, not before. By the way, I cannot abide being addressed as Mrs Ferguson, because the late mister of that name was a drunken curmudgeon of whom I am well rid. I prefer to simply be called Hester.' Mrs Ferguson went out and closed the door softly behind her.

11

Annabel changed into the sky blue pelisse and café-au-lait gown she had traveled in the day before. Overnight she had refreshed both garments by brushing and smoothing them carefully, and had then hung them on a picture rail close to an open window, with lavender bags pinned inside. Now they felt and looked good enough for a drive in London.

Toby did not know of Hester's colorful history, and on being told was of a mind not only to forbid Annabel to go out with the former convent-keeper, but to remove to another inn as well. Annabel wouldn't countenance such things, and told him so in no uncertain terms. She reminded him that the fix was his fault in the first place, and that she was not prepared to let him persist in confounding all attempts to rectify the situation. This silenced him, although as she left the rooms, he was still muttering darkly about a complete lack of propriety.

Hester's town chariot was very smart, with fine maroon lacquer and highly polished brass embellishments that would not have been amiss on a carriage belonging to the nobility. Drawn by two high-stepping black horses, it drew a number of admiring glances as it emerged from the Dog and Duck yard into Piccadilly, but instead of turning east for St James's Street as Annabel anticipated, the coachman turned west toward Hyde Park Corner. She immediately turned to Hester in surprise. 'Aren't we going the wrong way?'

'For St James's, yes. For Hyde Park, no.'

'Hyde Park? Oh, but — '

'But me no buts, my dear, for it is where the most sought-after high impures are to be seen, both riding and driving. I was once the toast of the park in my bright yellow vis-à-vis, with a reputation for being the most furious whip of all, not, I hasten to add, because I beat my horses, but because I cut a dash to end all dashes. I was a fast woman in more ways than one! Ah, those were indeed the days.' Hester gazed out at the street with a wistful look in her fine dark eyes.

'I would have liked to see you then,' Annabel said.

Hester smiled. 'I would have given today's beauties a run for their money, I can tell you. Except perhaps Juno Wyatt. Now *she* is a great impure, but I cannot approve of some of her practices. She may be regarded as today's princess of procuresses, and a courtesan *par excellence*, but she has a heart of stone. However, that does not detract from her beauty. She has the most fiery red hair I ever saw, and to go with it the palest, most flawless of skins. Not a freckle to behold. It's a pity her eyes are not green, for that would have been perfect, but she has to make do with a sort of tawny hazel that can look quite dull in certain lights.'

'Will you show me her address?' That it was in King's Place Annabel already knew, but not which house.

'Of course, but all in good time. Heavens, these sewer works are tiresome. I vow the authorities always make a point of waiting until the weather is hot before commencing dirty, smelly excavations.' Hester was seated opposite Annabel, and wore a navy blue pelisse and oyster gown. On her head there was a jaunty wide-brimmed hat tied on with wide navy ribbons, and she looked every inch a lady. Certainly it was impossible to tell she had such a shocking history. Now she surveyed Annabel seriously. 'When we join the parade in the park, I will point out any lady of interest, that you may see the sort of lovelies who haunt the more superior houses. Do not for a moment think they are anything like the common streetwalkers of areas like Whitechapel, for nothing could be further from the truth. These are ladies to their pretty finger-tips, fascinating, witty, and very, very skilled at what they do. Why else do you imagine London's gentlemen are prepared to pay so handsomely for their time?'

Richard's face flashed before Annabel's eyes.

Hester continued. 'Ah, we are at the corner. I have instructed my man not to enter the park at this point, but to drive up Park Lane to the Grosvenor Gate. The indoor Gloucester Riding School is situated just inside. Ladies of the kind in which we are interested are particularly given to preening there.'

The chariot went north along Park Lane to the gate, where a considerable number of other vehicles and riders were arriving and leaving. Once inside, the formal display of fashion began almost immediately, although in the mornings it was not quite so lavish as in the afternoons. Nevertheless, a brilliant procession moved into the railed way that led south again between the boundary wall and the riding school Hester had mentioned. The school was an impressive brick and slate building some one hundred and twenty feet long, and on its far side there was a circular reservoir owned by the Chelsea Water Company. The reservoir was surrounded by a double avenue of elms that had been planted in the time of Queen Anne, and shaded the railed way as well as the water.

Four-in-hands, landaus, barouches, and curricles were well represented, all of them glinting in the sunshine, all of them drawn by excellent horses. There were phaetons, too, mostly driven by bucks and dandies, but some had ladies at the ribbons. These ladies Annabel now saw in a rather different light. Hester's information also made her more cautious about the lady riders, especially those around the riding school, for the prettier and more stylish they were, the more likely it seemed that they too might be fashionable courtesans.

As soon as the chariot had joined the throng, Hester pointed out one of these equestriennes, a dainty figure in a white riding habit trimmed with bright blue braiding, mounted on a pristine white horse. She was a brunette with a heart-shaped face of quite exquisite beauty, but a certain coolness of expression. Her figure, pinched in at the waist and pushed out at the bosom, was all that was enviable, and she wore her little beaver hat at such a jaunty angle that Annabel wondered how many pins were required to prevent it from sliding off.

'That is Petra Fenston,' Hester said. 'She

commenced her fortunes in a small seraglio above a haberdashery in Pav'd Alley. But then someone, Juno Wyatt is suspected, reported the premises to the authorities — an important member of which just happened to be one of her own most ardent clients! Juno claimed there was something particularly disgraceful going on there, and a great fuss ensued. It ended with the haberdashery being obliged to confine its activities to the sale of ribbons, buttons, and so on. It was all sheer jealousy on Juno's part, because Petra was attracting the attention of a gentleman in whom Juno herself was interested.'

Annabel listened intently.

Hester continued about Petra Fenston. 'Then she was discovered by Lord Craven, who made her his mistress, although now I gather she is too old for him and he is casting his net for a new inamorata, preferably of about fifteen.'

Annabel deplored the idea that any man could desire such young girls. She gazed at the figure in white. 'But she is so extraordinarily beautiful that I cannot imagine she would lose her place to anyone, let alone a fifteen-year-old!'

'Miss Gresham, it is not only for beauty that a man takes a mistress. I gather Petra is not exactly, er, passionate, shall we say. She is rumored to be as cool as she appears.'

'Oh.'

Hester smiled. 'I am embarrassing you, am I not? But I fear that the world about which you are now so interested is very different from the one that you have inhabited hitherto. Very different indeed.'

'I am beginning to understand that, Hester. I am a very green country girl, I fear.'

'That is not to be regarded as a fault, Miss Gresham. Now then, if you look over there, just beyond the trees, you will see another young lady, this time in scarlet on a rather unusual piebald horse. Do you see her?'

'Yes, of course.' The lady had coal black hair and a figure that could only be described as resembling an hourglass. The neckline of her riding habit jacket plunged shockingly low, and her snowy chest seemed about to leap to freedom. Hester eyed her thoughtfully. 'Hmm, she is a brash piece, and no mistake. I do not know who she is, but I can tell you that without a doubt her favors can be purchased.'

'Maybe she is just a lady of questionable morals,' Annabel pointed out.

Hester chuckled wryly. 'My dear, it takes a fee-charging whore to know one.'

The chariot moved slowly south toward Hyde Park Corner, which was the main

117

entrance to the park, where the crush became even worse as more and more people joined the parade. Annabel was so intent upon watching it all that she almost forgot the reason she was here, but suddenly Hester touched her arm.

'There is Juno Wyatt herself!'

'Where?'

'In that rather amazing pink vis-à-vis. I haven't seen it before — it must be new. Bright pink, what a master-stroke.'

Annabel stared at the phaeton, which was drawn by two chestnut horses in pink leather harness. Juno Wyatt herself was as eyecatching as her vehicle, if not more so, for she scorned to wear a hat and her flame red hair fell about her shoulders. She wore pink to match the vis-à-vis, and was altogether the brightest of sights as she maneuvered the light vehicle expertly past other vehicles into the carriage road. Then she gave a flick of the whip and tooled the team away at speed, setting the dust flying.

Hester pursed her lips. 'Ah, the woman knows well how to put on a great show.'

And how to hold disgraceful auctions, Annabel thought.

The other noticed the expression flit briefly over her face. 'What is it, my dear?'

'Oh, nothing . . . '

'Come now, it is clear that something is on your mind. Does it concern Juno?'

'Well, yes.' Annabel told her about the auction, which she had omitted to mention when she had first confided in Hester.

'Ah, an auction. I have never approved of such things, and I certainly never held one at my establishment. Sir Richard Tregerran was the highest bidder, you say?'

'Yes.'

Hester pursed her lips thoughtfully. 'It does not sound like him, but if Mr Gresham was there, he must know.'

'Toby is quite clear on the point. Sir Richard and Mr Boskingham were bidding against each other until Mr Boskingham's funds ran out.'

'Then it must be so.'

'Hester, how well do you know Sir Richard?'

'Oh, reasonably well, I suppose. He dines at the Dog and Duck occasionally.'

Annabel was embarrassed to ask the next question, but she wanted to know. 'Did he come to your, er, premises?'

'From time to time, but he did indeed come to play faro and hazard. I vow some of my girls would have given him their favors *gratis* just for the pleasure of his attentions. He is the sort of fellow who will never lack female company.'

'That is how I would have thought of him, but nevertheless he indulged in an auction,' Annabel said.

'So it seems.'

'Toby thinks him all that is noble and to be admired,' Annabel said.

'Well, I cannot say I disagree with your brother, Miss Gresham. Sir Richard may have fallen from grace concerning this auction business, but apart from that I think him one of the most excellent fellows in town. Juno Wyatt set her cap at him a while back, but he was not interested. Now, if you will forgive the vulgarity, she slips between the sheets with your half brother, Mavor.' Hester glanced out of the chariot window and spotted Juno Wyatt driving back toward them. 'Ah, here she comes now. I am of a mind to prod her a little, for it's such excellent sport. Pay attention, Miss Gresham, for you are about to learn how to become the most of a feline in creation.'

Before Annabel knew it, Hester had leaned out of the chariot to instruct the coachman to halt. Then she waved to the dashing courtesan, who immediately stopped the pink vis-à-vis alongside.

12

Annabel's first impression was that Toby was right to say Juno Wyatt looked at least ten years younger than her true age. She was all in pink, an unbuttoned spencer over a matching gown that had a neckline that threatened to banish respectability altogether. And to draw even more attention to her admittedly splendid bosom, a jeweled gold watch was pinned to the center of what passed for the gown's bodice. Her red hair seemed ablaze in the bright sunshine, and there was rouge on her cheeks and lips. She was a very lovely trollop, Annabel decided, well able to believe that Juno attracted someone like Roderick.

Clearly not expecting a pleasant conversation, Juno's tawny hazel eyes rested warily upon Hester. 'Well now, I trust this day finds you in fine feather?' Her gaze moved to Annabel, who made sure her head was at a tilt so that her hat cast as much shadow as possible.

'Fine enough, Juno, fine enough,' Hester replied sweetly. 'How goes it *chez* Wyatt?'

'Excellently.'

'Is that so? Fame has it that you are now reduced to parading with your stable in the St James's Park enclosure. Times must indeed be bad.'

'I have never paraded in St James's Park!' The mere suggestion clearly stung very sharply indeed.

Hester evinced surprise. 'Really? As I recall, that is where you commenced your career. Up against a tree in the Mall like any desperate milliner.'

Juno gave her a poisonous look. 'The trees in the Mall were worn away in ages past by *your* exertions, Hester,' she fired back.

'Well, what a thing to say. *Ages* past? Fie on you! There are two years between us, if that. In my favor, too, I fancy.' Hester brushed an imaginary speck of dust from her spotless sleeve.

Still the acid flowed. 'How you do flatter yourself, my dear,' Juno replied. 'You may be sound in wind and limb, but you are an old nag now.'

'An old nag who was wise enough to retire while she was still a favorite, and still able to remain in full command. Whereas according to one scandal sheet, you are now reduced to pandering the uncommon diversions for those of, er, rare taste.'

'And what, precisely, do you mean by that?'

'Well, de Sade would feel quite at home in your salon, would he not?'

'That is a monstrous lie!' cried Juno, nostrils flaring with outrage.

'Oh. Then it must be the other scandal sheet that has the real facts.'

'Real facts?'

Hester smiled. 'Yes, my dear. It printed a hilarious anecdote concerning your exploits with that regular order you've placed with Gunter's for whipped fruit creams. I understand that spoons and dainty glass dishes are not required for the way *you* consume them.'

Juno colored unexpectedly. 'That too is a monstrous lie,' she said, but far from convincingly.

Annabel was filled with intense curiosity. How on earth did she eat fruit creams? she wondered naïvely.

Hester was enjoying herself immensely. 'So it's another monstrous lie? Come now, Juno, that is one too many. You know how they say horses for courses? Well, you and your fillies have completed almost every course imaginable, so it won't only be fruit creams!'

'I'll have you know that unlike yours, *my* salon is all that is proper!' Juno retorted.

Annabel lowered her glance. My, she thought, how these abbesses liked to pretend they were eligible for Almack's!

Hester sat forward a little. 'Proper? So it isn't true that you held an auction a night or so ago?'

Juno gazed at her. 'Quite untrue.'

'And Sir Richard Tregerran didn't make the highest bid?'

'I don't know what you're talking about. Oh, he removed one of my best girls to his house in Marylebone, for which I am very cross with him, but there was certainly not an auction.'

Hester raised an eyebrow. 'Removed her to his house? Your vanity must be pricked.'

'Whatever makes you say that?' Juno inquired airily, although Annabel noted how her fingers tightened on the reins.

'Everyone knows you still pant for Sir Richard,' Hester replied crushingly.

'That's utter nonsense.'

'Oh, what a barefaced fibber you are, Juno Wyatt. You and I both know that it was solely due to your failure with Tregerran that you turned your attentions to satisfying Lord Mavor's dubious desires.'

How horrid, Annabel thought, shuddering at the thought of a mere peck on the cheek from her elder brother, let alone anything more!

Hester was smiling. 'Ah, yes, no doubt you surrender yourself in the vain hope of getting a wedding band out of him.'

To Hester's surprise, the remark brought a smile to Juno's lips. 'My dear Hester, it is not a vain hope. He *will* marry me, make no mistake of that. I even have his word on it.'

Hester stared at her for a moment, then laughed. 'If Mavor has said that, you may be sure it is gammon. Thanks to his incompetent gambling, his finances are no longer as comfortable as he imagined, so it's an heiress he requires, not a faded whore who hasn't had the wit to put something by for the proverbial rainy day.'

Annabel could see that the barbs were finding a target, and she was almost sorry for Juno, but the feeling was short-lived. The auction loomed large, therefore the King's Place abbess did not warrant kind thoughts, any more than did Sir Richard Tregerran.

'Tell me, Juno,' Hester continued, 'is it true that you intend to celebrate Mavor's forthcoming birthday with another of your scandalous *bals d'amour?*'

Juno's simmering glance ought to have turned her to stone. 'Only half of that is true.'

'Which half? That you are to celebrate his forty-second birthday with a *bal d'amour*, or that your last such ball was shocking beyond belief?'

'Oh, I intend to celebrate his birthday in

style — in two days' time as it happens, when he will return from the Marine Pavilion in Brighton simply to spend the night with me.' Juno could not resist mentioning the Prince of Wales's fine seaside villa in the fashionable south coast watering place, for she wished to convey the impression that such a very proper connection with royalty brushed off upon her as well. She was, of course, well acquainted with the Prince of Wales, and indeed with all the other princes, but in a decidedly improper way. 'There is not to be a *bal d'amour* on this occasion, Hester. As to whether or not that last one was shocking beyond belief, well, I can only hope so, for that was most certainly the intention.'

'It was a disgraceful orgy, an exercise in licentious vulgarity that made even the scandal sheets squirm with embarrassment.'

Annabel was privately agog.

Juno's hand had crept to the gold watch, and Hester not only observed the gesture, but pounced upon it, 'Tut, tut, Juno, how could you be so remiss as to wear the hallmark of your profession in such an obvious way? Even Seven Dials streetwalkers aspire to such a bauble.'

'Clearly you forgot to pick up yours from the dressing-table this morning after your favorite ostler sneaked out. Was it lost behind the bucket of rhubarb pills?' Juno responded. Then her eyes moved to Annabel, who was too late in averting her face. 'Who is this, your latest vestal? Hm, a pretty enough piece, but hardly outstanding, and her clothes seem all that is proper, but what is she really? A dairymaid you've scrubbed clean of the byre?'

Annabel forgot anonymity for a moment to glare furiously at her. How dared the creature speak of her in such a way! Then she was immediately angry with herself as well because Juno had now seen her face rather too clearly for comfort, and — domino or not — that might prove awkward if the secret scheme was undertaken.

Hester flicked her sleeve again. 'Such spleen can only mean that my friend here would be a welcome new addition, Juno, for you know quality when you see it, even if you are far from it yourself.'

Juno parried taunt with taunt. 'If you are showing a new girl around, it can only mean that the Dog and Duck is after all nothing more than a common bawdy house. Well, I always knew its veneer of respectability would soon be proven thin to the point of transparency.'

Hester did not rise to the bait. 'That is all behind me now, Juno.'

'Our kind never retire, Hester. Once a

demirep, always a demirep.'

'This demirep is now a veritable Scripture reader,' Hester replied. 'I have given up whoring for a more agreeable life.'

'Agreeable?' Juno gave a mocking laugh. 'More likely it is a second-best life, resorted to because your looks paid the price of too much good food.'

'At least I no longer have to invite all and sundry to my bed to pay the bills.'

'No, because your great girth so fills said bed that all and sundry could not squeeze in!' Juno gathered her reins, then bestowed a favorable glance upon Annabel. 'My dear, you should come to me if you wish to go far. My door is open to you, for the Beldame Ferguson has long since lost her touch! Come for Lord Mavor's birthday, for on that night it will indeed be the more the merrier!' With that she flicked her whip, and in a moment the pink vis-à-vis had disappeared toward Hyde Park Corner.

Hester sat back, pleased. 'Oh, I do enjoy twitting her, for she is a very annoying creature. A superb whore, but a spitfire who needs the occasional dousing.' She gave a low chuckle. 'My dear Miss Gresham, can you imagine her as your sister-in-law! The stir she would cause in the polite society of Gloucestershire can only be imagined!'

Annabel smiled, but said nothing because she was thinking about Juno's casually issued invitation. Go to King's Place on the night of Roderick's birthday? Now there was a thought. But it would be too risky. Another night maybe, if she could find out when Roderick himself was elsewhere.

Hester didn't notice her pensive expression. 'It is good to unsheath my claws once in a while, especially when my adversary is someone like that.'

'I suppose it must be.' Annabel had found the catty confrontation quite an education, and considered both women to be equally formidable. Juno Wyatt had also shown herself to be quite capable of the auction she so blatantly denied. She and Roderick deserved each other. But when Juno said that Richard had taken one of her nuns to his Marylebone house, Annabel suspected she was telling the truth. No doubt he would have his acquisition hidden away there tonight while he wined and dined his guests, and when his guests had gone, he would enjoy his night revels.

Hester was thinking about the conversation. 'It seems I struck a nerve with the fruit creams,' she murmured.

'What *does* she do with them?' Annabel asked ingenuously.

Humor glinted in Hester's eyes as she beckoned to Annabel to lean forward, then whispered in her ear.

Annabel's breath caught with shock. 'Really?'

'Oh, yes. Believe me, my dear, you should try it sometime. Er, when you're married, of course.' Annabel sat back feeling very green and flustered.

She had no idea such things were done.

The chariot moved on again, and was soon driving beside the glittering Serpentine, where people were out in pleasure boats. It was there that the second park encounter took place, this time with Sir Richard Tregerran himself, who was enjoying a ride away from the crush of Rotten Row. The moment he saw Hester's chariot, he made a point of riding over.

13

Hester observed Richard approaching. 'Well, think of the devil and he is sure to appear,' she murmured.

Annabel hadn't seen him yet. 'What do you mean?' she asked.

'Sir Richard is coming over, and I can tell that he means to speak.'

Annabel was horrified, for he was bound to recognize her clothes from Pav'd Alley! 'Oh, no! Hester, I don't want him to see me! Please tell your coachman to drive on quickly!'

It was a foolish request because the chariot was temporarily caught up in a jam, which persuaded Hester to put another interpretation upon Annabel's panic. 'Be easy, my dear, for I am respectable now. Besides, Mr Vernon knows, so it is quite in order for you to be with me.'

'Please don't misunderstand, Hester, for this has nothing to do with you. I . . . I just don't wish to speak to Sir Richard, that's all. I don't want him to know who I am.'

'Not know who — ? My dear, he already knows you, so what difference does it make if you to speak to him now?'

'That's the point, Hester, he *doesn't* know me. I know he came to see Toby yesterday, but I hid in my bedroom before he could see me.'

'Why on earth did you do that?'

'Because I did not approve of the auction and feared I would give him a piece of my mind.'

Hester smiled then. 'I grant you have spirit enough for that. Well, it is going to be impossible to completely avoid him now.'

'I shall do my utmost!' Annabel fumbled with her hat, tilting it as far forward as she could without looking ridiculous. Why was fate so intent upon thrusting her into Sir Richard Tregerran's company at every turn? Luck had been with her yesterday — at least, she hoped it had — so to risk it again now was surely to test her luck a little too far!

Hester was all breezy brightness as Richard reined in. 'Why, Sir Richard, how very agreeable to see you!'

He smiled and doffed his tall hat, his body flexing to the capering of his impatient horse, a large black thoroughbred that looked fit to gallop all the way to Marylebone and back several times without pause. He wore white corduroy breeches and was dressed in the pine green riding coat that was *de rigueur* for gentlemen of *ton*. It had a velvet collar and velvet-covered buttons, and was worn with great elegance and style. A neckcloth of the palest green silk blossomed at his throat, with a tasteful gold pin on the knot, and shades of gold were picked out in the intricate pattern of his waistcoat.

'Well met, proud Hester,' he said with a warm smile, then his glance encompassed Annabel for a moment. Well, he thought, if it wasn't the highly intriguing *incognita* of Pav'd Alley, who had also, as he now belatedly remembered, been in Toby Vernon's rooms yesterday. At least, her hat had been in said rooms, so presumably the lady herself had been there, too. It now seemed more unlikely than ever that she could be Toby's sister from Gloucestershire, which left a rather more questionable alternative. It seemed she could not be a lady after all.

'I trust I find you well, Sir Richard?' Hester inquired.

'Very well indeed, as I see you are also. You don't grace the park often enough these days, Hester.'

She laughed. 'That is the price of propriety, Sir Richard. Earning a good character requires my almost constant presence at the inn.' Then to Annabel's horror, she went on. 'Allow me to introduce Miss Brown. My dear, this is Sir Richard Tregerran.'

Richard bowed forward to Annabel. 'Miss Brown,' he murmured.

'Sir Richard,' she replied in the same hoarse voice as the day before.

Hester gave a startled tinkle of laughter. 'Dear me, what a veritable corncrake we have here. I am afraid Miss Brown has a very sore throat, Sir Richard,' she explained.

'I'm sorry to hear that. I trust it is soon a thing of the past. Good authority has it that garlic is the best cure for such an affliction. Four or five raw cloves a day.'

Hester laughed again. 'Good heavens, Sir Richard, one would not wish to go anywhere near someone who had consumed so much!'

'That would certainly be a difficulty,' he agreed. Especially for a whore, he thought.

Annabel drew a deep breath, and forced herself to be objective about the situation. Even if he had seen her hat at the inn he was unlikely to associate her with Toby's sister, to whom he would expect to be politely introduced. Because she had hidden, he was more likely to think she was a demimondaine Toby had been entertaining! What else could he think after subsequently finding her first on a notorious St James's corner and now driving in the park with a former abbess! The Miss Greshams of the world did not do such things; at least, they ought not to! Annabel swallowed, hardly able to credit that she actually preferred him to think she was a denizen of somewhere like King's Place! Please let this be a nightmare, she thought, and let me wake up in a moment and find it hadn't happened at all.

To her relief Hester moved on to another subject. 'How is dear Miss Hensleigh keeping?' she asked Richard.

'Catherine? Well enough.'

Annabel wondered who Miss Hensleigh was, for the brevity of his reply indicated a desire not to talk about her.

Hester did not notice. 'Will she be coming out this Season? After all, she is such a great beauty, and an heiress as well, so I vow she will be the absolute belle of the year.'

'My sister-in-law has no desire to come out at the moment,' he replied.

Well, that explained who Catherine was, Annabel thought.

He continued. 'As it happens she has gone to stay with friends in Ireland.'

'*Ireland?*' Hester was taken aback. 'But I thought you said . . . Oh, no matter.'

'I know I said she was eager to take London by storm this summer, but she has changed her mind. A woman's prerogative, I fancy.'

'Indeed so, but it is a shame, for I was looking forward to following her progress. You must be very proud to be her guardian, for I am sure she will snare a duke at the very least. She must be all of eighteen now, yet when I think of what a shy little thing she was when I observed her in Bath . . . '

'As I recall, she was only twelve on that occasion.'

This time his tone was decidedly unencouraging, and at last Hester took the hint. 'Er, indeed, so. Well, who else have you encountered in the park today?'

He summoned a smile of sorts. 'Not quite the entire *monde*, but very close. Including your former arch-rival, Juno Wyatt. As it happens, I have just observed her, tooling the ribbons of her vis-à-vis like a crack whip on the Brighton road.'

'Yes, and very much in the pink as well,' Hester replied wryly.

His smile warmed. '*Une fille en rose*,' he murmured, then went on. 'Apropos of Juno, you will never guess who called upon her yesterday, with *Cuisse de Nymphe* in lieu of a pipe of peace.' He paused in some embarrassment, glancing again at Annabel, of whose morals he could not be entirely certain because the evidence that damned her was purely circumstantial. 'Maybe I should not speak of such things in front of . . . ?'

Hester was all reassurance. 'Oh, you may speak as you please, Sir Richard, there are no shrinking violets here.'

And he would make what he would of that statement! Annabel thought crossly, only just refraining from kicking her new friend on the ankle. But in truth she could not be entirely angry because she wanted to know more. For instance, what could Sir Richard possibly mean by *Cuisse de Nymphe*, which translated as 'nymph's thigh?'

Hester bade him continue. 'Who was Juno's caller?'

'A certain young woman who thought it necessary to purchase an entire florist's shop of Juno's favorite roses.'

Annabel's lips parted. Was the veiled woman about to be identified?

Hester was puzzled. 'Don't keep me hanging, Sir Richard. To whom are you referring?'

'Why, Molly Simmonds, of course.'

Annabel was absolutely thunderstruck. *Molly Simmonds?* Surely this could not be another person of that name? No, of course it wasn't, for the more she thought about it, the more she knew that the veiled woman was her Molly. The figure and mannerisms were all the same, and it was only because the maid had always worn plain and simple clothes at Perton House that the connection had not been made. And if the curricle man was indeed Boskingham ... The train of thought was severed as Hester suddenly uttered that very gentleman's name.

'Is Molly still Boskingham's *amour?*'

Richard shrugged. 'She said she had continued to see him after Mavor set her aside, but that it was now over with him as well because he had gone into exile to escape duns.'

Annabel listened with very startled ears indeed. Molly with Boskingham was bad enough, but to learn that the creature had been associated with Roderick as well was almost too much to cope with. Just what was going on? She pondered. Unsettling new facts seemed to be virtually clamoring on all sides!

'Do you believe her?' Hester asked him.

'I have no reason not to.'

'Molly Simmonds tell the truth? That will be the day, sir, that will be the day. You see, I too understood he had gone into very hasty exile, yet yesterday I heard of a gentleman in a green curricle who has been taken for him.'

'Yes, I've heard of this fellow as well, but I am convinced Boskingham is long gone.'

'Perhaps you are right. It would explain why Molly is seeking to worm her way back into Juno's favor. She needs a new protector.'

'Probably. Would you believe she had been employed as maid to a rather prim and dowdy gentlewoman somewhere in the wild hinterlands? I don't know who this woman was.'

Annabel's lips pressed furiously together. How dared Molly describe her in such a way! Still, it was some consolation that the creature hadn't actually mentioned her by name.

Hester was taken aback. 'Molly Simmonds a ladies' maid? I cannot believe it.'

'Nor I. However, she says she now longs to serve Venus once again. I warned her that another convent might be a wiser choice because Mavor and Juno are most definitely united, but she was set upon taking her chances. Nothing would do except that it was Juno's.'

Annabel's eyes were virtually fastened to the floor.

Hester gave a short laugh. 'I cannot imagine anyone less suited than Molly to be a ladies' maid, except perhaps Juno herself. Molly is far too impertinent and artful to be acceptable for such a position. Was she successful at Juno's?'

'I have no idea, for I left her on the doorstep.' Richard made to bring the meeting to a close. 'Well, I must toddle along, for I have an appointment in half an hour.' He doffed his tall hat again. 'À bientôt, Hester.'

'À bientôt, Sir Richard.'

He inclined his head to Annabel. 'Miss Brown.'

'Sir Richard,' that corncrake replied.

He wanted to be able to dismiss her as no better than she should be, but he couldn't. There was something about her that drew him, even when she adopted such a ridiculous false voice! He knew it was false, and as much an attempt to conceal her identity as her damned hat! So instead of simply riding off without another word, he addressed her again. 'I sincerely hope that when next we meet your throat will be full recovered.'

'You are too kind, sir.'

'And may I also venture to say that I hope that meeting will not be too far in the future?'

Hester looked quickly at him, and then at Annabel, for there was no mistaking the interest in his voice.

Annabel heard it, too, and felt her heart tighten with excitement. The urge to look him fully in the eyes was almost too much to withstand, but somehow she succeeded.

He tugged his hat on once more and rode

off, and Hester immediately glanced at her. 'I perceive there is a great deal you still have to tell me, miss,' she murmured, then leaned from the chariot to instruct the coachman to continue driving.

14

Annabel was no longer able to concentrate on the original reasons for the drive — the candlesticks and missing documents. She hardly heard anything Hester said as the chariot returned to St James's, where it completed a very comprehensive circuit of the houses of ill repute before finally drawing up at the curb in King Street, right next to the archway to King's Place.

Only then was Annabel able to direct her thoughts fully to the matter in hand. Because the chariot had halted, she thought they were going to alight, but Hester shook her head. 'No, my dear, for I can tell you all you need to know from here. Every house you see through this archway is dedicated to Venus, and the one with the green door — can you just see it? — is the Abbess Wyatt's convent.'

Annabel studied the house into which Molly Simmonds had been so reluctantly admitted. It seemed such an ordinary residence, yet it was really rather extraordinary. Everything recently had been extraordinary. Yet there was a thread, if only she could pick it up to follow, like Theseus in the Labyrinth.

But who was the Minotaur? Mr Boskingham? Molly? Roderick? Mayhap even Richard . . . ?

Hester was still speaking. 'Juno's entire house is given over to, er, business, except the top floor at the front, where her private rooms are. The arch hides them from here, but if you look carefully, you can just see the sills.' She chuckled. 'Oh, that enterprising lady has arranged some goings-on, I can tell you. For instance, if you wondered about my *bals d'amour*, let me say that they were puritan sermons compared with the ball she once held at the Roman Rooms in Oxford Street.'

'What happened?'

'Once inside the building, all persons who attended took off every stitch of clothing, except the orchestra, which played with its back to the floor to spare everyone's blushes.'

Annabel stared at her. 'Really?'

'Really.'

Annabel was speechless for a moment, but then thought of something else. 'Hester, you know when you spoke of Petra Fenton you mentioned a haberdashery in Pav'd Alley? What else do you know about it?'

'Know? Well, that it is much used for the collection of letters. Many of the girls from King's Place and other such addresses have their letters sent there because they do not wish their families and so on to know their true occupation. You see, even the most proper gentlemen are inclined to recognize addresses they should not, so the girls claim instead to work for Mrs Smith, or that she is a relative. It is such a wide-spread practice that identification numbers have to be put on the letters to ensure they are received by the correct person!'

'I thought so!'

Hester raised an eyebrow. 'Clearly you are about to tell me something,' she observed. 'Would I be right in presuming it is connected with Sir Richard?'

'No, as far as I know he has nothing to do with the haberdashery, but there is something about him that I haven't told you.' Annabel shifted a little guiltily.

'You and he had met before today after all, hadn't you?'

'In a manner of speaking, although I'm certain he doesn't know who I really am. It happened last night, but not at the inn. You see, I was following the veiled lady we now know is Molly Simmonds, when I — '

Hester held up a hand. 'You were *following* Molly? Do I take it that you were alone?'

'Yes.'

The older woman was appalled. 'Why on earth were you so foolhardy? What could Mr Vernon have been thinking of!'

'Toby didn't know because he was asleep when I left.'

'Anything might have happened to you alone in London, Miss Gresham, so you must promise you will never do anything so reckless again.'

'I promise,' Annabel said, trying not to think of the domino.

'Very well, please go on. You were telling me how you met Sir Richard.'

'Yes. It came about because I followed Molly. I had to follow her, Hester. She seemed so familiar that I couldn't help myself. I now know why she was familiar. You see, she is my maid, and is supposed to be back in Gloucestershire!'

'*Your* maid?' Hester's eyes widened as she recalled what Richard had said about Molly's country mistress.

'Yes, I am the person to whom she apparently referred to so disparagingly as the rather prim and dowdy gentlewoman somewhere in the wild hinterlands. She has been — or rather was — with me for about a month.'

'I . . . I don't know what to say.'

'There is nothing to say, except that she was a very impudent creature. Why, she even gave Toby a letter to take to the haberdashery, for all the world as if *he* was the servant!

145

Anyway, it's beside the point, for I was explaining about my meeting with Sir Richard. I was following Molly when Roderick apprehended me on the corner of Pav'd Alley and St James's Street, and — '

Hester threw up her hands in fresh dismay. 'You loitered on that corner? My dear, the only women found there are streetwalkers!'

'I realize that now. However, that is how I met Sir Richard. He rescued me from Roderick, who ran off at the first chance. I remained, and was obliged to speak to Sir Richard for a while. But I did not let him see my face, and I spoke in the same croaky voice I used in Hyde Park, so I'm certain he has no idea who I really am. After I had left him, I saw Molly again and followed her. She came through this alley, where I saw her talking to him, just as he described in the park.'

'Is there anything else you are omitting to tell me?' Hester asked a little dryly.

'No. Truly.'

'I'm relieved to hear it, for to be sure your conduct has not been praiseworthy.'

'I know.' Annabel met the other's eyes for a moment, then lowered her gaze again.

'Well you might look penitent, miss, for you took a great many risks yesterday. However, there is nothing to be gained by lecturing you even more, for I am sure you now see the error of your ways.'

'I do.'

Hester sat back. 'Hmm, let us consider things for a moment. Until recently, Molly was mistress to both Boskingham and Mavor, and was therefore party to most of their schemes. Then the two men quarreled, and Mavor cast Molly aside in favor of Juno, who promptly threw her out. Boskingham remained Molly's lover, and they both nursed a grudge against Mavor.' Hester drew a long breath. 'The man in the curricle must be Boskingham, which means he is still in this country, despite all the signs to the contrary. Molly was employed at Perton House for a month, you say?'

'Thereabouts, yes.'

'That is about how long it is since the quarrels. It is my guess that Boskingham and Molly saw the advantage of stealing the codicil, which they would be bound to know about from their closer days with Mavor. Boskingham is always in need of money, for he is the most incompetent son of faro I have ever known, second only in gambling genius to Mavor himself, who has been frittering his way through his inheritance like sands through an hourglass. Boskingham would know only too well how important the codicil would be to Mavor's future purse strings, and therefore how lucrative it would be to acquire it to sell for a price. Presumably, you chose this convenient moment to advertise for a new maid?'

'Yes.'

'So Molly promptly hied herself to Gloucestershire to see what could be done about the codicil. Hmm. I'd like to know her thoughts when she arrived and found it already missing.'

'She certainly joined in the general search for it,' Annabel remembered, 'and when Father suddenly produced it the other night, she was so startled she almost dropped a jug of cordial.'

'And after that she asked Mr Vernon to deliver the letter to Mrs Smith of Pav'd Alley?'

'Yes.'

'There was only one letter, and it was addressed to Mrs Smith?'

Annabel was mystified by the question. 'Yes, with the figure fourteen on it. Why do you ask?'

'Oh, I just wondered if she sent one to her cousin as well.'

'Her cousin?'

'Fragrant Freddie, the male assistant behind the counter at the haberdashery.'

Annabel's lips opened, then closed again.

She was almost beginning to be resigned to the succession of surprises.

Hester continued. 'So, the letter was delivered, and miracles of miracles, Boskingham immediately turned up out of the blue at the Dog and Duck. *He* was clearly the recipient. She must have told him everything in the letter, so he would know Toby had the codicil and new will.'

Annabel drew a deep breath. 'Hester, I believe you have fathomed it all.'

'Except why Molly returned to Juno's yesterday with a peace offering of pink roses. It cannot after all be because she requires a new protector, for we can now be sure that Boskingham has been here all along, and until yesterday at least, we know they were still together.'

Annabel looked toward the green door. 'I could tell she wasn't a welcome visitor. The footman was most reluctant to admit her, but in the end he did.'

'Ah, yes, the inestimable Claudius. Juno will have barred Mavor's former mistress, but Claudius always had a soft spot for Molly Simmonds. The pink roses would have been a peace offering for Juno.'

'Maiden's Blush,' Annabel said with a smile.

'Hmm?'

'The roses. They are called Maiden's Blush.'

'In polite circles, no doubt. I daresay she purchased them from the florist in Pav'd Alley. I go there because they have the most excellent blooms all the year round from their hothouses and gardens in Chelsea, and I like to have flowers in the bedrooms at the inn. I also need my nosegays, of course.' Hester smiled then. 'Anyway, they sell that particular variety of rose because it is so very fashionable in all the nunneries, where I assure you it is not known as Maiden's Blush. The nuns and abbesses call it *Cuisse de Nymphe*, or nymph's thigh.'

So *that* was what Sir Richard meant, Annabel thought. She hoped her cheeks would not let her down with another blush to match the roses in question!

Hester drew a long breath. 'Well, the roses are by and by, for we should concern ourselves with the candlestick.'

'It's one of a set of four,' Annabel replied.

'Really? You hadn't mentioned that before.'

'Hadn't I? Well, according to Sir Richard's information they are probably Indian. Each one stands upon a different creature from that subcontinent, an elephant, a tiger, a monkey, and a crocodile, and — What is it, Hester?' She broke off, for the other's face had suddenly assumed a startled expression.

'My dear Miss Gresham, if only you had described them before! You see, I believe I know where those candlesticks are to be found!'

15

Annabel was shaken. 'You ... you know where the candlesticks are?'

'Yes.' Hester pointed through the archway toward King's Place. 'I believe they are located in Juno's private apartment, because I saw her purchasing them. It was only last week, at a warehouse in Upper Thames Street that specializes in items of eastern origin. There was a sale in progress, and I am always ready to toddle along to such occasions to see if there is anything that might be of use at the Dog and Duck. Well, Juno was there, too, and she acquired candlesticks that were precisely as you describe. I will tell you who else was there, with a mignon friend — Fragrant Freddie!'

'Really?' Hester was proving such a mine of information that Annabel was almost dazed.

The other sat forward slightly. 'My dear, as Freddie is Molly's cousin, and has his immaculately kept finger constantly on the world of bawdry's ignoble pulse, I feel sure that the first thing she and Boskingham will have done on arriving in London is repair to the haberdashery. It is my hunch that they mentioned the candlesticks, and that he told them what I have just told you. *That* is why Molly went to Juno's. When you saw her from the window of the Dog and Duck, she had most probably just left wherever it is she and Boskingham are now lodging. They could not stay with Freddie and his, er, male companion, because the latter is far too jealous and possessive to countenance Boskingham as a guest.'

'Why?'

'Because Boskingham leads with the other foot from time to time.'

'That is how Toby described him, too.' Annabel glanced at the older woman. 'I think I understand what it means. Would I be right in thinking of David and Jonathan?'

Hester smiled. 'You would.'

'I've learned more in the past few hours than ever before.'

'Unfortunately, it is the sort of education that will not be found in the curriculum of an academy for young ladies.'

'Perhaps it should be, for then there would not be so many shocks later on,' Annabel replied dryly. 'Well, I suppose it is rather pointless to continue my search for the codicil. If Molly gained admittance to Juno's yesterday, by now she is almost certain to have absconded with the documents.'

'Do not jump to that fainthearted conclusion, my dear. You see, Juno's private apartments are her holy of holies, an inner sanctum where no one else goes, except possibly Mavor now that she is under the illusion he will put a ring on her finger. Oh, and I recall that for some reason it is her habit to use her rooms to conduct initial interviews with new nuns. Otherwise she keeps the door locked at all times with the key upon her person. So even if Molly did manage to worm her way back in, which I doubt, she will have a very hard — if not impossible — task gaining entry to those rooms. In my opinion, Juno will have had her ejected again almost as soon as she entered the house, for that lady is not known for her capacity to forgive. Molly was not only Mavor's former inamorata, but on being thrown out before had some very cutting things to say about Juno being an old ewe dressed lamb-fashion. It did not go down well with the old ewe, as you may imagine.'

Annabel began to feel a little more hopeful, but something puzzled her. 'Hester, if Juno doesn't let anyone into her apartments, save for initial interviews and most likely to, er, entertain my brother, how did Mr Boskingham manage to not only get in, but actually sleep on the bed?'

'That mystifies me as well. I am equally confounded as to why Boskingham would go to Juno's at all after he had fallen out with Mavor.'

They were both silent for a moment, then Annabel addressed her new friend again. 'So you really think the documents might still be there?'

'There is a strong possibility. It has to be faced that Molly *may* already have succeeded in her aim, or that she still might. We simply do not know how she went on after Claudius admitted her.'

They both gazed through the archway into the daytime peacefulness of King's Place, then Hester gave Annabel a sideways glance. 'So you observed Sir Richard here with Molly, mm?'

'Yes, but then he is a familiar face in this area, is he not?' Annabel replied a little acidly.

Hester chuckled. 'Maybe so, but it has never been my experience that he comes for the same reason as the likes of Mavor and Boskingham. You know, Miss Gresham, you are very fortunate indeed that Sir Richard came to your rescue yesterday. However, at least I think I now understand your anxiety not to meet him in the park. Your clothes are the problem, are they not?'

'Yes. I wore them when I came out

yesterday evening, and he had already seen my hat when he visited Toby. Then he came to my aid on that infamous corner, and now he has happened upon me again, this time driving with you.'

Hester laughed. 'So he probably imagines you are a lightskirt whom Mr Vernon was, um, entertaining?'

'I daresay,' Annabel answered, flushing at the thought. 'Not that you have helped dispel the general misapprehension regarding my morals,' she added.

'Me?'

'Yes. You didn't exactly insist to Juno that I was a young lady of faultless morals, and then you told Sir Richard there were no shrinking violets present, which he must interpret as meaning I was no better than I should be.'

'I was swept along a little, I fear. What Juno thinks does not matter, but I am sorry where Sir Richard is concerned. However, I was convinced you would successfully remain anonymous to all but myself, and I wanted to hear what he had to say about Juno, so I took the obvious way to reassure him it was in order to speak in front of you.'

'Yes, well I wanted to hear as well, so I suppose it ill becomes me to grizzle.'

Hester smiled. 'One way or another you have much to grizzle about, my dear.

However, in spite of the hat being in Mr Vernon's rooms, I do not think Sir Richard will associate you with Miss Gresham.'

'I pray you are correct, because Toby and I are to dine with him tonight at Tregerran Lodge,' Annabel said with feeling.

'Would I be right in believing that you find him unconscionably attractive?' Hester ventured.

Annabel colored. 'You certainly would not!' she declared.

Hester raised an eyebrow. 'Methinks the lady doth protest too much,' she murmured.

Annabel looked away, wishing she could disguise her feelings a little better.

'Well, no matter what your feelings are in the matter, he is certainly intrigued by you.'

'You think so?'

'Yes, as do you, miss. There was no need at all for him to express a wish to meet you again in the none-too-distant future. You have aroused his interest.'

Annabel could not prevent her eyes from beginning to shine. 'Do you really think so?'

'My dear, a gentleman like that would not say it otherwise.'

A gentleman like that? The auction broke into Annabel's pleasure. 'I shall not permit myself to encourage him in any way, for I cannot respect anyone who participates in — '

'Auctions?' Hester interrupted. 'Ah, yes. Would that I had asked him about it in Hyde Park, for I am sure there is more to it than seems on the surface. He will have had good reason to do what he did.'

'I doubt it,' Annabel replied, believing she knew his reason only too well, for he had removed it to Tregerran Lodge to enjoy to the full!

'Do not prejudge him, Miss Gresham, for I find it virtually impossible to believe he acted for base reasons. However, since the subject is a trifle contentious, let us move on a little. If you are dining at Tregerran Lodge, you will go past the Peach Tree tavern.'

'The Peach Tree?'

'The hostelry and tea gardens I will be taking over at the end of the summer.'

'Oh, yes.'

'As soon as you see it, I know you will understand why I so wish to have it. To eventually retire there, in the country air of Marylebone, is my dream.'

Annabel smiled, and dismissed the uncomfortably direct remarks about her supposed feelings toward Sir Richard.

Hester went on, 'And you must also be sure to tell me all about Tregerran Lodge. It was originally a fifteenth-century hunting lodge for the royal park, but fell into ruin.

Then Sir Richard purchased it about four years ago, and rebuilt it as a very modern and newfangled house. I'm told that every room on the ground floor has French doors to the gardens.'

'Four years ago? That must have been just before Lady Tregerran died.'

'Yes.' Hester gave a sad sigh.

'Did you know her?'

'My dear, the likes of Hester Ferguson do not 'know' the likes of Lady Tregerran, although strange to say, she and I were distantly related. Very distantly.'

'What was she like?'

'Breathtakingly beautiful. Vivacious and dainty, elfin almost, with large dark eyes and dark hair that she wore very short, *à la victime*.'

All that I am not, Annabel thought.

'Her younger sister, Catherine, is just the same; eighteen years old and quite exquisite.'

'And Sir Richard is her guardian?'

'That is so. She recently became a very considerable heiress, so safeguarding her future is a great responsibility for him.'

Annabel didn't comment, for it seemed to her that a man who behaved as Richard did was not fit to have care of anyone, let alone an eighteen-year-old heiress.

'The story of Sir Richard's marriage is a sad one, I fear. Elizabeth fell ill at about the time he acquired the lodge. It was her house, designed by her and for her in every way. Oh, how he adored her. Theirs was a love match par excellence, and it broke his heart when she passed away only weeks after the house was finished.' Hester took a brisk breath. 'Well, that is the story of Tregerran Lodge, and I have never seen it because it cannot be observed from the highway, so I am relying upon you to enlighten me, Miss Gresham.'

'I will be sure to tell you all.'

'And you can also tell me if your opinion of Sir Richard remains as low as at present.' There was a twinkle in Hester's eyes.

'You think it will not?'

'I am sure of it.'

Annabel considered for a moment. 'His character will quite clearly never be to my liking, but I have to concede that his looks are all that must be admired.'

'Ah, yes, the answer to a maiden's dream, is he not?'

'Not this maiden.'

Silence fell, then Hester spoke again. 'Well, now that I have shown you a little of the world that has your missing documents clutched tightly to its unvirtuous bosom, what do you intend to do next?'

'I don't know,' Annabel replied untruthfully, for now that it seemed only too likely that the candlesticks belonged to Juno Wyatt, that lady's half-joking invitation to Roderick's birthday celebrations had become almost irresistible. She was even able to persuade herself that with the domino there would be little chance of her odious half brother recognizing her.

To go would be foolhardy in the extreme, and if she were discovered, it would be the end of her reputation, but recovery of the codicil was of overriding importance . . .

16

Richard's town carriage arrived at the Dog and Duck at half past eight precisely, and for a last time Annabel examined her reflection in the looking glass. She wished the aquamarine silk were a finer garment. The cut was good, and the silk and stitching quite excellent, but the style was rather humdrum. All of a sudden, she wished she had not been so mulishly set against clinging white muslin, for that material no longer seemed pallid and fit only for the French or wrapping around cheeses. If she were wearing something bang up to the mark and diaphanous, she would be feeling a good deal more poised right now! As it was, she felt provincial.

But not even a white muslin gown would have relieved her troubled mind. Toby had been told about events in St James's as if they had happened to Hester, and he had given his word not to mention to Richard that his sister had been the lady in Hester's chariot. Thus Annabel hoped to cover her improper tracks satisfactorily, but she was only too aware of becoming enmeshed in half-truths and subterfuge. By telling one person this and another person that, sooner or later there was going to be an awkward tangle.

She gazed at her reflection again. Even her hair looked countrified, she thought with a dismay that verged on the panic-stricken. What on earth had possessed her to purchase a posy of lily of the valley from the flower woman in the yard and fix them to her comb? They were quite ridiculous!

'Oh, do hurry, Annie,' Toby called from the next room. 'The carriage is waiting, and we don't wish to be later than necessary. Remember, it will take me an age to get downstairs!'

The lily of the valley would have to stay. With a resigned sigh she smoothed her elbow-length white gloves, picked up her velvet reticule and lace shawl, and went to him. Five minutes later, they set off on the mile and a half drive to Tregerran Lodge in Marylebone Park.

The way took them north along Old and New Bond Street, then over Oxford Street into Marylebone Lane, beside which ran the Tyburn stream. Here grew the famous elms, the Tyburn trees that had once served such a grim purpose. Soon after passing through the village of Marylebone, with its parish church and manor house, they reached the New Road. This highway had been built less than fifty years earlier to avoid the congestion of the capital by traversing the northern limits from Paddington Green to Islington. It was busy and beginning to be developed on either side, but beyond it lay Marylebone Park, once a forested royal hunting ground, now a vista of rolling farmland dotted with farms, inns, and villas, where the Tyburn meandered toward the Thames. There were still some stands of trees, all that was left of the original forest, and to the north of it rose higher land, including fashionable Hampstead, and Primrose Hill, renowned for its wildflowers and panoramic views. Now the former royal preserve supplied hay for the capital's countless horses, and milk for thousands of kitchens.

The scene of rural tranquility came suddenly upon the eye as the carriage crossed the New Road and struck into a leafy lane that might have been many miles indeed from the largest city in the world. Birds sang in the hedgerows, flowers and tall grass grew sweetly in the meadows, reeds waved on the banks of the Tyburn, and cows grazed in lush pastures. Annabel found it so welcome after the bustle of Piccadilly that she lowered the window to enjoy the air, except that enjoyment was not exactly possible because of the evening ahead. A formal meeting with Richard was only minutes away now, and her confidence was on the ebb. She had to confront the moment during the struggle by Pav'd Alley, when he had seen her face. It could only have been a glimpse, over in a split second, but it might be all that was needed.

Waves of trepidation washed over her, but then Toby interrupted with an observation about the weather. 'We're in for rain.'

'Rain?' She pulled herself together. 'Why do you say that?'

'Because Primrose Hill looks so clear and close.'

'Yes, I suppose it does. I hope you're wrong.'

He smiled and glanced out of the window again. Evening wear became him, she decided, approving of his black corded silk coat, oyster satin waistcoat, and white silk breeches and stockings. On the seat beside him lay his tall hat, gloves, and cane, and his fair hair shone in the evening sunlight. It had to be said that Toby Alexander Vernon was a very attractive young man; the least said about the horrid other brother, the better!

He noticed something ahead. 'Did you say Mrs Ferguson is taking over the Peach Tree?'

'Yes.'

'Well, there it is.' He pointed.

Annabel twisted around to look. Far from being an isolated country tavern, the Peach

Tree stood among a number of buildings, including various dwellings and two small manufactories. According to the large letters painted on the wall of one, it produced the japan lacquer and copal varnish that was used to protect coach paintwork against minor scratches. The other announced itself as a maker of hair powder.

The tavern itself comprised several attractive white-washed buildings with gables and twisted chimneys, and was set among trees at one end of a small boating lake. In the tea gardens to one side there were two semicircular wooden loggias covered with roses. They faced over a patch of grass where grew the peach tree from which the tavern took its name. The loggias contained alcoves with tables and chairs, where suppers could be enjoyed al fresco, and on an evening such as this they were all fully occupied. Nearby there were several skittle alleys, and through the open carriage window came the rumble of the wooden balls before they struck and scattered the skittles. Fine carriages were drawn up under the trees, as well as traps, curricles, phaetons, and at least a dozen saddle horses. The sound of laughter drifted on the air, and it was as summery a scene as could be imagined. Annabel could quite understand Hester's eagerness to take over the lease.

Richard's coachman drove on along the lane, over the Tyburn by means of a small humpbacked bridge, and shortly afterward came to the open gates of Tregerran Lodge. A gravel drive wound through a small park of about one hundred acres, where fine old trees cast leafy shadows. As the carriage came within view of the new house, the calls of peacocks were a fond reminder to Annabel of Perton House, which right now she fervently wished she had never left!

The lodge was a gothic villa, castellated, asymmetrical, and utterly charming. The ground-floor windows were arched with elegant French doors, so it was possible, as Hester had said, to go outside whatever room one was in. There were arched windows upstairs, peeping out of towers and turrets that might have belonged to a medieval castle. As much sunlight as possible was welcomed in, and the outer walls were bright with climbing roses and clematis. To one side extended a wing that Annabel thought must house the servants' quarters, kitchen, laundry, and so on. All the windows of this wing faced away from the lawns, and against the lower wall there was a fine conservatory, one of two, for there was a smaller one jutting into the lawns on the south front.

Annabel found herself wondering in which

part of the house Richard had installed his King's Place nun. It seemed very wrong indeed to bring such a person to the home planned and furnished by his late wife. Did the demirep merit a bedroom in the main house? Or had he salvaged his widower's conscience by relegating her to the servants' quarters?

The studded main doors of the house were flung open as the carriage drew up at the porte cochère, and a senior manservant came out to attend the guests. He was a robust, rawboned man in his early forties, with freckles and auburn hair that he had tied back with a black silk ribbon. He wore fawn breeches and a light brown coat, and after he had lowered the rung and opened the carriage door, he bowed respectfully.

'Welcome to Tregerran Lodge, sir, madam. I am Sir Richard's man, Mordecai Penworthy.' His pleasing Cornish accent made Annabel conclude that he must have come from Sir Richard's estates in that far western county.

'Good evening, Penworthy,' Toby answered, alighting with such difficulty that the man hastened to assist him. Once safely on the ground, Toby stretched for a moment because he was awkward and stiff, then he turned to extend a hand to Annabel.

She took it very reluctantly, for in a few moments now she would know whether or not Richard had seen enough of her face before to recognize her. The scent of roses drifted on the light evening breeze, and oaks in the park were beginning to be tinged with warm gold as the sun commenced its descent toward a horizon that was faintly darkened by clouds. The rain Toby had forecast, she thought as she composed herself for the imminent meeting.

Penworthy bowed to them again. 'If you will please follow me, I will take you to Sir Richard.'

But as he led them into the square outer hall, which had a red-tiled floor and walls of cream and gold, Richard himself came toward them from the little circular inner hall. He wore a velvet coat of the deepest purple, white silk breeches, and a silver brocade waistcoat. Lace spilled from his cuffs and adorned his neckcloth, where shone an amethyst pin. His glance met Annabel's, but his expression gave nothing away.

Her blood quickened, and her heart lurched as if it would turn right over. He affected her so much that it was almost like a pain running through her. Never would she have believed that she, sensible Annabel Gresham, would be so stricken with . . . with what? Love? Was *that* what she felt for this astonishingly attractive man? It couldn't be. She wouldn't let it be! He did not deserve such an emotion. And yet ... Her lips seemed to tingle with the kiss that had never been, the kiss she wished had been.

His gaze moved to Toby, to whom he held out a hand in greeting. 'I am honored to welcome you to Tregerran Lodge.'

'And we're delighted to be here,' Toby responded, gladly shaking the proffered hand. Then he turned to bring Annabel forward slightly. 'May I present my sister, Miss Gresham? Annabel, this is our host, Sir Richard Tregerran.'

This was the moment that would tell, she thought, aware that her quickened heart had now frozen with anxiety, waiting to beat safely again when danger was past. 'Sir Richard,' she murmured, and as he raised her gloved hand to his lips, she somehow summoned the willpower to at last look him properly in the eyes; not a mere glance, but a true gaze, steady and unequivocal.

'Miss Gresham,' he replied softly.

The air seemed to tingle around her, and time itself stood still as she stepped helplessly over the edge and plunged headlong into the arms of love.

17

So many wild emotions were darting through Annabel that she needed all her wits not to let them show in her eyes. She had to drag her concentration back from the realms of love and fantasy to the present, because her own emotions did not count right now; it was what Richard was thinking that really mattered. Did he know her? To her relief she perceived no suggestion of recognition on his face, no shade of puzzlement, as if he thought he might have seen her somewhere before. She immediately relaxed so much that she was guilty of a smile that was perhaps a little too bright and warm for the situation. 'Your house is very beautiful, Sir Richard,' she said, wishing she could think of something more witty and entertaining.

For a moment he did not respond, but continued to gaze into her eyes. Then he returned her smile. 'I'm glad you like it, Miss Gresham. It is by Nash, but to my late wife's exact wishes.'

Toby was impressed. 'Nash? Nothing but the very best, eh?'

'Only the best would do for Elizabeth,'

Richard murmured, then cleared his throat. 'Er, Miss Gresham, I fear that my French cook, who is more of a tyrant than Bonaparte, will not brook any delays before the serving of his masterpieces, but afterward perhaps you and Toby would like to be conducted over the house? Its lack of symmetry makes for great interest.'

'I would like that very much,' she replied, privately concluding that the nun must be in the servants' wing, otherwise such a tour would not have been suggested. She was angry with herself having such a thought, after all it was no business of hers what he did in his private life; indeed, only a fool would expect such a man to lead a celibate existence. But she just could not help herself. Deep in her heart, where lurked her irreparably romantic soul, she wanted him to be as perfect as he looked.

He continued. 'As there are only three of us dining tonight, I have decided upon a modest choice of dishes for dinner. I trust that is in order?'

Toby nodded. 'Oh, yes. What is it to be? I vow my appetite is disgustingly hearty tonight.'

Richard smiled. 'Asparagus soup, fillet of sole, breasts of chicken in white wine sauce, with salad and new potatoes, and then apricot tart.'

'Oh, excellent!' Toby cried, for he was very partial to apricots.

Richard turned to Penworthy. 'Mordecai, if you will inform Gilbert that we are at his disposal?'

'Very well, sir.' The Cornishman bowed, then walked away through a side door that opened to the long wing that Annabel had noticed on approaching the house. Richard then conducted them through the little circular inner hall, intending to go directly to the dining-room, but a large portrait on the half-landing of the split staircase caught Toby's eye so much that he halted in admiration.

'Oh, I say, how truly captivating . . . ' he breathed.

Annabel halted as well, and Richard turned reluctantly. 'My wife and her younger sister,' he said.

Annabel gazed at the late Lady Tregerran, who was all that Hester had said, and perhaps a little more. Elizabeth and her sister, who could only have been about twelve when the portrait was painted, were seated in a cliff-top pergola with a little brown pug dog at their feet and the sea behind them. They had been gathering the honeysuckle that bloomed freely over the pergola, and the flowers were so exquisitely painted that Annabel could almost smell their heady fragrance.

Elizabeth, Lady Tregerran, was so very dainty and lovely that she seemed ethereal. She wore a pink silk gown trimmed with tiny bows, and on her lap there was an upturned gypsy hat filled with honeysuckle. She had piquant features, with blue eyes and short dark hair. Annabel almost expected her to twirl the spray of honeysuckle she held between her fingers and thumb. Beside her, young Catherine was delightful, too. She shared her elder sister's looks, and was attired in a cream muslin gown with a wide blue sash around her waist. Her dark hair fell in loose tresses about her shoulders, and she was teasing the pug with the ribbons of her little straw bonnet. Her eyes were brown instead of blue, and she had an appealing smile that seemed to reach out of the canvas.

Toby was in raptures over Catherine, whose eyes and smile entranced him. 'Miss Hensleigh was an angel then, and must now be a divinity,' he declared.

Annabel lowered her eyes with a hidden smile, for it was not often that he was so overcome by a pretty face that he waxed poetic. Then she glanced at Richard, and to her surprise saw a withdrawn expression descend over his face. She wondered what he was thinking. Was it simply that he was affected by looking at his late wife's portrait? A stir of compassion began to rise through her, but subsided again in a moment as she thought he could hardly be breaking his heart for Elizabeth if he was keeping a demirep here! Then she was angry with herself again. Clear, logical thought seemed impossible where he was concerned. One moment she sympathized with him, the next she despised him, then she was drawn to him so much she hardly knew what to do! She was mortified to admit that jealousy prompted her outrage over the nun. If anyone had told her she could be like this, she would have scoffed. Yet it had happened, and right now it could not be more inconvenient.

Richard shook off his transient mood and smiled briskly at them both. 'Come, let us adjourn to the dining-room before Gilbert takes up a cleaver,' he said, and spread his arms to usher them toward a door.

The windows of the rectangular dining-room occupied two walls of the house, east and south, and stood open to the summer evening, allowing in the scent of flowers. To the east one could look across the park to the boundary trees, mostly elms, and then the rich meadows between the lodge and the Peach Tree tavern. To the south, through the second conservatory she had noticed on arriving, the view was toward the village of Marylebone. The smaller conservatory contained comfortable chairs as well as a proliferation of exotic plants. A place where Elizabeth intended to sit, Annabel thought.

The walls of the dining-room were a shade of deep carnation with panels of cream and gilt plasterwork, and the ceiling was coffered in the same colors. On the shelf of the white marble fireplace stood a garniture of exquisite porcelain jars from the Orient, and there was a fine display of plate on the sideboard. A longcase clock stood in a corner, and its slow ticking fell comfortably into the quiet of the summer evening.

A lavishly laid table, white-clothed and decorated with candlesticks and flowers, had as a centerpiece an epergne that tumbled with early hothouse grapes. The candles had already been lit because the room was away from the sun at this time of the day, and the flames swayed idly in the draft from the open windows. It was all very pleasing, and Annabel knew that if the late Lady Tregerran were still alive, she would be very pleased indeed to be hostess at such a table; indeed, there were four chairs, almost as if her ladyship would soon join them.

Richard noticed the fourth setting with some disapproval. 'I fear the servants have not yet become accustomed to my sister-in-law's temporary absence,' he explained as he drew out one of the chairs for Annabel.

Toby looked at him, 'Will Miss Hensleigh be away for long?' he inquired in the obvious hope that she would not.

'That I cannot answer. It is in the lap of the gods, as they say,' Richard replied.

The meal that followed proved to be very good indeed. Richard was a genial and entertaining host, and an excellent raconteur. Conversation ranged upon many topics, including, of course, the missing documents. Everything that was new to Richard was spoken of as if it had come from Hester, and Annabel's involvement remained the secret she hoped. As they talked, she was conscious once or twice of Richard regarding her. It was a curious gaze, perhaps quizzical, perhaps something else, but interpretation was impossible.

The evening darkened considerably as the meal progressed, foreshortened by the advancing clouds, which had now crept very close indeed and from which thunder could be heard now and then. After dinner they adjourned to the candlelit drawing-room, where Mordecai served sweet liqueurs and strong Turkish coffee. Annabel inspected the room with approval. Every ground-floor chamber at Tregerran Lodge was a different shape, but all were beautifully decorated and furnished. It was a cream-and-gold chamber, with sage green chairs and sofas, and watercolor landscapes that conveyed the joys of every season. Annabel felt she would have liked Elizabeth, for how could one not warm to a woman whose taste was so very like her own?

Much after-dinner amusement was had from a telescope that stood on a tripod by one of the open windows. Through its powerful lens it was possible to watch peacocks parading in the gloaming at the far end of the drive, and squirrels playing in the elms on the eastern boundary. Annabel could make out the lights of the Peach Tree tavern and its nearby houses, and to the south the lights of London itself. Toby was in high spirits due to the excellent wines he had sampled during dinner, for to be sure he had given each one more than ample opportunity to prove itself. Now that he sipped liqueurs as well, his face was rosy, his smile beaming, his chatter constant, for tonight he had set aside the worry of all that had happened since he left Gloucestershire.

When they at last tired of the telescope, the promised tour of the rest of the house took place. Thunder was audible as Richard picked up a lighted candelabrum to show them upstairs first. Toby tackled the ascent of the stairs with gusto, but had to be helped by the others, and as he reached the little landing where the portrait hung, he bestowed more praise upon Catherine Hensleigh. Annabel was sure he was almost in love with her, even though he had yet to see her in the flesh.

The bedrooms at Tregerran Lodge were all as pleasing and individually shaped as the ground floor, with arched windows that displayed fine views of the grounds, which had become very dark indeed now the advancing storm was so near. In Catherine's room, which was octagonal because it was directly above the drawing-room, Annabel made the acquaintance of Percy, the pug in the portrait. Elderly now and decidedly wheezy, he was asleep on the window seat, and looked up with a hopeful little whine as the door opened. Seeing Richard, he jumped down and trotted over. His reward was to be picked up and fussed.

Annabel was enchanted. 'What an adorable pug. He was in the portrait, wasn't he? Does he belong to Miss Hensleigh?'

'He does now, yes. He was Elizabeth's originally,' Richard replied.

Percy took a fancy to Annabel, and strained and wriggled until he had his way. Richard held him out to her. 'I trust you like him well enough to hold him, Miss Gresham, for clearly nothing else will do.'

'I would be honored,' she replied, and gladly took the little dog, whose delight was only too evident from the frantic wagging of his entire posterior. 'Why didn't Miss Hensleigh take him to Ireland with her?' she asked.

'Er, I believe he wasn't well,' Richard replied.

'He is certainly in fine fettle again now,' Annabel said, laughing as the pug squirmed in her arms and tried to lick her face.

'He appears to approve greatly of you, Miss Gresham.'

'And I approve of him,' she replied.

Percy remained in her arms as they went next to Richard's room, which was directly above the dining-room. It was the only first-floor room that had French doors to the outside, and this was because the roof of the small conservatory served as an extended balcony. Toby elected to sit down inside for a moment because climbing the staircase had taken more out of him than he cared to admit, but the other two went outside with Percy.

Lightning flashing against the heavens, and as a roll of thunder followed, Annabel was very conscious of Richard's closeness. The wind stirred, warm and humid, and the night scent of flowers seemed to drift almost tangibly through the air. It was one of those strange moments that she knew would stay with her forever — the balcony, the storm, her feelings and thoughts, Sir Richard Tregerran . . . All combined into a painting she would keep in the scrapbook of her life.

Richard's voice interrupted her thoughts. 'Perhaps we should go inside, Miss Gresham, for it is about to rain.'

'Yes, of course.' But still she stood there with Percy snuggling happily in her arms.

The first raindrops fell, and she raised her face to them and closed her eyes. But those eyes flew open again with a start when Richard spoke again, very softly.

'Come inside, Miss Brown, for this is yet another corner where it is most unwise to linger.'

18

Annabel was so shaken that the thunderstorm was suddenly forgotten. He had recognized her after all! She couldn't look at him; indeed she didn't know what to do. She felt alternately humiliated and angry. He had toyed with her from the moment she arrived, probably enjoying a great deal of amusement at her expense.

'Miss Gresham? If you wish to remain out here and become drenched, that is your prerogative, but I don't think poor Percy deserves a soaking as well,' Richard said quietly.

She glanced down at the unfortunate pug, which was regarding her with mournful reproach as the rain tamped on his little face. 'Oh,' she said lamely, and hastened back into the bedroom just as such a cloud-burst commenced that Richard very hastily had to close the windows.

The rain made Toby get up from his chair in astonishment. 'Good Lord, the heavens have opened!'

Richard looked out. 'With luck it will not last long,' he said.

'I certainly hope not,' Toby replied, thinking of the journey back to the Dog and Duck.

Annabel glimpsed herself in a mirror. She realized she was the color of beetroot! If Toby were to notice, he would think she was burning up with a fever. Richard was looking at her, but she steadfastly ignored him. Instead, she made much of poor Percy, who was so frightened by a particularly loud thunderclap that he buried his head beneath her arm, his little body quivering. As she stroked and fussed him, she stole a glance at the rain on the glass, willing it to stop, for she felt so dreadful that all she wanted was to escape from this place.

Richard spoke to her again. 'Miss Gresham, if you make too much of that pug, I warn you he will play to the gods, for he is a terrible ham.'

'I . . . I am sure Percy will behave like a gentleman,' she replied, and at last looked at him. Let the pug not be the only one to behave like a gentleman her eyes entreated, but his face gave nothing away.

Toby was still observing the downpour. 'This has a feel of being in for some time,' he said.

Richard nodded. 'Yes. I hope it isn't, however, because it does not take much to flood the lane that leads here. If the rain goes on like this for any time, I'll send Mordecai out to see how things are. You can always stay here tonight.'

Annabel's lips parted in horror. *Stay here? No! Never!* If she had to wade through that waterlogged lane up to her waist, she would do it! Anything rather than remain beneath this roof.

It was still pouring with a vengeance as they returned to the candlelit drawing-room, where Mordecai had closed the French windows against the weather. Toby expressed a desire to play cards, but Annabel elected to sit on a sofa with Percy, who would not leave her for even a moment. She watched Richard as he dealt the cards. But for his words on the balcony she still would not have known that he recognized her, for he gave no further sign. He certainly showed no inclination to apprise Toby of her misdeeds, but of course that did not signify that he wasn't going to, just that he chose not to as yet.

For an hour the two men played cards, laughing and talking together as the storm continued relentlessly. The deluge descended as if the clouds themselves were in spate, a damp draft sucked down the chimney, making the bowls of flowers in the hearth shiver, and now and then there came a thunderclap so savage that the windows shook. Water ran in the gutters and drain-pipes, and sluiced over the paving right against the house. There were puddles forming on the lawns as well, and Annabel's spirits sank further each minute, for she could almost feel the lane flooding.

Toby felt the same. 'I say, Richard, how will the lane be now?'

'Not good, I fear. To be frank, my advice is not to attempt to leave tonight.'

'And to be equally frank, I'd rather not try when Annie's safety is at stake,' Toby admitted.

She spoke up quickly. 'Please do not concern yourselves about me, for I am quite prepared to return to the Dog and Duck.'

Richard shook his head. 'I will not hear of it. What manner of host would I be to permit my guests to depart in such conditions?' He got up to go to the bell rope. 'There is an excellent guest room on the ground floor that I am sure will suit Toby nicely, and Catherine's room is more than at your disposal. I'll instruct Mordecai right now.'

'But — '

He was reproving. 'The matter is settled, Miss Gresham. Besides, Percy insists. He says you will be very welcome company for him in the absence of his mistress.'

The pug whined and wagged his rear end on hearing his name, and Toby grinned. 'There, Annie, how can you refuse?'

Very easily, she thought, but gave a resigned smile. 'Well, for Percy,' she murmured.

'It is best,' Richard said. 'Please feel free to use anything of Catherine's, for she would insist upon it if she were here. Would you like the services of a maid?'

'No, thank you,' she replied, and he pulled the bell rope.

It was almost midnight when Mordecai came to inform them that their rooms were in readiness. Rain was still falling heavily, but at least the thunder and lightning had begun to move on as Richard performed the courtesy of escorting his guests to their rooms. This of course meant that Toby was shown to his first, because it was only just off the inner hall. He declared that it was just to his liking, and that he would sleep very soundly indeed, which was the truth because he always did sleep soundly; even more so when he had overindulged of an evening!

Then Richard conducted Annabel up to Catherine's chamber. She cuddled Percy close, taking comfort from him, and she didn't raise her eyes to Elizabeth's likeness as they passed. Her heart was thumping as she anticipated Richard's next move, for to be sure, in this particular instance she was very much the pawn.

It wasn't until they reached Catherine's door that at last he confronted her. 'Right, Miss Gresham, we are now private enough for you to tell me firstly what you were doing on the corner of Pav'd Alley, and secondly why you were in Hester Ferguson's chariot masquerading as the unshrinking violet Miss Brown.' He held the candelabrum so that her face was fully illuminated.

She raised her chin defiantly. 'I do not think it is any business of yours, Sir Richard.'

'I have made it my business.'

'That does not mean I will meekly tell you what you wish to know,' she replied.

'Either you tell me, Miss Gresham, or I will tell Toby, who cannot possibly know all that you have been up to.'

She recoiled at the threat. 'Quite the gentleman, are you not?'

'Can you assure me that you are quite the lady?' he countered.

'How dare you say such a thing!'

'Miss Gresham, *ladies* do not loiter on corners in St James's. Nor do they assume false names and then drive around Hyde Park with former abbesses.'

Her eyes flashed. 'How quickly you leap in

to judge me, sir. Could that perhaps be because you are so well acquainted with the demimonde that you think everyone else must be as well?'

Anger darkened his face. 'And what, pray, is that supposed to mean?' he demanded.

'Simply that I think it very rich indeed that *you* should question *my* respectability when you purchased a woman at an auction!'

'Ah, so that's it. You appear to have adopted the moral high ground, Miss Gresham, but do you belong there, that is the question.'

'I fancy I belong there far more than you, *Sir* Richard! Where is your purchase now? In a stable loft?'

For a long moment he looked piercingly into her angry eyes, then his lips twitched into something that might have been a smile. 'Oh, she is ready and waiting in my bed, Miss Gresham, where she will pander to my unimaginable vice.'

'That does not surprise me in the least, sir!' Still holding Percy she strode into the room and slammed the door behind her.

Richard rapped angrily. 'Miss Gresham?'

'Go away,' she said, and turned the key.

'Miss Gresham!'

'If you do not go away, sir, I will ring for Penworthy to rescue me from your despicable advances.'

'My despicable *what?*' There was silence. 'Very well, I will go, but I promise you this is not done with yet. I will have a sensible explanation from you, or you will know the consequences!' With that he walked away.

Annabel blinked back tears as she went to the window to look out at the rainy night. All she wanted was the safe return of the documents so that she and Toby could lodge them with Sir Humphrey Smythe-Castle and then go home to Gloucestershire. Instead, the documents were as out of reach as ever, and she had fallen hopelessly in love with a man who now revealed himself to be capable of an odiousness that came close to matching Roderick's!

She rested her cheek against the pug's silky head.

'Oh, Percy, how am I going to get out of this?' she whispered.

Percy gave a little whine that sounded like sympathy.

19

Annabel forced Richard from her mind as she prepared to go to bed. She didn't want to use Catherine's belongings without her permission, but really had no choice, and as she sat at the dressing table, she noticed that Catherine did not seem to have taken much with her to Ireland. Combs, brushes, pins, cosmetics, ribbons, and jewelry were all still there. Annabel's curiosity was aroused, and when she went to look in the wardrobes she found them filled with so many clothes that she could not help thinking Catherine Hensleigh had gone away with only the clothes she stood up in!

Still, it wasn't something to dwell upon, so after donning a pretty cotton nightgown trimmed with lemon ribbons, Annabel climbed into the bed. Percy immediately jumped up onto the coverlet and lay down by her feet, as was clearly his custom with Catherine. Annabel thought she would be too agitated to sleep after the contretemps with Richard, but eventually Percy's gentle snores and the noise of the rain lulled her.

She awoke suddenly at three in the

morning. The rain was still falling, but all of a sudden it stopped and there was an eerie hush. Why had she awoken? she wondered. No, it was more than just awakening, for she was positively alert, alarmed even. Something had disturbed her. But what? Slowly she sat up in the bed, pushing her hair back from her face as she glanced around the room. Where was Percy? There was no sign of him. 'Percy?' she whispered. Nothing. 'Percy?' This time she said the name a little louder, but still there was no response. An uneasy finger passed down her spine as she pushed the bedclothes aside and got up. The pug *had* to be in the room because the doors and window were closed. Was he unwell? 'Percy? Where are you?'

If the rain had still been falling, she would not have heard the faint sound, a little like a squeak, a little like a snuffle. It came from behind the drawn curtains. The pug was on the window seat, she thought, remembering that was where he had been earlier, but just as she was about to investigate, she noticed the curtain twitch slightly, not low where she expected, but higher up. Someone was hiding there!

Again the finger moved down her spine, but icily this time. What should she do? She glanced around and saw a candlestick on the mantelpiece. She hesitated, then hurried toward it, but before she could pick it up, the curtain had been wrenched aside and a man in a hooded cloak leapt out. Holding Percy fast under his arm, he thrust Annabel aside as he made for the door. Knocked off balance, she instinctively grabbed at his hood, which came away in her hand. For a split second she found herself looking at the curricle man, then she fell heavily against the mantel.

Opening the door, the man fled toward the staircase, setting the night candle on the landing dancing in the draft he made. It wasn't until she heard Percy whining in fear as he was borne down the staircase two steps at a time that Annabel found her voice. 'Help! Help! Thief!' she screamed, but already the intruder's steps rang in the hall.

Richard erupted from his room, dragging on his blue paisley dressing gown. 'What in God's own name is going on?' he cried as she stumbled out on to the landing.

'Percy has been stolen!' she cried, pointing at the staircase as came the sound of the front door being flung open.

Delaying only long enough to pull on a pair of boots, Richard gave chase. She heard him run out of the house after the intruder, then there was silence again. The servants had not heard anything from their wing, and Toby slumbered on unawares. Annabel dithered. Part of her was afraid, but part of her was incensed as well. How *dared* anyone steal Percy! It was the latter emotion that swiftly triumphed. She dashed back into Catherine's bedroom for her evening shoes, grabbed a cloak, then ran after Richard.

The air outside was cool and damp, and the cloud was breaking up sufficiently for a little moonlight to cast a pale sheen over the grounds, where here and there storm water had collected to form shallow pools. Part of the drive was a ribbon of silver, and as she paused beneath the porte cochère to see which way Richard and the intruder had gone, she could hear water dripping from the eaves.

Her heart was pounding as she cast this way and then that. Suddenly, she heard Percy yelp and begin to bark, and she turned sharply toward the sound. In the moonlight she saw two wrestling figures. Richard had caught up with his quarry near the elms on the boundary, and was trying to apprehend him while Percy stood nearby barking furiously. As she watched, the two men stumbled into one of the pools of rainwater, struggling and splashing like demons.

To her dismay she saw that, whether by fair means or foul, the curricle man was successfully dealing blow after blow with his clenched fist, and that Richard was forced to raise his arms over his head in defense. Gradually, she realized that his opponent was holding a weapon of some sort, a stone maybe.

She ran forward, screaming in alarm. 'Stop it! Oh, stop it!' But the man took no notice. She knew she had to do something! Suddenly, she halted, clasped her hands together, and held them out as if she had a pistol. 'Stand away from Sir Richard or I'll shoot!' she warned.

The man froze.

'Stand away I say!' she cried, her hands still clasped convincingly in front of her.

But instead of conceding capture, the man scrambled to his feet and made off across the park with Percy in pursuit, still barking. Annabel immediately ran to Richard, who was sitting up a little dazedly in the puddle.

'Are you all right?' she cried, not caring about the water as she knelt beside him.

'I . . . I believe so,' he replied, but the moonlight showed a red trickle on his forehead.

'Oh, there's some blood!' she gasped, reaching out to it.

'He had a stone,' he replied, and wiped his forehead with the back of his hand.

She looked intently at his pale face in the

silver light. 'Are you quite sure you're all right? Maybe we should send for a doctor . . . ?'

'There is no need for that,' he answered, and struggled to his feet. Then he helped her up as well. 'You saved me from a far worse drubbing, and for that I am very grateful,' he said, and drew her hand briefly to his lips.

'There is no need to thank me, sir, for I am sure you would have done the same for me.'

A flicker of humor lit his eyes. 'If I had the presence of mind to invent a pistol I did not have, I most certainly would, Miss Gresham. How very resourceful you are.'

'I trust that was a compliment?' she queried, not entirely sure that it was.

'What else could it be?'

'Who knows?' she replied, for it was hard to forget the antipathy of their previous meeting.

If he noticed, he gave no sign. 'Well, at least we now know that Boskingham is definitely still here in England.'

'So it *was* Mr Boskingham?'

'Oh, yes, I'd know him anywhere.' He ran his fingers through his wet hair, wincing a little as he touched a place where his assailant's stone had found a mark. 'Thank heaven I have a good thatch,' he murmured.

Annabel gazed in the direction the man had gone. 'We also know that Mr Boskingham and the curricle man are the same person.'

'You're sure of that?'

'Oh, yes. I pulled his hood off and saw his face quite clearly.'

Richard sighed. 'Oh, damn it all, I don't know what to think. I anticipated many a thing, but not Percy's abduction. Tell me exactly what happened.'

She explained, then added. 'And please do not think I am party to anything, because I'm not.'

He smiled. 'I don't imagine you are, Miss Gresham.'

'No? You do surprise me. I expected you to conclude that anyone who pretends to be Miss Brown must be less than honest,' she replied a little tartly.

'Miss Gresham, please do not willfully misunderstand me.'

Her eyes flashed in another brief moment of moon-light. '*I* willfully misunderstand you? Well, that is indeed rich! Can't we simply be honest enough to admit that we don't trust each other?'

'And why, pray, should you not trust me?'

Her eyes flickered. 'Because, sir, wherever there is woodwork, you crawl out.'

'And you do not, I suppose?'

She drew back slightly. 'That's different.'

'Well, you *would* say that, wouldn't you? So I am expected to obligingly place faith in you

196

when you haven't even seen fit to tell Toby you were lurking on a corner in St James's like a Cyprian, or that you cavorted around Hyde Park under a false name with a former King's Place duenna?'

'I didn't lurk *or* cavort!' she cried indignantly.

'Oh, yes you did, madam!'

She was furious. 'And what of you, *Sir* Richard? Were you not in King's Place yourself in warm and attentive conversation with Mr Boskingham's doxy?'

'That was all innocence!' he snapped.

'Oh? As, I suppose, was your participation in that abominable auction the night Toby lost the documents?'

'So we are back to that, are we? Miss Gresham, Toby may have been a firsthand witness to what happened on that occasion, but he certainly doesn't know anything!'

'Well, you would say that, wouldn't you?' She adopted his tone of a few moments earlier.

A nerve flickered at his temple as he found it difficult to contain his temper, then he drew a long breath. 'Look, this is not getting us anywhere, and besides, I see little point in standing up to our ankles in cold water while we argue. I suggest we return to the house, change into dry clothes, have a drink of something restorative, and argue in comfort.'

She hesitated. 'Very well.'

'Good.'

She glanced around for the pug. 'Where is Percy?' she asked, suddenly realizing that they hadn't heard the little dog for some time.

Richard cupped his hands to his mouth. 'Percy! Come here, boy!'

But there was only silence.

Annabel's hand crept to his wet sleeve. 'Oh, no,' she whispered.

Richard shouted again and again, but Percy did not return. Too late they realized that while they had been arguing Boskingham had succeeded in his purpose after all.

20

It was to be dawn before Annabel and Richard confronted each other in the promised comfort of the drawing-room, because he decided first to search the grounds for the missing pug. He aroused Mordecai and the other menservants to comb the area as best they could in the darkness, but both he and Annabel knew in their hearts that Percy had been kidnapped. Miraculously, Toby slept on. His unerring ability to do this had always amazed his sister, who was inclined to awaken easily, as had been proved during the night.

Boskingham had left footprints in the soft ground, but they disappeared into a particularly large puddle alongside the elms, and could not be found emerging again, no matter how diligently the area was searched. The lane was barely passable, even on horseback, and certainly would have been too hazardous to attempt in the dark. However, there was a low, narrow causeway that traversed the meadows to the Peach Tree. It wasn't suitable for a vehicle of any description, but a man on foot or horseback could certainly risk using it, even on such a night. Boskingham must have come and gone along this way. But where had he taken Percy? And *why?*

As the searchers returned, Annabel waited for Richard in the drawing-room. She had changed into her aquamarine gown once more, but borrowed a pair of Catherine's little slippers because her own were soaked through. She had also borrowed a warm shawl because the early morning air was surprisingly cool after all the rain, and the lace one she had brought with her was not sufficient. Her hair was twisted up in a rather makeshift knot on top of her head, and she was deep in thought at the window where Richard's telescope stood.

She had gone over and over the increasingly mystifying situation so far, and had now moved on to the chancy business of how to insert herself in Juno's private apartment. The method of gaining entry to the house in King's Place was obvious enough, for she would present herself at the door as invited by Juno herself, but the rooms on the top floor were another matter. And even if she succeeded, she wondered how she was going to get out again.

The door opened behind her, and Richard entered. He wore a plain sage green coat and leather riding breeches, and half-buttoned shirt. His neckcloth was nowhere to be seen, and he looked tired. He made no secret of his surprise to find her still waiting. 'Forgive me for keeping you so long, Miss Gresham. To be honest, I thought you would have returned to bed.'

'We decided to talk,' she reminded him.

He smiled at that. 'To argue, I think,' he corrected, then went to a small table on which stood decanters and glasses. 'I'm not sure if this is very late or very early, but I intend to partake of a very large cognac regardless. Can I offer you one as well?' He didn't wait for her to answer, but commenced to pour two anyway. 'Well, there isn't a whisker of either scoundrel or pug. Oh, the felon's footprints lead across the grounds, but disappear in a large puddle, and that is that. It is my opinion that he came here on horseback across the meadow causeway, and then escaped that way, too.'

'Meadow causeway?'

'The Tyburn used to flood the low land between here and the site of the tavern, especially in winter, so a causeway was built to allow royal huntsmen and their ladies to ride to the old lodge.'

'Why would anyone want to take a pug? It just doesn't make sense.'

'I fear it does, Miss Gresham. At least, it does to me.'

She looked curiously at him. 'What do you mean?'

'I do not know whether I should tell you.'

She bridled again. 'If that means you still do not trust me, I — !'

He held up a protesting hand. '*Pax*, Miss Gresham, thrice times *pax*! This is a private family matter that has nothing to do with not trusting you. Besides, it is quite obvious that you do not trust me, so we remain equal on that score.' He paused, then gave a tired sigh. 'Oh, perhaps I should tell you anyway.'

Suddenly, she saw the worry in his eyes. It had been there all along, yet she only noticed it now. It affected her, as did just about everything about him; indeed he aroused her every sense bar the common. 'What is it, Sir Richard? I can see there is something very weighty on your mind.'

'There is.' He swirled his cognac, then drank it all. 'Please let us be seated, for I am very tired.' He waited until she had taken an armchair, then poured another glass of cognac and flung himself on a sofa, where he leaned his head back and closed his eyes. 'Miss Gresham, before I expound my theory concerning Percy's disappearance, I must first explain that although I have no proof, I nevertheless have every reason in the world to believe that your brother Mavor has abducted Catherine.'

Annabel was astounded. 'Roderick has what . . . ?' Her voice trailed away as she remembered the conversation in St James's. 'It was *Catherine* you and he referred to at Pav'd Alley?'

'Yes, it was. I have absolutely no idea where she is, except that she most certainly is *not* in Ireland with friends. Mavor has no intention of making Juno Wyatt his bride — he's merely enjoying her favors. He wants Catherine, and I fear he will go so far as to force her to marry him.'

Annabel was so shocked that she got up from her chair and went to the window. 'How long has she been missing?'

'Just over a week. She went out for a ride one morning, and neither she nor her horse returned. Just as I was about to raise a hue and cry because I feared she had met with an accident, a message came that she was well and I was not to report her missing or she would cease to be.'

'Who sent the message? Roderick?'

'I believe so. It was shouted to one of my gardeners by a stranger on horseback. The gardener had no description to offer, just a man on horseback, rough and ready, and wearing drab clothes, so it certainly wasn't Mavor in person, nor can it have been Boskingham, even supposing the quarrel had been patched. The man's horse was just a hack, certainly not a blood animal like Mavor's, so I think he must have been someone hired to deliver the message.'

'What have the authorities to say about it?'

'I haven't told the authorities because to raise the alarm under such circumstances would be to risk Catherine's life. Two days of agony passed after she first disappeared, and because there was no ransom demand forthcoming I began to realize it was no ordinary kidnapping. Then Mordecai discovered that in recent weeks Mavor had been meeting her on her rides. Inquiries revealed many whispers in the neighborhood that she was meeting a lover. I was dismayed that she had not even mentioned Mavor to me, for it suggested that she might have welcomed his attentions. As for Mavor himself, I have since learned that he explained away his frequent visits to Marylebone by telling Juno he was inspecting the Peach Tree inn with a view to acquiring the lease for her. She is apparently keen on acquiring the tenancy in order to spite Hester Ferguson.'

Annabel was dismayed for her new friend. 'Hester thinks the matter is as good as settled.'

'I fear it is far from that. Anyway, the Peach Tree doesn't matter, for Mavor's real reason was clearly to dance sly attendance on Catherine. If he has harmed a single hair of her head . . . '

Annabel felt a little awkward. 'Sir Richard, can you be quite sure that she was abducted? I mean, maybe she had gone with him voluntarily.'

'No. She took nothing with her, not even Percy. Perhaps it would be better to say especially Percy, for she adores that silly pug and wouldn't leave without him. I believe Mavor did his utmost to persuade her to elope, and abducted her when she wouldn't. Marriage is his purpose, because he wants to lay hands upon her fortune. If he cannot persuade her to consent, I know he will resort to force.'

21

Annabel was appalled, but knew Roderick was capable of anything. She lowered her gaze as Richard continued to speak.

'Catherine's cooperation is preferable, of course, because it will be better for him socially if he can present to society a Lady Mavor who agreed to the match. I do not know where he is holding her, except that it is certainly not his London house or his country seat, for I have had secret but thorough searches made of both. *Ergo*, he has her somewhere else. I have men searching for her horse as well. It is a rather distinctive animal, an exceedingly pale golden chestnut mare with a very wide white blaze. She calls it Xanthe.'

'Xanthe is Greek for yellow, isn't it?'

'Yes. Anyway, the mare has disappeared without trace as well. Time is running out, Miss Gresham. That is why recent days have found me so much in evidence at Juno Wyatt's seraglio. She is Mavor's creature, and while he certainly would not tell her about his designs upon Catherine, he might neverthe-less have let something slip. For instance, a seemingly innocent remark about driving down to Bath might suggest that he had taken Catherine there. Oh, it's only an example, but you know what I mean. He is certainly at the Marine Pavilion at the moment because the invitation was issued some time ago and he crowed mightily. Everyone in town knows that is where he is.'

She nodded. 'He bragged to me as well. Sir Richard, I cannot fault your reasoning or indeed your actions, but one thing hasn't been mentioned. Why would Mr Boskingham steal Percy? He certainly isn't Roderick's friend anymore, so he can't have done it for him.'

He raised his head from the sofa to look at her. 'Miss Gresham, if there is a chance of making a penny or two, Boskingham is always quick to exploit a situation. That will be why he purloined the documents, and no doubt is also why he stole Percy. You know the sort of thing — 'Give me a good price for the codicil and will or I will sell them back to Perton House', or, 'Pay me for the pug's safe return or he'll end up in the Thames'.'

'Oh, please don't say that,' Annabel gasped, finding the latter scene a little too vivid.

'Forgive me, but it is the sort of threat to make in situations such as these. Anyway, the fact that Boskingham has gone into hiding suggests to me that he knows Mavor won't take kindly to any of this. That is why he didn't risk returning to Juno's, but sent Molly instead. Once he has recovered the documents, he knows that if Mavor won't pay up, then your father will. Stealing Percy will be a way of getting further money, out of me this time.'

'Do you think Boskingham knows where Catherine is?'

'No. Believe me, if he did, he would have offered to sell me the information by now. I know Boskingham.'

'Sir Richard, I will do all that I can to help you,' Annabel promised fervently.

'And I am doing what I can to help you, Miss Gresham, so it would seem we are now accomplices.'

'Yes, and so is Toby. I do not think we should keep all this from him.'

'That is understood, Miss Gresham.'

Annabel looked at him. 'Hester Ferguson is our accomplice, too, Sir Richard. I will tell her that Juno is her rival for the Peach Tree, but I also think she should be told about Catherine. If Juno is involved in any way, Hester may be able to find out.'

He nodded. 'If that is what you think, then I have no objection.' He leaned his head back again. 'I still cannot figure some of what has gone on. Boskingham's quarrel with Mavor is well known, yet he still frequents Juno's salon. She is Mavor's mistress, so why does she allow Boskingham to go there? She appears to permit the fellow an unconscionable amount of latitude. I do not think they have ever been lovers, but there is definitely something odd between them. He has been unpleasantly in drink on her premises, yet he has not been ejected. Many a better man has been requested to leave on far less. Now she has gone so far as to let Boskingham sleep it off on her bed. An intriguing puzzle, *n'est-ce pas?*'

'Indeed.'

'Come to think of it, I have never seen Boskingham and Mavor there on the same night. It is always one or the other. No, wait a moment now . . . ' He sat up with a start. 'The cold light of dawn is evidently good for the memory, Miss Gresham, for I suddenly realize that by having Boskingham taken to her rooms, Juno was keeping him out of Mavor's way! I was playing cards as usual that night and saw the fracas when Toby was ejected. I only had half an eye on events because play had reached a particularly critical point at my table, but I realize with hindsight that Boskingham didn't leave at all, but stayed on. He was so drunk he may think he went elsewhere for a time, but I would swear an oath that he didn't. He became more and more unpleasant, and eventually passed out. Just as that happened, I noticed Mavor arrive unexpectedly. There wasn't time to send Boskingham safely off in a growler, so Juno had her footmen carry him up to her rooms. She knew it was very unlikely indeed that anyone else present would mention Boskingham to Mavor because of the quarrel, and Mavor stayed only about an hour anyway. When he had gone, she would have sent someone to bring a growler from the rank in Pall Mall to take Boskingham back to his lodgings. I left shortly after Mavor, and came upon Toby lying on the ground. The rest you know.'

Annabel sighed. 'I wonder why Juno is so indulgent where Mr Boskingham is concerned? Do you think he knows something about her and uses it to his advantage?'

Richard nodded philosophically. 'A dark secret? Yes, you're probably right, for I would hazard a guess that there is much in Juno's past that she would prefer did not become public knowledge. Things she might pay to keep quiet, and when it comes to extorting money, Boskingham is the very man.'

'Many of us have secrets, Sir Richard,' Annabel observed, thinking of her wish to conceal her own activities since coming to London.

'Dark secrets we would pay to suppress? I cannot imagine that you harbor such a skeleton in your cupboard, and I know I do not. Boskingham, however, *does* have such a secret. He is married, and his wife is very much alive. It is something he keeps very close indeed, and I only know because I was fortunate enough to travel from Windsor with him one night when he was once again completely in his cups.'

'Where is his wife now?'

'I have no idea, for he didn't get that far in the saga before he lost consciousness on the carriage floor. He doesn't even remember that he told me, so I imagine I am the only person who knows. Your good self now excepting.' He gave a quick smile. 'He spoke of Mrs Boskingham as 'an arrogant, ambitious, bright-haired Venus who thought herself too good for him'.'

'Bright-haired? Could it be Juno?' Annabel ventured.

Richard paused. 'I had not thought of *that*. It would explain her tolerance where he is concerned. If she has hopes of Mavor, she would certainly allow an inconvenient spouse considerable latitude *and* pay him to hold his tongue.'

'Juno has more than mere hopes of Roderick, Sir Richard. She is certain that he will marry her. I have heard her say so.'

'Then she is either not Mrs Boskingham, or she will happily commit bigamy. She's a fool to hope anyway, because Mavor has his eye upon far richer pickings than she will ever be.' In spite of thinking of Catherine again, he managed a wry smile. 'I almost hope Juno *is* Mrs Boskingham, and that she is correct about Mavor's intentions toward her. A bigamous wife would serve Mavor right. The *monde* would chortle for months at his expense. It couldn't happen to a nicer fellow, eh? Oh, I know he is your brother, but he is without a doubt the most vile maggot it has ever been my misfortune to meet.'

'Please do not feel obliged to apologize, Sir Richard, for I am in hearty agreement. You will not hear protests from my father or Toby either. We would probably chortle as well.'

He put his glass aside and got up, then came to join her at the window, standing just behind her. 'On another matter, and while we are on cordial terms, Miss Gresham, I would like to make it clear that although I certainly did outbid Boskingham at that damnable auction, I did it to secure the girl's freedom, nothing more. I purchased her, brought her here, gave her some money, and let her go. If

I had an ulterior motive, it was to question her all I could for a snippet that would indicate something about Catherine's whereabouts.'

'Did you learn anything?'

'The business of Juno's interest in the Peach Tree.'

'And that was really the only reason you participated in the auction?'

Humor curved his lips as he glanced down at the sweet line of her neck and shoulder, so slender, pale, and infinitely kissable. 'Yes, Miss Gresham, it was.'

'And . . . and she isn't here now?' Annabel couldn't help the question.

'The girl? Certainly not.' He laughed then. 'My, my, how very persistent you are on this point. You really did come here under the impression that I had a demirep in residence, didn't you?'

Annabel colored. 'Yes, sir, I did.'

'Then you could not have been more wrong.'

'I . . . I realize that now.' She wished the ground would open up and swallow her.

'Believe me, I have never had to pay for a woman's caresses in my life. Maybe I will have no choice in the matter when I am in my dotage, but until then I will continue to charm my way between the sheets.'

'I can well believe that, sir,' she replied,

knowing she was going even more pink. Oh, how she wished she had not pressed the point.

Her mortification was most becoming, he thought. Everything about her was becoming. He had thought so in Pav'd Alley, and again in Hyde Park, and the time she had spent here had only served to increase his interest. She was a woman he enjoyed being with, a woman he wanted to know far, far more . . . He yearned to hold her, to steal the kiss that eluded him before. 'Would you like a demonstration of my skills?' he asked softly, provocatively. Her fragrance tantalized him. If he bent his head now, he could kiss her naked shoulder.

'That is no question for a gentleman to ask a lady.' She closed her eyes, for she could feel his breath upon her skin.

'Perhaps not, but nevertheless . . . '

'To even say such things would compromise me in company, sir.' She trembled deep inside, for she wanted him to go further. There was seduction in the air, her seduction, and her heart and senses were excited in a way they had no business to be.

'So it would, but we are not in company, are we?' He turned her to face him. 'Let us be very, very frank with each other, Annabel. I desire you, oh, how I desire you, and I am certain that you desire me. Oh, yes, it is there in your eyes, a darkening of that wonderful clear gray, a widening of the pupils. And there is a glow upon your skin, a warmth that tells me you are conscious of me in the same way I am conscious of you. Kiss me, Annabel, and test the veracity of the feelings you are experiencing now. Maybe this is just a dream, and you haven't awakened at all.'

She stared at him, caught by the allure of his voice and the incredible excitement that thundered through her body.

'Kiss me,' he whispered, and took her by the wrists to link her arms around his neck. She closed her eyes as he pulled her to him, body to body, desire to desire. She lifted her lips, and at last put them to his. Her breath caught, and she drew back slightly, but then touched her mouth to his again. Just a touch, a caress of parted lips, a taste of unfulfilled passion, a promise of ecstasy. His fingers curled luxuriously in the warm hair at her neck as his body responded to everything about her. He experienced a need that had lain dormant for too long, an urgent need that only this woman could satisfy. Making love to her would release him from the shackles of the past, and let him live again, love again . . .

The door opened behind them. 'I say, what's going on?' Toby asked with a yawn.

22

Annabel and Richard leapt apart as if scalded, but they need not have been concerned because Toby was too sleepy to notice anything much. Still yawning and stretching, he came into the room in a fine ruby-colored dressing-gown belonging to Richard. He walked with noticeably more ease than the day before.

'Have I been sleeping through something?' he asked. 'I heard voices in the grounds and looked out to see two groups of men coming back toward the house.'

Annabel was still so overcome by what had just happened that she couldn't say anything. It was left to Richard to reply. 'I fear you have slept through a great deal, my friend,' he said, somehow managing to sound admirably collected.

Toby collected himself. 'What's happened? Is something wrong?'

'Sit down and we'll tell you,' Richard said, and went to pour another glass of cognac, which he thrust into Toby's startled hand.

Toby gaped at it, then sat down on the sofa. 'So early in the morning? Is it bad news then?'

'That depends upon your viewpoint,' Richard murmured as he handed Annabel to her chair again. His manner was all that was proper, with no vestige of the incredible moments that had just passed between them.

Her fingers shook in his. Had it really happened? Or had it been a dream after all? she wondered.

Still Toby did not observe anything, because he was intent upon Richard. 'Right, what's all this about?'

'Are you fully awake?'

'Oh, yes. I may sleep like a log, and occasionally be as unintelligent as one, but you have me all ears and wits now.'

Richard took up a place before the fireplace, one foot upon the polished fender, and told him about Catherine's disappearance, probably at Roderick's hands, and about Percy's abduction by Boskingham. Toby had drunk his cognac and demanded another by the time Richard finished. 'If that blackguard Mavor has done this vile thing, I vow I will call him out!' he breathed. 'As for Boskingham . . . '

'We will bring them both to rights,' Richard promised.

'But how? If the candlestick is in Juno's inner sanctum, I do not see how we are going to lay hands upon it, and as for rescuing poor

Miss Hensleigh . . . '

Richard toyed with the edge of the mantelshelf. 'Catherine's plight torments me greatly, but if possible I wish to accomplish her return without jeopardizing her safety or reputation. I cannot call Mavor out because he would certainly force her into marriage before any dawn confrontation, and if I attempt to seize him, I feel certain he will have some arrangement with whoever is keeping her for him. It will be something along the lines of a message having to be received from him within so many hours, otherwise she will be . . . well, I do not have to paint a picture . . . '

A heavy silence descended upon the room, during which Annabel and Richard shared a long, long look. He smiled a little, and she saw that she had not made a fool of herself at all in his eyes. Hesitantly, she returned the smile, and more words were spoken in those lingering seconds than might have been said in a whole sermon.

Toby interrupted again. 'Damn it all, I can never think on an empty stomach.'

'Oh, Toby!' Annabel chided, for now hardly seemed the time to contemplate food.

But Richard smiled again. 'Toby's right. We'll be useless wilting of hunger. Whether we feel like it or not, I suggest we make some attempt at breakfast.' He went to the bellpull.

Toby got up awkwardly and made his way to the window, then wrinkled his nose as he gazed out at the waterlogged grounds. 'Good lord above, there was certainly a lot of rain last night,' he observed. 'Will Annie and I be able to return to the Dog and Duck, do you think, Richard?'

Richard shook his head. 'On horseback maybe, but I don't think your bruises are quite ready for that. It's my guess that the lanes will be passable by tomorrow, but only provided there isn't more rain. You are most welcome to stay on another day.' He glanced at Annabel as he said this.

Toby was philosophical. 'I shall quite like to stay on. What do you say, Annie?'

'Well, I, er . . . '

Richard looked at her. 'I thought you and I could ride along the causeway a little later, Annabel. Maybe in daylight we will find some of Boskingham's tracks. You can wear Catherine's other riding habit. I know she has two.'

Toby urged her to accept. 'Oh, do say yes, Annie. You'll enjoy it.'

Enjoy being alone with Sir Richard Tregerran? She was rather afraid she would, far too much! Apart from that, however, what if there was more rain, resulting in a stay of a further day again? How could she carry out her domino plan?

Toby was still speaking to her. 'Who knows, on your ride you may run Bosky to ground, and possibly rescue Percy as well! Would that not be splendid?'

Richard smiled. 'It's settled then,' he said before she could decline. 'Ah, here's Mordecai . . . '

The Cornishman came in. 'You rang for me, sir?' he inquired.

'Please tell Gilbert that we require one of his finest breakfasts.'

'Certainly, sir.' Mordecai withdrew again.

It had been such a stressful night and a momentous morning that Annabel suddenly felt the need to be alone for a while. 'I . . . I think I will pin my hair again. It doesn't feel quite right at the moment,' she said, and hurried from the room in Mordecai's wake.

The moment she had gone, Richard turned to Toby. 'May I have a word in strict confidence?'

'Eh? Yes, of course.'

'I'm afraid I haven't been entirely open with you and Annabel, for I have a plan that might well rescue both Catherine *and* the documents.'

'You do? Why on earth didn't you say so before?'

'Because I didn't really wish to explain it in front of Annabel. It is a little, well, indelicate is perhaps the word I seek.'

'Indelicate? What on earth do you have in mind?'

'Well, let us discuss the documents first. *Cuisse de Nymphe* or not, I agree with Hester that it is very unlikely indeed that Molly regained admittance to Juno's seraglio, and I certainly do not think she entered the private apartments. It therefore seems very likely that the codicil and will are still where Boskingham hid them. Do you agree?'

'Yes.'

'It is my intention to revisit Juno's at the earliest opportunity.'

'I see. But with all due respect, dear fellow, I cannot see what is indelicate about this, unless you mean to bed every nun in the place!'

'Here me out. Not long ago Juno entertained a certain, er, *tendresse* for me that I most certainly did not return, but now I wonder if the time is ripe for a change of heart?'

'To what purpose?' Toby asked without thinking.

Richard groaned. 'For heaven's sake, Toby, do I have to spell it out? What is the most likely way I am going to gain admittance to her private rooms?'

Toby reddened. 'Oh! Oh, I follow you now . . .'

Richard smiled. 'It is time to discover if my powers of persuasion are as good as I think they are.'

'I daresay they are, damn your handsome eyes,' Toby replied. 'When do you think you will do this?'

'Well, it's Mavor's birthday tomorrow.'

Toby's jaw dropped. 'Eh? You can't be serious!'

'Never more so. A short while ago, just as I was returning from searching for Percy, the letter carrier brought a note from a friend of mine in town. We are both members of Brooks's, and I confided in him an interest in being informed of anything he discovered concerning Mavor. Late yesterday he heard that Prinny has invited Mavor to stay on at the Marine Pavilion for another night, and that Mavor has accepted without telling Juno. Imagine her fury when the birthday king himself fails to attend her little gathering. I rather fancy she will be amenable to my advances, don't you?'

Toby exhaled slowly. 'Yes, I suppose she would, but what if all this information isn't true?'

'Oh, I'm pretty certain it is. The person who told my friend is a reliable source. Dear Roderick will definitely not be returning to town until the day after tomorrow.'

'Then you will be able to pursue Juno at your leisure tomorrow night.' Toby gave a heavy sigh. 'I feel so damned useless!' he declared. 'All I seem fit for at the moment is sitting around discussing it all. When it comes to action, you and Annie have done everything.'

'It's hardly your fault.'

Toby watched him. 'I don't see why you couldn't bring Annie in on your plan. You don't have to tell her the, er, more awkward details.'

'I would just prefer she didn't know,' Richard replied, bending to look through the telescope.

'But — '

'She might think less of me if she finds out, Toby, and I really do not want that to happen,' Richard interrupted, straightening again. 'Damn it, man, I like her, I like her a great deal, and the last thing I want is for her to find out that I have been flattering Juno Wyatt, even in this good cause. If I retrieve the documents, I intend to spin a whitewashing yarn about how I achieved it. Now do you follow my meaning?'

'It's plain as a pikestaff. You have a fancy for my sister.'

'It's more than a fancy, Toby, I love her with all my heart.'

'Good God.' Toby was astonished.

Richard drew a long breath. 'I intend to ask for her hand, Toby, but first I wish to be certain Perton House — and its valuable contents — are hers. Once she is safe in her rightful inheritance, and therefore mistress of her own future, I will propose. I want her to feel safe if she accepts me, safe if she does not. She must have every choice in the world. Do you understand?'

'I . . . think so.' Toby understood one thing very clearly — whether or not she yet knew it, Annie had snared herself a title!

23

It was midmorning, there wasn't a cloud to be seen, and the sun was high in the heavens as Annabel and Richard set out on their ride. Pools and puddles seemed to be everywhere after the torrential rain, but the air was fresh and clear. Catherine's second riding habit did not fit Annabel all that well because she was taller than Richard's missing ward, but it was very modish and of a particularly becoming shade of light blue. The horse she had been provided with was a pretty roan with an even temperament, which was as well because Annabel did not count herself among the world's most accomplished equestriennes. Adequate was more the word she would have used to describe her riding ability.

They rode down the drive of Tregerran Lodge toward the lane, where they meant to inspect the extent of the flooding. Water lay very deep in the expected place, but Richard said he could tell it was already beginning to drain slowly away. He was certain that if the rain held off now, she and Toby would be able to return to the Dog and Duck in the carriage the following morning. With King's Place and the recovery of the documents in mind, Annabel privately hoped this prediction would prove correct. With matters of the heart in mind, she hoped it would not, for she longed to stay with Richard. Contradiction therefore beset her on all sides, with nothing clear or simple to guide her, and no sensible way to proceed — especially when he made no mention of what happened between them earlier. His silence dismayed her, for she did not know what it signified, and insecurity robbed her of confidence.

Still nothing was said as they left the lane and proceeded to the causeway, which led east toward the Peach Tree. The causeway had been raised alongside a tiny brook that was usually little more than a trickle of water, but was today chuckling and gurgling as it hurried to join the Tyburn. There were cows in the meadows on either side, sometimes up to their hocks in water, sometimes finding an area that was just a little raised. Buttercups, clover, and other wildflowers bloomed brightly, having survived the night relatively unscathed, and willows whispered in the breeze, their leaves sometimes silver, sometimes fresh and green. There were hoofprints on the causeway, indicating that this was indeed the route Boskingham had used the night before.

A wooden bridge spanned the Tyburn, and

as the horses were coaxed across, Annabel saw that the little river was much higher now. The muddy water sucked against the banks and dragged audibly through the reeds, a far cry indeed from the clear, gentle flow of the evening before. But then everything was a far cry from the evening before, she thought, stealing another hesitant glance at Richard. He wore the clothes he had on in Hyde Park, and rode the same large black horse. She doubted if there was a gentleman anywhere in England who was more handsome, or more able to break hearts. Would her heart be among them? Perhaps it already was . . .

Ahead rose the group of buildings that included the Peach Tree. While driving toward Tregerran Lodge, Annabel had been mostly intent upon the tavern itself, and perhaps the two manufactories, but now she was at liberty to study the dwellings as well. There was a row of laborers' cottages, some occupied by families employed at the manufactories or on surrounding farms, others housing families whose men looked to Richard for their livelihood. Apart from these cottages there were several houses, the oldest being a redbrick building of Tudor origin, with a tower from where Annabel guessed the hunting in the royal park had once been observed. Now it was in a dilapidated state, covered with ivy and inhabited by a large flock of white doves that suddenly fluttered noisily skyward, as if startled by something. Strahan's Lacquer and Varnish Manufactory was hard at work, and the smell of its products drifted over the meadows, but Tye's Hair Powder was clearly no longer in production. This was only to be expected, she decided, now that Mr Pitt's tax on hair powder had caused that item to fall out of fashion.

The pool in front of the Peach Tree had swollen so that it now ventured a little way into a meadow where a number of horses and heifers grazed among buttercups. A light breeze rippled the surface of the water, and the willows and poplars around the shore cast leafy shadows over the inevitable fringe of reeds. A serving girl from the tavern was tossing crusts to some noisy ducks, and a boy was tarring an upturned rowing boat. All the other pleasure craft were moored to a small jetty close to the entrance to the tea gardens. Where the causeway ended the ground had been scattered with gravel, and Boskingham's tracks immediately disappeared. With them went all hope of a swift recovery of Percy.

Richard reined in by the entrance to the tea gardens, where the loggias were deserted. He glanced around approvingly. 'I can understand Hester's desire to take over here,' he said, removing his tall hat so that the breeze stirred his hair.

'Yes, so can I.'

'Shall we take some refreshment before we ride back? On a day like this I think a sip of sparkling perry might suit?'

'I would like that.'

He hesitated, as if not knowing how to broach an awkward subject, then suddenly he leaned across to put his gloved hand to her cheek. It was a questioning gesture, uncertain, and oddly moving. 'Annabel, do you regret anything that has passed between us?'

The question caught her off guard, even though it was the very one she had wanted to ask him. 'Regret? I . . . '

'If you do, please say so, and I will not transgress again.'

She gazed into his eyes. 'I don't regret a single thing,' she whispered.

He relaxed and smiled, stroking her skin with his thumb. 'Nor I, my darling, nor I,' he said softly. 'Oh, if only you knew how relieved this makes me, for I was afraid I had ruined everything . . . '

'Never.' But then her fingers moved anxiously to enclose his. 'You do mean this, don't you? I . . . I mean, you aren't sparing my feelings, or — ?'

He interrupted swiftly. 'I mean every word,

Annabel. You have awakened me from a very lonely slumber.'

'Can that really be so?' Her fingers remained over his, seeking rescue from vulnerability. 'You are a gentleman of fashion, sought after and eligible, whereas . . . Well, I am nothing.'

He caught her hand and drew it urgently to his lips. 'Never think of yourself that way, for to me you have very swiftly become everything.'

Tears pricked her eyes. 'Those words will remain in my heart forever, and I will hold them close even if you never say them again.'

'But I *will* say them again,' he promised, then dismounted and rested his hat on the saddle before reaching up to her. She slid gently down into his arms, and their lips came together even before her feet had touched the ground. They embraced passionately, cleaving close to share a second kiss to seal their love — and their hearts.

Desire flared between them, intense, imperative, and invigorating, and it swept them up so completely that for these few seconds she did not feel earthbound. It was as though she soared with the larks that sang so wonderfully overhead.

Richard had to end the kiss, for the feeling had become too much to bear. He pulled away, his face flushed. He had never expected to experience again the passion he had shared with Elizabeth. But there was no mistaking the need that throbbed through his loins, or the joy that filled his heart; or the deeper realization that, if anything, what he felt now transcended all he had known before.

Suddenly, the doves again fluttered noisily into the sky, and Annabel's attention was immediately snatched toward the tower, where for a split second she saw a man looking down at her from the only window, high up by the eaves. Whoever it was immediately withdrew out of sight.

'What is it?' Richard asked, following her gaze.

'There is someone up in the tower.'

Richard turned. 'I see no one.'

'He drew back as soon as he saw me looking.'

'It will be old Barling, for it's his house and he lives alone. There have been some accusations from the cottages that he spends too much time up there spying upon the womenfolk. I doubt if it is the women particularly, just everything in general, for he is an inveterate busybody.'

Richard tethered the horses to a post provided for the purpose, then turned to draw Annabel's hand over his arm. He was happier than he had been in a very long time, and all because of this delightful innocent, whose kisses were so sweet with wanton pleasure that he was in her thrall. Until Annabel, he had been wandering through the days, with Catherine's welfare his only real concern, and he had not done well at *that!* Now it was all so wonderfully different that he seemed to have exchanged all his old dull senses for dizzy new ones. The blood coursed exuberantly through his veins, and his eyes had opened again to find a brilliant world, the existence of which he had almost forgotten.

They walked arm in arm into the tea gardens, and when they were seated at a table in one of the alcoves, the girl who had been feeding the ducks came to wait upon them. She was a buxom creature, fresh-faced and forward, with plaited fair hair worn in loops on either side of her head. Her brown linen dress was neat and clean, and her apron and mobcap were crisply starched.

'How may I serve you, Sir Richard?' she asked pertly, her warm glance making it clear that 'serve' could be interpreted how he wished.

'Perry, if you please, Kitty, and not from the taproom. The barrel in the cellar is much more cool and refreshing.'

'Certainly, sir.' The girl's glance moved

impertinently toward Annabel, then with a toss of her head she hastened away.

'I don't think I am very popular,' Annabel declared.

'You are popular with me, and that is surely what counts,' he replied with a smile.

Kitty brought two brimming glasses of perry to the table. One she placed invitingly in front of Richard, the other she placed abruptly before Annabel, almost as if hoping it would splash. But it was delicious however it was served, for it was pale, bubbling, and fragrant with pears. Sipping and talking, the two were lost to everything but each other. They laughed at the same things, shared the same spontaneous thoughts, and held the same views.

As they were leaving, Annabel noticed Catherine's Xanthe; at least, she could only think that it was Xanthe. Richard was just about to lift her back on to her own mount when there was a squabble among the horses in the meadow at the end of the pond. She looked instinctively toward the disturbance, and her attention fixed upon one of the animals, a very pale golden chestnut mare with a wide white blaze. Wasn't that exactly how Richard had described Catherine's horse? she thought.

'Look over there,' she said, pointing as the

mare kicked up her heels and cantered away through the buttercups.

He turned. 'Well, I'll be damned, it's Xanthe!' he breathed, and began to run around the pond toward the meadow.

Annabel followed.

24

A closer examination of the mare revealed that she was indeed Catherine's Xanthe. Someone had dyed her singular white blaze to match the rest of her coat, but reckoned without Mother Nature's cleansing deluge. Who had done it? they wondered. And where was Catherine herself?

The meadow belonged to Mr Barling, owner of the tower house, who charged a number of people for the privilege of grazing their horses with his heifers. When there was no reply at his door, Richard and Annabel went into the Peach Tree to see if he had gone there while they were in the tea gardens. He had not, indeed it was believed he had gone away because he had not been seen for some time. No one could shed any light on the mare, although now that her blaze was suddenly visible again she was recognized as Catherine's.

Richard decided to go to Mr Barling's house again, and he and Annabel were followed by everyone from the tavern, even the maid. The doves cooed and fluttered around the ivy-clad tower as he stepped beneath the low stone porch and knocked again at the door. The sound echoed through the hallway beyond, but still no one came. Richard turned to one of the men from the tavern, a lanky, sallow-faced fellow called Harry Croswell, who happened to be one of his grooms at Tregerran Lodge. 'Does Barling live alone here?'

'Oh, yes, Sir Richard.'

'Well, we know that *someone* was here earlier on,' Richard muttered as he stepped back slightly to look at the upper windows. A curtain twitched, or so he thought. Annoyance darkened his face, and he thundered his fist upon the door. 'Barling? This is Sir Richard Tregerran. Open up this instant, or so help me I'll break your door down!'

For a moment there was still no sound from within, but then they all heard footsteps on the stone floor of the hall. Bolts were drawn, a key turned, and then the door opened slowly, creaking on hinges that needed attention. A bearded man of about fifty peered reluctantly out. He was pale and drawn, and wore clothes that looked as if they had been slept in for more than one night.

Richard regarded him coolly. 'Mr Barling, I wish to ask you about one of the mares you have in your meadow.'

'I know nothing of any mares,' the man replied.

'It is your meadow, is it not?'

'Yes.'

'And there are a number of horses, including mares, grazing in it. Are you telling me you don't know anything about any of them?'

Barling stared at him, seeming at a loss for what to say. Then he gave an odd start, as if someone had jabbed him. 'I . . . I mean, I . . . ' He trailed into silence, staring at Richard like a trapped rabbit.

What was wrong with him? Annabel wondered. Something was certainly up, for he seemed nervous enough to faint clean away. Richard thought so, too. In fact he thought Barling *had* been jabbed, so on impulse he pushed him aside and kicked the door with such a force that it swung violently back against the wainscotted wall. There was a grunt of pain, a knife clattered into sight on the floor, and then came a soft thud as someone collapsed.

Barling had stumbled back when Richard pushed him, and now leaned weakly against the wall, his eyes closed with relief. 'Thank God, oh, thank God,' he breathed.

Richard stepped into the hall and moved the door in order to look down at the semiconscious man who lay there. Then he glanced at Barling. 'Who is he?' he demanded.

'I . . . I don't know who he is, Sir Richard,

except that his name is Coogan.'

Richard swept the knife well out of reach with his toe. 'What's been going on here?'

Barling was alarmed. 'It was none of my doing, Sir Richard! I've been a prisoner in my own house!'

'Who is holding you? Lord Mavor?'

Barling blinked. 'I . . . I don't know, Sir Richard. All I can be certain of is that I've been confined here since the day before Miss Hensleigh was kidnapped. She's being kept here, too, sir, but I haven't been able to do anything about it.'

There were gasps among the other men, and Annabel pressed her hands to her lips, hardly able to believe that they had found Catherine.

Richard took Barling by the lapels. 'Where is she?' he breathed.

'Upstairs, sir, the room at the end.'

Richard turned to the other men. 'Tie Coogan up,' he ordered, then dashed upstairs two at a time. Several of the men followed, while those who remained set about Coogan with a coil of twine that hung conveniently on a wall peg next to Barling's well-worn hat and coat. Coogan began to groan and regain consciousness.

Richard shouted Catherine's name as he ran along the passage on the floor above.

Annabel gazed up the staircase and thought, please let Catherine be all right, *please* . . . . Another door was kicked open, and she heard a young woman's cry of joy. 'Richard! Oh, Richard!'

While the remaining men plied Barling with questions, Annabel put a shaking hand on the newel post and waiting in trepidation as the footsteps on the floor above returned much more slowly toward the stairs. Then Richard appeared, carrying Catherine in his arms. She still wore the beige riding habit, and her short dark hair was tousled and uncombed. She was sobbing with relief, her arms around his neck, her face buried against his shoulder. He brought her gently downstairs, then brushed past everyone in the hall to take her into the low-ceilinged parlor, where he laid her gently on a deep settle by the inglenook fireplace.

'You're safe now, sweetheart,' he said gently, smoothing her hair back from her forehead.

Annabel had followed him into the parlor, and he glanced up at her. 'Some water, if you please, Annabel.'

'Yes, of course.' Catching up her cumbersome skirts, Annabel hastened toward the kitchen at the back of the house. She saw an immense dark wood dresser laden with blue-and-white crockery, including a number of jugs, and in another corner stood a pump over a low stone sink. Soon she had drawn a jug of water and taken it back to the parlor with a cup.

Catherine Hensleigh was no longer sobbing, and smiled gratefully up at her as she accepted a drink. 'Thank you, thank you very much,' she whispered, and drank thirstily. She was the very image of her sister, the late Lady Tregerran, with that same delightful elfin loveliness that was so much the vogue. Beside someone so beautiful, dark, and dainty, Annabel felt all that was plain, pale, and uninteresting.

Richard knelt by the settle and took one of Catherine's little hands between his. 'Are you all right, sweeting?'

She nodded. 'I'm just so very tired, and I've been more frightened than you can begin to guess. I don't know who has been holding me . . . '

'We think it is Mavor.'

'Oh.' Catherine looked quickly away, her cheeks assuming a dull, guilty pink.

'Why didn't you tell me about him?'

'Well, I . . . I knew I shouldn't have let him talk to me, but he seemed to be there every time I rode out, no matter which way I went.' Catherine looked timidly at Richard. 'He was so very charming, and always such a gentleman, that I began to enjoy seeing him.'

'Mavor is a snake,' Richard said shortly.

She bit her lip. 'I . . . I did not find him so, and anyway I had let things go on too long and was afraid to tell you in case you were angry with me.'

'Oh, Catherine . . . ' Richard drew her fingers to his lips.

'Are you quite sure he is involved in this? He hasn't come here at all, nor have I even heard his name mentioned. In all the time I have been here, the only people I've seen have been Mr Barling and the man called Coogan.'

Harry Cresswell pushed into the room from the hall, where the hapless Coogan was now conscious enough to be questioned. 'I've been having a little word with Coogan, Sir Richard. It seems that Lord Mavor you asked about is behind all this.' As he spoke he tapped the knife in his palm, leaving little doubt as to the nature of the 'little word.'

Richard gave a grim smile. 'Prod some more, Harry. I want to know as much as possible. And while I think of it, please impress upon everyone the need to keep all this as quiet as possible. Not only do I wish to protect Miss Hensleigh's good name, but I do not want stray words to reach Mavor either. He must be properly caught, with all the damning evidence I can gather. Tell them I will make it worth their while to hold their tongues until he is under lock and key, at which time I will reward their silence.'

'Very well, Sir Richard.' Harry went out into the crowded hall again.

Richard turned back to Catherine. 'Are you quite sure you are all right? No one has . . . touched you in any way?'

'Touched me? Oh, no, not in that way at least.' She went pink again. 'I was bundled here like a sack of coal, but since then I've had the freedom of my room, food that was edible if not exactly delicious, and even some books to read. Coogan kept watch from the tower. I used to hear him going up there.' She remembered her horse. 'What happened to Xanthe? Do you know?'

'Xanthe is fine and well, and has been in Barling's meadow all along.'

'Really?'

'Someone, presumably Coogan, dyed her blaze.' Richard gave Catherine a perplexed look. 'Why didn't you call for help? The window overlooks the cottages, so surely — ?'

'I didn't dare,' she interrupted. 'I was told that you and Percy would be harmed if I made a sound. How is Percy? I have so missed him.'

Richard exchanged a glance with Annabel,

then looked regretfully at Catherine. 'I'm afraid he too has been kidnapped.'

Catherine's eyes widened. 'Oh, no! Oh, my poor, darling Percy! Was it Lord Mavor's doing as well?'

'No, it seems not.' Richard kissed her hand again. 'It is a complicated story, sweeting, and I will tell you all when we get you safely home. We'll rescue Percy, have no fear of that.' He said these last words with more confidence than he felt, as Annabel knew only too well.

Catherine suddenly burst into tears, sobbing so much that her whole body shook. Richard rescued the cup from her hand, then scrambled anxiously to his feet and turned distractedly to Annabel. 'What shall I do?' he cried.

Annabel swiftly took his place by the settle and gathered Catherine into her arms. 'I'm sure all will be well again soon, Miss Hensleigh. Sir Richard will do everything he possibly can to see Percy returned to you. No one would take a pug unless for money, and any such demand will be met.' She looked inquiringly up at Richard, who nodded.

Catherine clung to her. 'Do . . . do you really think that is how it will be?'

'Yes.'

With a shuddering sigh, Catherine struggled to regain her composure. Then she looked apologetically at them both. 'I . . . I'm sorry for being such a baby. Discovering that poor Percy has suffered as well suddenly made it all too much to bear.'

Annabel smiled. 'That is quite understandable,' she said sympathetically.

'What happened to Percy? When was he taken?'

Richard leaned down to stroke her hair. 'It's too long a tale to tell you here. We'll go back to the lodge in a few minutes, once I have settled things here. I'll just go out and have words with everyone in the hall, especially friend Coogan.' He went out of the parlor and closed the door behind him.

Catherine regarded Annabel a little curiously. 'Unless I am mistaken, that is my riding habit you are wearing, and yet I don't even know who you are.'

'My name is Annabel Gresham, and I know Sir Richard through my brother, Toby Vernon.'

Catherine managed a little smile. 'I suppose you are part of Richard's long story?'

'I fear so.'

Within minutes Richard returned to the room. 'Well, I have discovered much of interest concerning Mavor. It seems he intended to play the hero by arriving here as a knight in shining armor, under the pretence of having discovered the vile plot. Coogan was to be permitted to escape in all the confusion. Mavor trusted to sweep you from your feet and into his marriage bed, Catherine.'

That young lady met his gaze for a fraction of a second, then averted her eyes in such a way that both he and Annabel realized Roderick's plan might well have paid the handsome dividend he sought.

Richard exhaled. 'Just how much progress did he make on your rides, Catherine?' he asked quietly.

'A . . . a kiss. Just a little one.'

'And you did not see fit to tell me anything?'

Catherine's eyes filled with fresh tears, and Annabel rose hastily to her feet to put a calming hand on his sleeve. 'Now is not the time, Richard. I am quite sure Miss Hensleigh is no longer under any illusions where Roderick is concerned.'

'Your cursed brother should be horse-whipped!'

'Yes, I quite agree.'

Catherine's sobs caught. 'Lord Mavor is your brother, Miss Gresham?'

'I fear I must admit to the unwelcome connection,' Annabel replied, then looked at Richard again. 'What will you do now?'

'As things are, I will have the devil's own job proving that Mavor has anything to do with it. Barling knows nothing, so all I have is Coogan, whose word will hardly carry much weight in a court of law. One of the justices of the peace in Marylebone, Sir Cainforth Winstanton, is a good friend of mine, and has an excellent lockup on his premises at Marylebone Manor. Coogan can languish there for the time being while I think what to do next. Judge and jury aren't likely to believe him against Mavor's inevitable protestations of innocence, so I need to set a trap.'

'What sort of trap?'

He gave her a rueful look. 'When inspiration strikes, you will be the first to know. For the moment, however, I just want to get Catherine safely home.' He assisted his distressed ward from the settle. 'Come, Catherine, you can ride double with me because I want to leave Xanthe where she is for the time being. Outwardly everything must appear in order. If it isn't, Mavor may have a chance to cover his tracks.' He turned to Barling, who was in the open doorway. 'I accept that you are innocent of willing involvement, but I suggest you stay elsewhere until this is over.'

'I have a sister in Isleworth, Sir Richard. I can go to her.'

'Good. I will see that word is sent to you the moment this is resolved.'

'Thank you, Sir Richard.'

'Right. Let's quit this house without further delay.'

Leaving Barling to hastily prepare to go to nearby Isleworth, they all left the house. The men hauled Coogan off toward the Peach Tree, where a pony and cart would be made ready to take him to Richard's friend, Sir Cainforth Winstanton, in Marylebone. As Catherine hurried to the meadow to snatch a moment or so with her beloved Xanthe, Richard caught Annabel's arm and made her stop. 'Annabel . . . ?'

'Yes?'

He cupped her face in his hands. 'Thank you for your sharp eyes. If you hadn't spotted Xanthe, we wouldn't have found Catherine.' He bent his head forward to kiss her on the lips. It was not a fleeting kiss, but long and lingering, filled with all the tenderness of newly acknowledged love, and as he drew away again, they both realized that everyone seemed to have witnessed it, including Catherine.

He smiled. 'There, Annabel Gresham, now all the world knows I love you,' he whispered, but he knew a sliver of conscience because of his intention to go to King's Place to seduce Juno Wyatt. His motives might be laudable, he thought, but would Annabel think that the ends justified the means?

25

The servants at Tregerran Lodge were overjoyed when Catherine was brought safely home; and so was a certain Mr Toby Vernon, who gazed at her with such rapture that he was rendered utterly helpless. No word was adequate for the way he felt on seeing in the flesh the adorable young woman he had admired on canvas. She exceeded his hopes in every way, and he gladly offered himself as her willing slave.

When Catherine had washed her hair and indulged in a warm bath scented with her favorite rose water, she changed into a white muslin gown sprigged all over with little navy blue flowers, and joined the others in the drawing-room. As she sat on the sofa, listening to Richard's lengthy explanation concerning all that had been going on, she looked so utterly enchanting that Toby stared quite unforgivably. Annabel quietly reprimanded him, fearing he would embarrass Catherine, but although he struggled to mend his new way, he did not succeed for very long.

He hardly heard a word that was said, and

was consequently ridiculously at a loss when Catherine suddenly addressed him. 'Do your bruises trouble you greatly, Mr Vernon?'

'Mm?'

'Your bruises. Richard has explained what befell you.'

'Oh, I, er . . . '

Annabel spoke for him. 'He is improving daily, Miss Hensleigh.'

Catherine looked at Toby again. 'I do hope you will be well again soon,' she said with a shy smile that sank him as completely as one of Lord Nelson's broadsides.

Annabel could not help smiling, for it was novel to see him in such a state. Toby had always been liked by the opposite sex, and he was far from inexperienced, but right now he seemed as gauche as a schoolboy! But then, Catherine Hensleigh was quite exquisite, a porcelain doll of a creature who was as charming and delightful as she looked. She was also innocent, sincere, unaffected, and possessed of the sort of smile that twinkled in her lovely dark eyes as well as on her lips. In short, to Toby, she was perfection.

Catherine turned to her. 'I am so glad that you and Mr Vernon are here, Miss Gresham. Please tell me that you intend to stay on, for it would please me greatly to have you here.' The lovely dark eyes implored. 'Richard does his best to keep me amused, but he is only a man.'

Richard was offended. 'Thank you very much.'

'Oh, you know what I mean. I am sure you would be delighted to indulge me with a discussion about ribbons, lace, and other such things. No, of course you wouldn't, but Miss Gresham knows exactly what I mean. Don't you, Miss Gresham?'

'Er, yes, I rather think I do.' Annabel smiled.

'So you *will* stay on? Both of you, of course.' Again the devastating smile winged Toby's way.

Annabel was in a cleft stick. She wanted to stay very much, but at the same time she had her domino plan for King's Place to consider. She still needed the codicil if she was to save Perton House, and going to Juno's from Tregerran Lodge would be impossible.

'But — '

'Annie and I will be glad to stay,' Toby said quickly, fearing his sister was about to sink his chance of progress with Catherine.

Richard looked inquiringly at Annabel. 'Is that in order?'

She summoned a smile. 'Yes, of course. I . . . I just didn't want to be an imposition.'

Catherine laughed at that. 'Imposition?

Miss Gresham, after the way I saw you kissing each other a little earlier, I don't think you could ever be an imposition to Richard!'

Toby sat forward. 'Eh? What's this?' He glanced at Richard. It is going that well between you and Annie? his eyes asked.

Richard cleared his throat and got up. Then to Annabel's surprise — and hurt — he denied the nature of the kiss question. 'Catherine, I think you misinterpreted a mere display of gratitude.'

'*Gratitude?*' Catherine repeated in disbelief.

Annabel kept her gaze fixed upon the floor, and was glad when Mordecai entered the room with a letter that had just been delivered. The Cornishman bowed. 'Forgive me, Sir Richard, but I rather think this may be urgent.'

'Who is it from?'

'I do not know, sir. A boy brought it, then ran off without waiting. I'd hazard a guess that it has something to do with overnight events,' the Cornishman replied, glancing at Catherine, who immediately sat up anxiously.

'Is it about Percy?' she asked as Richard broke the unmarked sealing wax and opened the letter. He scanned the few lines, then nodded to her. 'Yes, it is a ransom demand,' he said quietly.

Catherine gasped, prompting Toby to completely forget his bruises in order to hasten to join her on the sofa, where he ventured to put a comforting hand over hers.

Richard read the letter out to them.

Tregerran. If you value the pug's life you will respond favorably to this demand. I want one hundred guineas to be carefully packed and left at Mrs Smith's Haberdashery, Pav'd Alley, identified only by the number fourteen. You are to take it there in person, no one else. As soon as this has been done, and the money safely collected, your property will be returned. Any attempt at trickery will result in the pug's certain death.

Catherine burst into tears, and Toby pressed his handkerchief upon her and murmured words of reassurance.

Forgetting her hurt for a moment, Annabel hurried to Richard's side to read the letter for herself. A mere glance told her that the author was an educated person. 'Fourteen is the number Molly put on the letter she asked Toby to deliver,' she said. 'This isn't her writing, so I think it must be Boskingham's.'

Richard nodded. 'I believe so, too, although it cannot be proved. It seems a little stilted, as if someone was attempting to disguise their real hand. Do you see the loops here and here? And the way the letters are joined here and here?' He pointed.

'Yes, the writer is taking too much care,' she agreed, then looked at him. 'What will you do?'

'I shall do exactly as instructed,' he replied, and turned to Mordecai. 'I'll leave right now. Please be so good as to have my horse saddled.'

'Sir Richard.' Mordecai bowed, then hurried from the room.

Catherine looked tearfully at him. 'Do you have that much money in the house, Richard?'

'Of course I do.' He smiled fondly at her. 'I am sure that Percy will be back with you very soon. Now, with your leave, ladies, sir, I will do the necessary.' Inclining his head, he went out.

Annabel followed him. 'Richard?'

He turned quickly, and with a smile. 'Annabel?'

She hesitated. How could she express the vulnerability his explanation of the kiss had again aroused?

He came quickly back to her. 'What is it?'

'Why did you say what you did to Catherine? About the kiss, I mean?'

'Is that why you look so solemn?'

'Yes.'

He tilted her face so that she had to look at him. 'My darling, I simply did not want Toby to think there had been any impropriety. That's all.'

'You are sure?'

'Of course.' He looked earnestly into her anxious eyes. 'Have you so little faith in me?'

She lowered her gaze. 'No, I have so little faith in myself. I look at Catherine and know she reminds you of Elizabeth. I look at myself, and know I cannot compare with either of them.'

'My darling, surely what matters is what I see when I look at you? I loved Elizabeth very much, and I always will, but you are the one I love now, and the embraces we have shared these past few hours tell me that my feelings for you are greater than any I've known before.'

'Greater?' Her glance fled toward the portrait, which seemed to be watching and listening.

'Oh, yes,' he whispered. 'You are the other half of my soul, Annabel Gresham, and the sooner you realize it — and *accept* it — the better. There are to be no more doubts, no more diffidence, no more fears. Will you promise me that?'

Tears shimmered in her eyes as she nodded. 'Yes, I promise.'

His lips brushed her again, then he left her in order to fulfill the ransom demands that would hopefully bring about Percy's safe return.

★ ★ ★

A little later, as chance would have it, Hester was walking through Pav'd Alley at the very moment Richard delivered the guineas to the haberdashery. He did not see her, however, for she was in the florist's shop where Molly had purchased the *Cuisse de Nymphe* for Juno. She was selecting fresh flowers for the Dog and Duck when a casual glance out of the window revealed Sir Richard Tregerran entering the haberdashery opposite with a small but clearly heavy package.

Flowers were suddenly of little interest as Hester moved closer to the window in order to peer across the alley. She could just see inside, where Richard was now handing the package to Freddie, who today was quite gorgeous in lilac satin. In a moment Richard left again, pausing outside to put on his tall hat. Then he glanced up and down the alley before striding away into St James's Street. Hester hurried out to watch him as he paid the boy who had been holding his horse. Then he rode swiftly off in the direction of Piccadilly.

Hester gazed after him, then back at the haberdashery. What was going on? she wondered. Was there a question mark over him after all? There was one way to find out! She swept back to the haberdashery and went inside to the counter, where Freddie immediately endeavored to appear as if he had not been examining Richard's package.

He gave her a wary look. 'Well, if it isn't the queen of Piccadilly,' he declared in his oddly effeminate voice.

'Well, if it isn't Fragrant Freddie,' she replied in kind, then wrinkled her nose. 'I perceive you are still the Viscount of Violets.'

'One likes to smell sweet,' he replied.

'Even though one isn't? Hm. Now then, Freddie, my laddo, are you going to tell me about this package, or do I have to remember certain unsavory details about your life that might prove of interest to the law?'

'Oh, you nasty vixen!' he cried, tossing his head and pursing his rouged lips. Then he glanced at the package. 'Feel the weight of it. There must be a hundred guineas in there, or I'm a Dutchman!'

Hester picked up the package. It was indeed heavy, and the jingle could only be of coins. 'I think you may be right about the contents, but it's the recipient I am interested in, and believe me, I am quite capable of carrying out my threat.'

He was flustered, but had no desire to test her resolve. 'Oh, very well,' he said petulantly. 'What do you want to know?'

'Who is it for?'

'Number fourteen, whoever that is,' he replied.

'Well, find out,' she ordered, 'although I fancy I already know.'

He reached under the counter and drew out a ledger. 'Let me see now. Twelve, thirteen . . . ah, here it is. Oh.'

Hester looked quickly at the ledger. As she suspected, the number fourteen belonged to Molly Simmonds. 'Well, now, Freddie, it is your cousin's number, is it not? Tell me what you know.'

'I don't know anything.'

'That will indeed be the day, sir. Tell me, or else.'

He considered refusing, but courage was not his forte. 'I don't know anything, really, except that Molly and her fellow are rather foolishly dabbling in Lord Mavor's affairs. That's more than I would do, I can tell you. I've tried to warn dear Bosky . . . '

'Bosky?'

Freddie's eyes lightened, and a wistful smile touched his rouged lips. 'Oh, he's such a darling, with hair a divine shade of corn, and the loveliest blue eyes I have ever gazed upon.'

'I'm not interested in Boskingham's claims to divinity, or in your wayward tastes, just what happens now regarding this package.'

'Well, it waits to be collected, of course.' Freddie examined his beautifully kept nails.

'When?'

'How should *I* know? It might be in five minutes — it might not be until next week.'

'Molly tried to return to Juno, didn't she? How did she get on?'

'She was thrown out, and came straight round here to dun me for a few quid.'

Hester was relieved to hear it, for that meant the documents were still in the candlestick. 'Where are Molly and Boskingham staying now?'

'I don't know.' Freddie held up his hands to prevent her from accusing him of lying. 'It's the truth, I have no idea at all where they are. They come to me — I've never been to them.'

'Very well, then you must do something for me, Freddie.'

He sighed and tutted. 'Do I have any choice?'

'Not if you wish to keep my wagging tongue at bay.'

'It's so unfair,' he declared theatrically.

'Unfairness is one of life's tedious little drawbacks, Freddie,' she replied with a cool smile. 'Now then, I do not doubt that one of your many mignon friends would be prepared to earn a little reward for following whoever picks up the package?'

'Following?' he repeated.

'Yes. Is it a word you do not understand?'

His nostrils flared. 'Oh, you do have a sharp tongue,' he complained.

She laughed. 'Sharp enough to carve you up into slices, Freddie. Right, I will leave it with you. I want the collector followed, and I want to be told the results immediately. Whoever brings word to the Dog and Duck will be handsomely remunerated for their trouble.'

'How handsomely?' he asked with interest.

'Enough to make it worth someone's while,' she said, and left the haberdashery.

As she made her way back to the Dog and Duck, she wondered what to do about the curious matter of the package of coins. What was handsome Sir Richard up to? Oh, she thought, if only Annabel and her brother were here instead of delayed by the weather out at Tregerran Lodge. At least, she presumed that was why they had not returned the night before. She knew the lanes of Marylebone often suffered after rain, so the storm was probably to blame. Still, the weather was fine again today, so no doubt they would be able to return very soon. When they did, she had a great deal to tell them!

26

It wasn't until the middle of the afternoon that Mordecai rode into the yard of the Dog and Duck to inform Hester that Annabel and Toby would be staying on at Tregerran Lodge. Hester was dismayed, for it meant she would no longer be able to convey to Annabel her suspicions arising from Richard's visit to the haberdashery. However, she found some consolation in making Mordecai Penworthy's acquaintance. The tall Cornishman was rather to her liking, and as he was by no means indifferent to her charms, he lingered at the inn rather longer than planned.

Hester had a lifetime of experience when it came to persuading men to do as she wished, and the usually taciturn Mordecai fell easy prey to her skills. They sat together in her cozy parlor, one cup of tea leading to another, and so great was the rapport she established that he was astonished to find himself taking her into his confidence about events at Tregerran Lodge. When she learned of the kidnapping of Catherine and Percy, and the reason for the package at the haberdashery, she was relieved to restore

Richard to his former lofty position in her estimation. It had been on Annabel's account that Hester had been so alarmed to doubt him, for there was no mistaking that young lady's futile struggle against falling for him.

Hester's immediate concern now was for everyone at the lodge to be told of her own maneuvers where the execrable Freddie was concerned. She realized how provident had been her presence in Pav'd Alley at the very moment Richard left the package, for now there was every chance that Percy *and* the hundred guineas might be safely recovered. She had no fear of Freddie taking the risk of double-crossing her, for her threat was a very real one. Legality had never featured prominently in his activities, and imprisonment certainly awaited if he were to be exposed in all his unworthy glory.

After telling Mordecai what she had done, she instructed him to relay every word, and he promised faithfully that he would. He thought she was a most admirable woman — a comely armful, as his father had always said — and he'd have stayed there drinking tea with her until the legendary cows had come home, except that he had to return to his duties at the lodge. As he was about to leave, he shyly requested permission to call upon her again. Hester was more than disposed to grant the wish.

She walked out into the yard with him, and there her glance fell upon a packhorse that had been requested earlier but not collected. Until then she had intended waiting until the lanes of Marylebone Park were passable to wheeled vehicles before sending Annabel and Toby's things to the lodge in a pony trap, but suddenly it seemed obvious to use the horse, which Mordecai could lead back right now. He thought it a sensible notion as well, so she called a maid and hastily repaired to Toby's suite to pack the things.

Thus it was that she opened a drawer in Annabel's room and discovered the domino concealed among the handkerchiefs, gloves, and similar such things every lady is always sure to bring with her. She stared at it. *A domino?* Now why would Annabel require such a thing? She had come to London because of the stolen documents, not to attend a masked ball! Hester was shrewd enough to know Annabel's rather impetuous spirit, and it did not take an enormous leap of imagination to suspect that Juno Wyatt was going to be taken up on her sly invitation!

While the maid continued to pack, Hester hid the domino beneath her apron and went pensively to the window. What should she do? Send everything to Tregerran Lodge *except* the domino? That was a possibility, but it still might not deter Annabel from her course. What else then? A word face-to-face seemed the best solution, but Mordecai had said that the lane near Tregerran Lodge was impassable to a carriage, which meant that the chariot was out of the question. Hester cleared her throat as she considered the disagreeable alternative — riding there.

It was a good long time since she had shown the *monde* she was as accomplished an equestrienne as she was at driving her vis-à-vis, and she was considerably larger these days, but she was still fit enough to mount a horse. One was required to be active in order to manage a large Piccadilly inn! She no longer possessed a riding habit, but would anyone really know if she wore her oldest gown under a voluminous cloak? It would be rather warm in a cloak, but that could not be helped. Getting there was not her only problem, for she did not feel able to call boldly at the lodge door. It was one thing for Sir Richard to acknowledge her here in London, and even dine at the inn, but it was quite another for a former abbess to appear on his private doorstep. Yet how else was she going to speak to Annabel?

Hester was in a quandary as she turned to watch the maid closing the last portmanteau.

Then she thought of Mordecai. Of course! If she went with him now, he was bound to know a suitable place at or near the lodge where a private meeting could take place, *and* he could tell Annabel she was waiting there. Without further ado Hester swept from the room and down to the yard again, where the Cornishman was leaning comfortably against the wall, enjoying a smoke of his long clay pipe as he watched the comings and goings at the busy inn. Hester did not tell him why she wished to see Annabel so urgently, but conveyed that it was an important private matter that required discretion. He was a little startled, but did not hesitate to cooperate, and Hester immediately went to change into her most dispensable gown and lightest cloak. Within half an hour, with the domino safely hidden in her cloak pocket, she mounted a sturdy Welsh cob to accompany Mordecai and the two packhorses north to Marylebone Park.

She was relieved to manage the entire ride without mishap, although it had to be said that her posterior definitely suffered a great deal! Mordecai took her along the causeway to the lodge, to the spot where the elms marked the perimeter of the grounds. After telling her he would not hear of her riding back unaccompanied, but would escort her himself, he continued the final two hundred yards to the house with the packhorse. He was to find that in spite of having delivered the package to Pav'd Alley all that time earlier, Richard had still not returned.

Although the poor cob had done most of the work, Hester was somewhat red in the face and out of breath as she waited for Annabel. She congratulated herself upon not having fallen in a ditch, or worse in the Tyburn itself! Never again would she get up on a horse she decided with feeling, as she dismounted, then dabbed her hot brow with a handkerchief. Mordecai and the packhorses disappeared beyond the servants' wing of the lodge, then all of twenty minutes passed before she saw him reappear with Annabel. He led his mount and the unladen packhorse while Annabel hurried anxiously ahead. 'What is it, Hester? Is something wrong?' she asked the moment she reached the waiting woman.

'Wrong? Well, I fancy there *will* be if you plan what I suspect you do.' Hester glanced past her to see that Mordecai was waiting discreetly out of earshot a little distance away. Certain he could not see, she held out the domino. 'What is the meaning of this?'

Annabel gazed at the offending article, then met Hester's critical gaze. 'I'm afraid I do not know what you mean,' she murmured.

'Oh, yes, you do, miss.'

Annabel summoned a light laugh. 'There is to be a masked ball at the Cheltenham Assembly Rooms next month, and — '

'Don't think to gull me, Annabel, for I have faced great mistresses of that particular art. Believe me, I *know* when a young minx is fibbing, and you, madam, are a great minx indeed.'

Annabel colored. 'There is no need to — '

Again Hester cut her short. 'No need? I suppose you are going to deny that the domino is for gaining entry to Juno's tomorrow night?'

Anna didn't reply.

'Ha! I thought so!'

Annabel looked guiltily at her. 'What do you intend to do? Tell on me for my own good?'

'I have never told tales in my life, and I do not intend to begin now,' Hester replied. 'All I want from you is an assurance that you will not go anywhere near Juno's seraglio.'

Annabel greeted this with a mutinous glare.

Hester sighed wearily. 'Oh, you foolish, foolish chit. Have you any idea what fate will await you once over that threshold? That auction the other night was not an isolated incident. Juno *enjoys* selling her new fillies to the highest bidder, and believe me, few of them are fortunate to be purchased by the likes of Sir Richard. Sliding between the sheets with him would not be a trial for any woman, but sliding between the sheets with a lecherous old goat who paws and dribbles is a very different matter.'

'Hester, I have no intention of letting things get to that point!' Annabel gasped, shocked that she should even think such a thing.

'And how, pray, do you imagine you will be able to prevent it? Once you are in, missy, you will not get out again until Juno is ready to let you go. You have sweet virgin written large upon your pretty face, and believe me, you will command a good price. Juno is in business, my dear, and she knows how to make a profit.'

'I . . . I would scream for help and throw myself on the mercy of a true gentleman!'

'You will not scream anything, my dear, because you will have been given a draft of something soothing to keep you quiet and malleable.'

Annabel stared at her. 'She would do that?'

'Oh, yes. Scruples do not loom large in her character.'

Annabel swallowed, and turned away.

'Hester, I really must have that codicil if I am to keep Perton House, and I know that if I go there as invited, I will most probably gain admittance to her private rooms.'

'Yes, you probably will. So far so good, but it's the getting out again that raises the difficulty, as I think I have demonstrated.'

'There must be a way of doing it. Maybe if we worked together . . . ?'

'We Annabel Gresham, my days of being a procuress are long since over, and if I assisted you in this, I would be no better than Juno herself! My conscience would not permit me to aid and abet an innocent like you to enter such an establishment.'

'I intend to be as innocent when I leave,' Annabel replied with a determined lift of her chin.

'I hear the baa-ing of a lamb on the way to slaughter,' Hester observed dryly.

'Hester, if there was a way of doing it safely, would you help me?'

'No.'

'Please, I beg of you.' Annabel came closer and took one of the older woman's hands in both hers. 'Please, Hester, for this is more important than you can begin to guess. Perton House is everything to me.'

27

'You are a horrid persuasive piece when you wish to be,' Hester complained, but did not snatch her hand away.

Annabel importuned again. 'Let us at least think. After all, you are my accomplice, aren't you?'

'For a sedate drive in my chariot, yes. For this foolhardy enterprise, no!'

'Look, if I can manage to get in, perhaps you can see that I get out,' Annabel said, speaking as the thoughts occurred. 'Maybe you could make a scene at the door, or . . . or send the constables in. Something of that sort?'

Hester gave an impatient groan. 'Send the constables? Oh, yes, what an excellent notion. You would then be locked in the stable with all the other fillies! How beneficial that would be for your reputation.'

'There must be a way, Hester, I just know it.' Annabel turned to gaze across the meadows, where the wildflowers were quite brilliant in the sunshine. Then a thought occurred to her, and she turned excitedly. 'Juno's private rooms are at the front of the house, are they not?'

'Yes, but I can't see what — '

'Once I have found the documents, if you are down in King's Place and I make signal from the window, you could come to the door and make a great fuss about Juno having lured me there for wicked purposes. You could beat on the door, threaten to send for the law, vow to see her in court! You could threaten all sorts of things, so that in the end she will be glad to throw me out.'

Hester stared at her. 'Is there no end to your capacity for recklessness?'

'It would work. I know it would.'

Hester sighed wearily. 'And while all this mayhem is going on, what of your brother Mavor? After all, it will be his birthday celebration, will it not? Do you imagine he will not recognize you?'

'Well, a great deal has gone on since last you and I spoke, and I now understand that he will not be there because he is staying in Brighton an extra day.' This very welcome news had been imparted in the drawing-room after Catherine's rescue.

'Juno will not like *that*!' Hester smiled at the prospect of her old foe's fury, then looked at Annabel again. 'You say a great deal has been going on? Are you referring to Miss Hensleigh's disappearance and rescue, and

271

the ransoming of her little pug dog? If so, I already know from the inestimable Mr Penworthy.' Hester glanced rather warmly toward Mordecai.

Annabel smiled. 'There isn't much more for me to tell you, oh, except that Juno is after the lease of the Peach Tree, just to spite you.'

Hester's breath caught. 'Is this true?'

'Sir Richard says so.'

'I see. Well, if she thinks she is going to do that, she will soon know her mistake. That tavern is to be mine, and only mine!'

'I hope you are right, truly I do.'

Hester gathered herself, and after a moment turned to another matter. 'Did Mr Penworthy have time to mention my visit to the haberdashery?'

'The haberdashery? No, he couldn't find me at first when he returned, and then he just said I was to come here to see you as a matter of some urgency.'

Hester told her about Freddie and the collection of the package, and Annabel was greatly impressed. 'How very fortuitous, and how sharp you were to think of such a thing.'

'Well, to be truthful, it was suspicion of Sir Richard that initially prompted me. However, once I had wheedled all the facts from Mr Penworthy, I realized that Sir Richard was still honorable after all.'

'So thanks to you, he may get his money back as well as Percy?'

'I sincerely trust so. At the very least we will discover where Boskingham has gone to ground, and where *he* is, so also must be Percy.'

A hopeful smile appeared on Annabel's lips. 'That should settle Mr Boskingham's hash — is that not the term they use in pugilism?'

'Most probably, although I am taken aback to hear a young lady employ it,' Hester replied.

'Oh, Toby has an interest in such things.' Annabel leaned back against one of the elms. 'How good it would be to sort all this out satisfactorily, and see the villains receive their just deserts. Sir Richard means to make certain of my brother Roderick's arrest and conviction for Miss Hensleigh's abduction by laying a trap of some sort. He says it will not do to rely solely upon the word of Coogan, the man they caught at Mr Barling's house.'

'What sort of trap?'

'That is the problem. I fear he has not fixed upon one yet.'

Hester turned away and paced up and down for a moment, then she regarded Annabel rather sleekly. 'I know how to snare Lord Mavor, my dear, and I will after all confound these scoundrelly fellows who think it their right to take the law into their hands,' she said quietly, then added, 'As for Juno Wyatt, it will be over my dead body that she takes over the Peach Tree tavern!'

★   ★   ★

When Mordecai escorted Hester back to London a little later, he found himself being begged to call on the way at the residence of Richard's friend, Sir Cainforth Winstanton, in whose lockup Coogan now languished. Mordecai did not demur, having very swiftly learned that she was not a lady to whom one ever said no. Not that he wished to refuse her, for when she explained exactly what she planned to do, he thought it all very neat, admirable, and clever.

Sir Cainforth, a dedicated bachelor and womanizer, was puzzled to receive a call from the former abbess, whose premises he had often favored, but when Hester explained her purpose, he immediately had Coogan brought from the lockup. On being questioned about how Roderick was to be contacted in the event of an emergency concerning Catherine, Coogan told them that a written message was to be dispatched, signed with the code name Mercury. He was constrained to pen such a communication, then returned to the lockup.

On leaving Sir Cainforth's house, Hester and Mordecai returned to the Dog and Duck, where she sent for the trustworthy Corbett, who had brought Toby's fateful letter to Perton House. He was given the note for Roderick, and instructed go to the Marine Pavilion in Brighton and see that it was delivered into that gentleman's hand the following morning. Corbett set off immediately, with sufficient money in his pocket to spend the night at an inn. Mordecai did not return to Tregerran Lodge, for he too had a part to play in Hester's stratagems.

★ ★ ★

Early that evening in Pav'd Alley, as the day's trade faded and business became very slow indeed at the haberdashery, Freddie was consumed with boredom. He yawned and stretched, then fluffed out his lemon neck-cloth and tweaked the elaborate cuffs of his royal blue coat. How he wished he had worn his emerald neck-cloth and coral coat today, for he really was not in a royal blue mood.

The doorbell tinkled, and he looked around. 'Oh, it's you, Coz,' he said airily as Molly came in. She was dressed in parchment muslin, with pink lace frills, and he supposed she looked well enough, but in his catty opinion she still smacked of the nunneries and always would.

She came up to the counter. 'Well, is that any way to greet your kith and kin?' she inquired, adopting a flirtatious manner because she knew he hated it.

He gave her a withering look, then pursed his lips. 'Er, how is Bosky?' he inquired.

'He's warming my bed very attentively,' she replied, 'so don't you go getting ideas.'

'Now would *I* get ideas about my own dear cousin's sweetheart?' he protested with a flutter of his long lashes.

'Yes, Freddie, you would, for you are the most unprincipled creature I have ever known. I'm well aware that you have a fancy for Bosky, but if you take so much as a single step toward him, you'll have me to reckon with.'

Freddie gave a trill of laughter. 'Oh, my dear, you have me trembling in my shoes. Let me just say this — when it comes to your Bosky, if all three of us were chicks in a nest, *you* would be the only one to be pushed out!'

'He has asked me to marry him,' she said then, and enjoyed the change that came over his painted face.

'Marry you?' he repeated. 'But he can't!'

'He already has.'

Freddie recovered a little, and gave her a knowing smile. 'My poor, dear Coz, I'm afraid he isn't free to marry anyone.'

Molly became very still. 'What do you mean by that?'

'You should do your home lessons where such a delectable morsel is concerned, my dear. I've done mine, which is how I know he is already married.'

Thunderstruck, she stared at him. Then she laughed. 'Oh, Freddie, you almost had me believing you . . . '

'It is the truth, sweetness.'

Suddenly she knew it was. 'Who is he married to? Where is she?'

He gave a laugh. 'My dear, it is more than my life is worth to tell you that.'

'Why?' she asked, unease entering her eyes.

'Because Lord Mavor is concerned along the line, and *he* is someone I certainly do not wish to tangle with. My advice is that you leave well enough alone, sweetness. Just realize that when Bosky promises marriage, he is playing you false.'

For a long moment she could only gaze at him, her lips slightly parted. Then anger and resentment clouded her eyes. She had been used!

28

Too bitter to speak, Molly turned on her heel to leave the haberdashery, but Freddie called quickly after her. 'Aren't you forgetting your package? That is what you came for, isn't it?'

She turned quickly, her mind racing. 'I . . . I quite forgot.'

'It's been here for hours now,' he said, repairing to the back of the shop to get it.

Molly came slowly back to the counter. She had realized she had been taken for a fool, offered empty promises simply in order to keep her sweet and induce her to help, but she was a fool no more! As Freddie placed the package in front of her, she smiled at him. 'Well, there is nothing like a dousing with cold water to bring one to one's senses. Of course you are right about who would be ejected from the nest, so I intend to cut my losses.'

'Very wise,' he replied, delighted to think his immediate rival was withdrawing from the arena.

She tapped the package. 'I think we both know what this contains, don't we?'

'Possibly.' He became guarded, wondering

what was she up to.

'If I do something for you, Freddie, will you do something for me?'

His nose wrinkled. 'My dear, I don't think there's anything *you* can do for me.'

'Well, I can make absolutely certain that Bosky calls here alone. You would be able to try your luck with him then, wouldn't you?'

He was interested. 'Go on. What must I do in exchange?'

'Just tell him that I came for the package and told you I was taking the Falmouth stage.'

'*Falmouth?*'

'He knows I yearn to go to America.'

'I see.' He studied her. 'And what will you really be doing?'

She gave him a knowing look. 'You don't think I'm going to tell you that, do you?' she said, sliding the package across the counter toward her.

He promptly slid it back again. 'Not so quickly, dearest, for I'm not sure about this . . . '

'What is there to be sure about? All I'm asking is a chance to get away.'

'With the money.'

'Yes, of course with the money. I'm hardly going to go without it!'

A calculating expression settled over his

visage. 'You can go without some of it,' he said.

She recoiled slightly. 'No.'

'Suit yourself,' he replied, tightening his hold upon the package with one hand and patting his hair into place with the other.

Molly was in a quandary. 'If I do give you some of it, can I be sure you will keep your side of the bargain?'

'You'll have to trust me, won't you?'

She would as soon trust Old Nick, but knew she had no choice. 'How much?' she asked.

'How much is there?' He weighed the package in his hands. 'A hundred guineas?'

'Eighty.'

He looked suspiciously at her. 'Well, we'll have to open it and see, won't we?' he said, and before she knew it, he'd ripped the brown paper and exposed the neat columns of gleaming coins. 'I spy ten little piles, each one of ten guineas,' he went on. 'Shame on you, Coz.'

'A girl can only try,' she murmured, and looked away.

'I'll have half.'

She gasped. 'Half! Never!'

'Take it or leave it,' he said, pushing five columns toward her.

'And you will say what I asked you to say?'

'Yes.' He scooped the other fifty guineas into a little box he brought from beneath the counter.

She seized her portion and put it quickly in her reticule, then hurried from the shop, but from the corner of her eyes she saw him signaling someone in Pav'd Alley. This person was a young man of about his own age, and effeminate without being rouged and curled. As she hurried into King Street, she realized that she was being followed. Determination steeled her, and she ran into Nerot's Hotel before the startled doorkeeper had time to blink. She fled across the vestibule and up the staircase, for she knew her way around the superior establishment, having at one time or another entered the room of many a lonely gentleman staying there.

At the top of the stairs she darted down the passage that led straight in front of her, then at the end she descended the back stairs used by the hotel servants. Halfway down was a landing, with a window that opened out on to the flat roof of a store. She climbed out, ran across the roof to the ivy-covered wall of the building next door, and scrambled down the ivy to the narrow court beyond. From there she ran through into Pall Mall, then across into Schomberg House, where was located the premises of Harding, Howell &

Company, a large shop that comprised numerous different departments set upon several floors. She scurried upstairs, then down again, finally emerging from the rear of the building and making her way through into the open acres of St James's Park.

Satisfied that she had managed to throw off all chance of being followed, she set off for the address in Oxford Street where she and the treacherous Boskingham were lodging. A determined expression had settled over her face. So Bosky thought to lead her along on a string, did he? Well, she would show him. And at the same time she would teach Cousin Freddie a lesson for stealing half the money from her. She walked quickly, spurred by anger, and in no time at all she had crossed Piccadilly by the Dog and Duck, covered the length of Dover Street, and reached the lodging house near the Roman Rooms, where Bosky awaited her in an attic room. Before going up to him, she was careful to hide the fifty guineas in a cupboard beneath the stairs, then she rubbed her right cheek until it was red and ran sobbing up to the attic.

Boskingham swung his legs off the bed in alarm as she burst tearfully in. 'What the dickens . . . ?'

'The money has been taken, Bosky!' she cried, hiding her face in her hands and sobbing still more.

He leapt up as if stuck with a pin. 'What do you mean?' he snapped.

'Freddie has it. He was just handing it over to me when he realized what it contained. He said he didn't see why he should pass over such a fine chance. I tried to get it from him, but he struck me.' She lowered her hands slowly to reveal her reddened cheek.

Bosky stared at her, his face becoming ugly with fury. 'I'll skin him alive! So help me, I will!' he cried, then dashed to a drawer. He pulled out a pistol, checked that it was loaded, then ran from the room.

Molly listened to his steps flying downstairs, then smiled coolly. 'At least I've kept my side of the bargain, Freddie, for he's coming to see you,' she murmured.

After that she wasted little time, grabbing all her things together in a battered old valise before going into an adjoining room where Percy was curled up forlornly on the floor with a bowl of water and some dry bread. A length of thin rope was tied to his collar, then to the leg of the bed, and he looked so sad that for a moment even Molly's heart was touched.

'Oh, I'm sorry, pug, but at least I'm going to let you go now. Better late than never, mm?' She untied him, then pulled the rope to coax him out on to the landing.

Percy dug his paws in a little, clearly not sure whether he was better off where he was, but at last she managed to cajole him downstairs, where she retrieved her money from the cupboard before taking the pug out of the house. Once in busy Oxford Street, which was as much thronged with people and traffic as Piccadilly, she put her things down again in order to remove the rope. 'Off you go then, dog.'

Percy gazed up at her, his tongue lolling.

'Go home!' Molly ordered. 'Well, go on!' She stamped her foot.

Percy flinched, then ran off as fast as his little old legs could carry him. Molly picked up her belongings and set off for pastures new. Fifty guineas wasn't much, but it would see her through to whatever lay ahead.

The pug kept running for several minutes, but then halted as he tried to get his bearings. He sniffed the air, calling up his instincts. Ah, it was *that* way! Turning, he trotted north into Marylebone Lane.

★　★　★

In the meantime Boskingham had run all the way to Pav'd Alley. He was in such a rage that he hardly noticed how far it was, or how hot the day. All he could think of was getting the money back and punishing Freddie for his impudence. But the moment he burst into the haberdashery, brandishing the pistol and causing two women at the counter to almost faint with alarm, Freddie took off like a greyhound into the rear of the shop. Boskingham gave a bellow of fury and leapt over the counter after him.

There followed a chase through the alleys and courts that separated King Street from Pall Mall, with Freddie squealing ever louder as he realized he wasn't going to throw off his furious pursuer. At last he reached the corner of St James's Square, where he hesitated. Savage with triumph, Boskingham halted and took aim. Freddie glanced back, screamed 'Murder!' and fled across the square toward the circular pool in the center.

Boskingham fired the pistol, and the shot winged through Freddie's hair, whining as it passed. Freddie kept on running, with Boskingham again on his heels. Soon they were both in the pool, grappling and struggling like demons until the constables' whistles sounded and both found themselves being manhandled out of the water under arrest. Accusation and counteraccusation was shouted, with Boskingham vowing that Freddie had stolen his money. A search of the haberdashery revealed at least half of said money being found in Freddie's private box, but if Boskingham thought he had won, he was mistaken, because he remained under arrest for the criminal act of having fired a pistol with intent to kill or maim. Both were set to appear before the magistrates first thing the following morning.

29

Annabel was preparing for the sortie to Juno's temple in King's Place. It had been agreed with Hester that at eight o'clock she would at last claim the terrible headache that had crossed her mind several times since arriving in London. She would then retire to her room, entreating the others not to disturb her. She and Hester had discussed everything in the minutest detail, except how the latter was going to corner and trap Roderick. All Hester would say was that when Richard returned at last from his errand to the haberdashery, he was to be assured that Lord Mavor was as good as shipwrecked.

Richard had not come back to the lodge until just before dinner. He explained his longer than expected absence by saying he had encountered an old friend, but this was not the truth. He was actually finding it difficult to face Annabel again because he felt bad about going to Juno's. He almost wished he had not thought of it, for then his cursed conscience would not now be plaguing him! But he had thought of it, and felt he had to proceed, even though there was a very great risk that Annabel might find out and would not accept such a circumstance.

Women did not regard these things in the same light as men. It was one of life's great ironies that a man could be unfaithful and swear — often truthfully — that it meant nothing, yet he could not accept the same behavior from a woman. Nor could he appreciate it when a woman did not understand his selfishly male point of view. Selfishness wasn't this man's motive now, and whatever ensued with Juno he would be able to say truthfully that it meant nothing, but Annabel wouldn't understand. And why should she? he thought. She gave her kisses because she meant them, so how could he expect her to believe that his were meaningful when bestowed upon her, but shallow if Juno was the recipient? If the shoe was on the other foot, and Annabel was the one to have kissed elsewhere, would he believe her? Eventually maybe, but the path to that conclusion would be very long and rocky — perhaps too long and rocky, he concluded.

All this was weighing on his mind when he entered the lodge, and it was immediately obvious to Annabel that all was not well. He assured her that it was, and she need not worry, but she was not comforted. Her dismay increased when at half past seven, directly after dinner and before she retired to her bedroom, he suddenly announced he had remembered some important business that required his immediate return to town. As he spoke, she was sure she intercepted a meaningful exchange of glances with Toby, but when she questioned her brother a few minutes later, he told her she had imagined it.

She now found Toby's manner odd as well, indeed it was almost furtive. Clearly he knew something concerning Richard that he was not prepared to divulge. Still being unsure of herself in this new experience of love, she could not help wondering if Richard had told Toby he wished he had not plunged in so deep with her.

After that it had been only too easy to plead the planned headache and escape upstairs, but as she crossed the inner hall to the staircase, Richard was coming down. He was dressed in evening clothes and did not look at all as if business was his purpose. She halted, almost feeling like fleeing back into the drawing-room.

'Annabel?' Her manner made him halt on the landing by the portrait. He was fiddling with the lace spilling from his indigo velvet cuff, and the light caught his wedding ring, which suddenly seemed to Annabel to be shining more brightly than before. She felt as if a gulf had opened between them.

His carriage was heard drawing up beneath the porte cochère, and all she could think of saying was, 'I . . . I trust your business is successful.'

'I hope so, too.'

He found it hard to meet her eyes, and she knew it. It was too much for her to bear, but she had to say something. 'Richard, I cannot endure this atmosphere. If you wish after all to distance yourself from me, I would prefer it if you simply said so.'

'Distance myself?' he repeated foolishly, for it hadn't occurred to him that this was the impression he might be conveying. 'Annabel, if I have caused you to think such a thing, believe me I didn't mean — '

'Your manner since returning from town has been so pointed that I cannot help but reach this conclusion. So I want to assure you that I will not cause any embarrassment. I will stay on here, but it will be for Miss Hensleigh's sake.'

He hurried down the last flight of the staircase and seized her by the arms. 'I love you and don't want anything to end between us! It's just . . . I have something weighing on my mind.'

'Whatever it is can clearly be confided in Toby.'

'I admit it, but I beg you to trust me, Annabel.'

'Trust you when you do not trust me?' She knew she was being unfair, because she herself had entrusted others with information she was at pains to keep from him, but in her unhappiness she could not help herself.

Green shadows deepened in his eyes. 'I cannot tell you, Annabel, but I nevertheless ask again for your trust.'

'How would you feel if I were the one leaving the house right now?' she replied, continuing her unreasonableness by overlooking the fact that very shortly she would indeed be leaving the house, and for a purpose she could not possibly confide in him!

He didn't answer, and she caught up her skirts to hurry upstairs.

'Annabel!'

She didn't stop or look back, but ran to her room with tears stinging her eyes. The chamber she had been given in lieu of Catherine's faced across the grounds toward the elms beneath which she and Hester had met earlier in the day. A few minutes later she heard his carriage departing, and went to the window to watch as the curve of the drive carried him briefly into view. The coachman had brought the team up to a smart trot, and she could just see Richard seated on the opposite side of the vehicle from her. His head was turned away, and she could see his arm resting along the sill. Then the drive carried the vehicle out of sight again.

She struggled to compose herself. This time a week before she had not even heard of Sir Richard Tregerran, let alone shared kisses with him, so if she had been able to exist then, she could do so again now. Besides, she had the recovery of the codicil to think about! Hester had promised to send the chariot to wait just a little way down the lane from the lodge, where the way widened sufficiently for such a vehicle to halt without impeding any other traffic. If the lane had remained impassable, the chariot would wait at the Peach Tree and a ride along the causeway would have been required. Thankfully there was no need to resort to that, nor would the chariot be there yet for Richard to see as he drove by.

She quickly got ready to slip from the house. There was no need for her to change clothes because she was already wearing the aquamarine gown from dinner, and her hair was combed and pinned into the best she could manage for an evening style. All she had to do was put on a cloak and some pattens that would protect her satin slippers, which had required a great deal of cleaning after the night of the storm. The train of her gown she would have to hold up safely by means of the little ribbons sewn in for that purpose. After all, every lady wished to be fashionable, and remain clean and tidy at the same time, which certainly could not be done if her train dragged through puddles and mud.

Minutes later, with the domino secure in her evening reticule, she secretly left the house out of sight from the drawing-room and made her way toward the lane. Hester's chariot arrived as she approached, and in hardly any time at all she was *en route* for the Dog and Duck, from where she would commence her attempt to enter the house in King's Place.

★   ★   ★

In his carriage ahead of her, Richard gazed out at the lengthening evening shadows for a long while, then lowered his eyes as he considered his strategy for the seduction of Juno Wyatt.

30

It was just gone half-past ten when Hester's chariot drew up by the archway. King Street was unexpectedly busy now that darkness had fallen. Bursts of male laughter issued from the open doorway of the Golden Lyon tavern, where a group of gentlemen in evening dress was in convivial spirits, but tonight also happened to be the occasion of a ball at Almack's. As a consequence of the latter there were a number of fine carriages arriving or turning around in the street. The windows of the one-hundred-feet-long ballroom on the first floor were open to the night, and even above the noise from the tavern the music of Mr Gow's orchestra could be heard playing a country reel.

However, Almack's could not have been further from the minds of the two ladies in the chariot as they gazed through the archway into King's Place, where Juno's house was ablaze with lights and Claudius the footman was standing guard outside the door, as always he did after dark.

Annabel wasn't as sure of herself as she pretended. 'Hester, if I do not appear at that window within half an hour, you are to make such a disturbance that Juno will fear her convent is on fire! You promise now, don't you?'

'Of course I will, you foolish chit! And do not fear that I will not be able to raise the necessary riot, for believe me, I have help at hand.' She nodded through the archway toward a tall figure standing in the shadows at the far end.

Annabel's lips parted. 'Mordecai?' she breathed.

'The very same. When he accompanied me back to town from the lodge, I acquainted him with our intentions. He will come to your rescue with force if need be.'

'But he might tell Sir Richard, and — '

'That he most certainly will not! Any gentleman I take into my confidence will always keep that confidence, my dear. You may count upon it that Mordecai Penworthy will be as silent as the grave itself where tonight's work is concerned.'

'So there is no chance whatsoever that Sir Richard already knows?' Annabel had a wild thought that this might explain his reserve toward her.

'Sir Richard knows nothing of this, my dear. You say he is on business here in town, and I must presume that is indeed the case.'

'Except that he was dressed fit for Almack's,' Annabel murmured, glancing toward the assembly rooms as another carriage drew up and a gentleman alighted. By the light of the lamp at the hallowed door, she saw that he wore a tight-fitting black velvet coat, white pantaloons and stockings, black pumps, and a white satin waistcoat that shone a little as he turned to speak to his coachman. Then he tucked his tricorn hat beneath his arm and disappeared into the rooms.

'Sir Richard will not have gone to Almack's, my dear, because I happen to know he does not care for the place since his wife died.'

'Oh.'

Hester looked gently at her. 'You love him, don't you?' she asked quietly.

Annabel saw no point in denying it. 'Yes, I fear I do. Much good it does me.'

'He doesn't return your affection?'

'He says he does, but I no longer believe it. I was a very passing fancy.' Annabel looked determinedly toward King's Place again. 'Well, I . . . I suppose I had best get on with it . . .'

'Only if you are absolutely certain you wish to.'

'I must regain the codicil, Hester, for it is my only hope for the future.'

'Your *only* hope? Oh, my dear, how wrong you are to hold such a low estimation of yourself. There is no doubt in my mind that you will soon make a very good marriage, and when that happens, Perton House will be neither here nor there to you.'

'I wish you were right, Hester,' Annabel replied, then donned the domino. In a moment her face was entirely concealed, her eyes by the mask, the rest by the little gauze veil. 'Would you know me now?' she asked.

Hester shook her head. 'Only by your gown and hair, but that is because I am acquainted with both. No one there tonight will recognize either.'

Annabel opened the chariot door and alighted in a rustle of taffeta. Hester climbed down as well, then glanced again toward the brightly lit house in King's Place. 'I would guess that Juno does not yet realize Mavor is going to disappoint her,' she said. 'Believe me, the festivities would be at an end if she did, for her temper would have sent everyone scuttling for cover.'

'Maybe she has just decided to continue as if nothing untoward has happened. That way at least she would save face.'

'Juno Wyatt doesn't stop to think of such things once something has upset her. She goes off half-cocked, as they say. Anyway, good luck, my dear,' she said, then lingered out of sight of Claudius as Annabel approached the fateful green door.

The other houses in King's Place had their curtains drawn discreetly upon what went on within, but every window of Juno's house was open and brightly lit. Annabel could see into the ground-floor rooms, where gentlemen in evening wear flirted with masked ladies in gowns so *décollete* they seemed perilously close to falling off. Chandeliers blazed, paintings of classical scenes of a rather improper nature hung on gilded walls, and a woman with a very pretty soprano voice was singing a naughty ditty to the strains of a cello, violin, and pianoforte. There was a murmur of conversation, with now and then a ripple of laughter.

Claudius straightened suspiciously as Annabel came toward him. 'Who are you?' he demanded, for only gentlemen were expected.

'My name is Miss Brown. Miss Wyatt invited me here tonight.'

'Oh? She didn't mention you,' he replied, still suspicious.

'Well, if you tell her I am here, I am sure she will wish me to be admitted. Tell her I have considered her advice, and have left my other abbess.'

He hesitated. 'You'll have to wait out here,' he said.

'Yes, for I understand you must make certain.'

He was a little mollified by her reasonableness, and went into the house. For a moment Annabel glimpsed the glittering hallway, where flowers and candles reflected in ornate oval mirrors. The sweetly seductive smell of eastern spices drifted on the air as Annabel glanced back. Mordecai was still by the narrow way that led through into Pall Mall, but Hester was keeping well out of sight beneath the arch. A rather discomforting quotation came back to her. *There is many a slip 'twixt cup and lip.* Oh, how true, she thought, for it could not be denied that anything might happen to her once she was inside this house.

She gave a start when the door was suddenly flung open. Juno stood there, startlingly immodest in a wisp of a Grecian gown that covered very little indeed of her magnificent figure. She was barefooted, and her fiery hair was caught up with strings of pearls. There was a little too much rouge on her lips and cheeks, and her eyes were painted in such a way that Annabel was put in mind of an illustration she had once seen of an Egyptian pharaoh.

Juno's gaze was guarded. 'Well now, what do we have here?' she said thoughtfully.

'I . . . I have decided it would be very foolish indeed not to take you up on your offer, Miss Wyatt.'

'My offer?'

'You said that if I wished to go far I should forget Mrs Ferguson and come here to you tonight.'

'Ah, yes, so I did. Take off your domino that I may see your face properly.'

Annabel obeyed, and Juno surveyed her critically. 'Hm, not too bad, not too bad at all. Tall, slender, and fair is not exactly what the *monde* seeks *à ce moment*, but you have a certain fresh charm. However, if that demure rag of a gown is your notion of seductive wear, I fear you have a great deal to learn. The neckline is far too proper!'

'It isn't that proper,' Annabel protested, for her father always chided her that this particular gown was too low!

'As far as my gentlemen are concerned, my dear, you lack only a wimple to make you a true nun!'

Annabel felt like turning and running away, but she reminded herself sternly that she needed the codicil, and thus made herself stay. 'This gown is the only one I possess that is suitable for evenings, Miss Wyatt,' she explained.

'Do I take it you would wear something

300

more inviting if you had the choice?'

'Yes, of course.'

Juno smiled. 'Very well, my dear. Do come in, for I am sure I have something appetizing tucked away in my personal wardrobe.' She stepped aside by way of ushering the newcomer inside. As Annabel crossed the threshold, Claudius resumed his place outside. Juno addressed him. 'Mind now, Claudius, I am to be informed the very second Lord Mavor arrives!'

'Yes, madam.'

Annabel waited close to the foot of the staircase. Through an open doorway at the end of the hall she could see the gaming-room, where gentlemen who wished to could enjoy hazard and faro instead of the more comely diversions elsewhere in the house. There was applause as the soprano ended her song in the front room, but in a second or so the singing began again, this time a Mozart lullaby to which the words had been rewritten — for to be sure Mozart himself could not have heard them!

The scent of spices was very strong indeed, and now that she was inside she saw that it came from little candles set beneath metal bowls in which scented oil had been poured. Annabel felt as if the brilliant, intimidating house were folding its frightening wings over her. There was still time to flee . . .

Juno closed the front door. 'By the way, my dear, I presume you are as virginal as you look?' she inquired.

Annabel's cheeks flared. 'Of course I am!'

'Ah, such maidenly color and indignation convinces me there is no need for an examination,' Juno murmured with some satisfaction as she walked past her to the pink marble staircase, which boasted newel posts formed of gilt cupids.

Annabel turned quickly. 'Examination?' she repeated nervously.

'My dear Miss Brown, you do not imagine that I believe every trollop who enters this house claiming to be intact? I would be a gull indeed. There are methods that fool callow boys, of course, but really experienced gentlemen are never tricked. Those same experienced gentlemen are prepared to pay a great deal for the privilege and satisfaction of being the first. Once I have you looking as required, you will be a great success tonight, my dear. Now then, follow me.'

31

Richard's carriage moved slowly west along Pall Mall toward St James's Palace. This was the third time the coachman had been ordered to do this because Richard was steeling himself for what lay ahead. The carriage halted once more outside Harding, Howell & Company, where nightlights burned in the windows and the doors were now locked for the night. The coachman alighted and came respectfully to the door. 'Do you wish me to drive around again, Sir Richard?'

'Er, no, I think not. Just wait here.'

'Sir.' Puzzled, the man climbed back up to his seat.

Pall Mall was never quiet, for there were many clubs situated along it. Several growler ranks ranged down its center, and there was always traffic passing by. Richard could hear snatches of conversation as people strolled along the pavements, a drift of music from a small concert hall, a street cry or two, and the seductively brazen importuning of the ladies of the night as they approached unaccompanied gentlemen.

He glanced at his fob watch by the light of

a street lamp. Eleven o'clock. Time to acquaint Juno with Mavor's change of plans? Yes, he thought, the moment was ripe. He opened the carriage door and alighted. Soon he had crossed the street and was walking toward the narrow entrance that led into King's Place.

★　★　★

At Tregerran Lodge, Toby and Catherine were concerned only with each other. They had opened the French windows to go outside, where Toby thought the climbing roses smelled sweeter and more romantic than ever now that Catherine was near. The western sky still bore the faint stain of the departed sun, and the peacocks were calling. For Toby it was a perfect moment, but for Catherine it was marred by the absence of her adored pug. 'Percy would always join me if I came outside like this,' she said with a sad little sigh.

'And he will again,' Toby declared vehemently, wondering if he dared place an arm around her shoulders. How he longed to do it, but he feared rejection. She might think him presumptuous, fast, or maybe even that he was a fortune hunter!

Catherine wished he would make an advance

of some sort, for she liked him far more than she imagined could be possible in so short a time. She was afraid to give an indication of favoring him in case he should think her forward. And why should he not, given her foolish behavior regarding Lord Mavor?

So neither of them said or did anything as they stood there side by side, gazing toward the remnants of the sunset. Then Catherine thought she heard a familiar little noise, a sort of wheezy panting . . . 'Percy?' she gasped.

Toby heard it too, and cast around in the fading light for anything that might be the pug. Then a pathetic whine ended on something resembling a sneeze, and the pug, footsore and exhausted, could be seen coming toward them from the direction of the elms. Catherine gave a sob of joy, and caught up her lemon silk skirts to dash across the grass. Toby hurried after her as best he could, and was almost in tears himself as he saw her sweep Percy up into her arms and cuddle him close.

'Percy! Oh, my darling, darling Percy!' she cried.

'Is he all right?' Toby asked as he reached them.

'I . . . I think so. Are you all right, Percy?' she asked, holding the pug up to look into his big round eyes.

Percy whined and stretched forward to lick her nose.

'Yes, he's all right,' Catherine declared. 'A little tired, maybe, but that can soon be remedied.'

Toby stroked the pug's head. 'I wish you could talk, boy, then you could tell us what happened.'

'The kidnappers must have brought him back on receiving the hundred guineas,' Catherine said.

Toby presumed so, too, and together they took the delighted pug into the house, where he was immediately treated to a drink of water and a plate of his favorite tidbits. Then he curled up on a comfortable chair and went to sleep. Catherine gazed at him, enraptured. 'Oh, isn't he sweet? Isn't he beautiful?' she breathed.

'It's certainly wonderful to have him back safe and sound.' Toby was forced to be diplomatic, for in his opinion pugs were rather ugly.

Tears suddenly shone in Catherine's eyes. 'Oh, I . . . I have b-been so desperately worried,' she whispered.

Toby gave in to temptation and pulled her tenderly into his arms. 'Did I not promise you that all would soon be well again?' he said gently.

'Yes, you did.' She raised her adorable face to look at him. 'Toby Vernon, if you do not kiss me now, I shall never forgive you.'

Toby thought he would die of happiness as he carried out her command. Wrapped in each other's arms, they contrived to make the kiss last a very long time indeed, certainly long enough to know how very agreeable an exercise it was. Agreeable enough to be tested again, and again . . .

It was therefore some time before it crossed Toby's mind to go upstairs to tell Annabel the good news about Percy, whether or not she wished to be disturbed. He hurried to her door and knocked. 'Annie?' Silence. 'Annie, wake up!' Still no sound from inside. 'For heaven's sake, *I* am the one who sleeps deeply,' he complained. Then he gave up. 'Oh, all right, sleep on if you must, but if you're awake and just too lazy to reply, I thought you would like to know that Percy has come home safe and well.'

With that he turned on his heel and walked away again, none the wiser that his sister wasn't even in the room.

★ ★ ★

Richard strolled across King's Place to Juno's door. The curtains at the lower windows had now been discreetly drawn, and by the noises emanating from within he could well understand why. The evening of dalliance and misconduct was clearly well under way. Claudius's face broke into a welcoming smile. 'Good evening, Sir Richard,' he greeted as he opened the door with a flourish.

'Good evening, Claudius.'

As Richard went inside, a dismayed Mordecai walked quickly to the archway, from where he and an equally alarmed Hester withdrew to King Street to discuss this new situation. She looked urgently at the Cornishman. 'Why didn't you tell me Sir Richard was coming here tonight?'

'Because I didn't know, of course. You don't think I would have held my tongue about something like this, do you?'

She was flustered. 'No, I suppose not. Forgive me. But what shall we do now?'

'Hanged if I know. Well, if he sees Miss Gresham, he sees her. There's nothing we can do about it. Anyway, we'd best keep an eye on those upper windows, for she might appear at any moment.'

They moved back beneath the archway, still being careful to keep out of Claudius's sight, but as they directed their anxious gaze to the top story, there was still no sign of Annabel.

In the interim, Richard had entered the

hot, sweet-smelling hall. An attractive nun wearing little more than a mask emerged giggling from a doorway. She was leading an eager baldheaded gentleman by a golden chain fixed around his neck. 'Come along now, there's a good dog,' she coaxed seductively, and as she conducted him upstairs, he uttered rather ridiculous canine noises. From the next floor there also came the sound of a whip, and a female voice berating 'a very naughty boy!'

Then a loud burst of laughter came from the room the nun and her dog had just left, and Richard glanced in to see there was a 'horse race' in progress, with six gentlemen on all fours being ridden by scantily clad female jockeys. The Bishop of Cranton was leading Major General Sir Conway Farrer-Plunkett by a short head. In the other room the soprano was still trilling, although now in a rather uneven tone. When Richard inspected the reason for this, he discovered she was endeavoring to concentrate upon 'Rule Britannia' while being fawned upon by three Tory Members of Parliament, all pillars of moral rectitude whenever they addressed the House of Commons.

While Richard stood downstairs watching the riotous assembly and wondering where Juno was, Annabel was seated on a pink silk sofa in that lady's rooms, sipping a glass of suspiciously sweet wine. She did not detect anything untoward about the drink; indeed she was far too nervous to think much at all. The domino and her too proper aquamarine silk lay on a nearby chair, together with her slippers. On her feet now she wore Roman sandals made of glittering gold string. Her gown had been replaced by one of cerise tissue with a matching slip, both of which shunned propriety, and her hair had been dressed anew into a deceptively loose knot on top of her head. It was the sort of knot that looked as if it would disintegrate at any moment, allowing her honey tresses to fall about her naked shoulders; the sort of knot, in fact, that suggested its wearer might be equally disposed to fall into becoming disarray. A loose knot for a loose woman, she thought in horror as she caught a glimpse of herself in Juno's elegant floor-standing glass.

Juno topped up the glass of wine. 'Drink up, it will make you feel better. My, my, Hester has been remiss, for she clearly hasn't prepared you for your new profession.'

'Can anyone really be prepared?' Annabel inquired, sipping the wine again as she began to find its sweetness quite pleasant. She glanced around the room, which was as pink and frilled as it was possible to be. A large vase of *Cuisse de Nymphe* — presumably

Molly's unsuccessful bribe — stood upon a table, beside another of the little bowls of spiced oil heated by a candle. There were a number of Indian furnishings and ornaments, among them a figurine of a rather grim goddess with at least twelve arms. She also noted two tasseled rose silk cushions, one embroidered with golden figures of naked dancing maidens, the other with couples making love in the most impossible positions. They were certainly not the sort of cushion one could present to one's elderly aunt!

The door into the adjoining bedroom had been closed since she arrived, for it so happened that Juno's dressing-room could be entered from the parlor. A number of gowns had been brought out for Annabel to see, all of them exceeding *décollete*, and now they lay on a chair in a rainbow of dazzling colors and trimmings. The cerise tissue suited Annabel's coloring surprisingly well, for it was not a shade she would ever have chosen. But the gown's immodesty made her look every inch the demirep, she thought, and hastily finished the glass of wine. If only Juno would go out for a moment, so she could get into the bedroom and see if the candlesticks were there! Always assuming the documents were still there, of course. Oh, please let them be there! she thought. It would be too cruel if they had already been removed.

Juno was replying to her last remark. 'Prepared for one's first time? Probably not,' she said, and came to replenish the wine.

'Am I not keeping you from your guests?' Annabel ventured hopefully.

'Mavor isn't here yet, and everyone is quite capable of enjoying themselves without my constant supervision.'

Mavor isn't coming, if you did but know it, Annabel thought, but she said, 'What is to happen now?'

'Happen? Well, when Mavor condescends to grace us with his presence, I have a novel diversion in readiness. I have found a fire-eating oriental woman who dances naked with a large python wrapped around her oiled body.'

Annabel's lips parted in horror. 'A . . . a python?' The fire-eating was bad enough!

'Yes. I shuddered, too, but it is a very sensual display.'

'I'm sure it is.' Annabel drank some more wine, and was glad of the warmth that was beginning to seep through her veins. Oh, how she wished she were at home in Perton House, curled up safely in her own bed!

'Now then, my dear, we must think of what to call you, for I doubt very much if your given name will do. My real name, for instance, is Dowsabel, which is hardly to be recommended.'

Annabel managed not to laugh, even though the wine already made her want to. 'Dowsabel? How very unusual.'

'Hmm, that is not what I would call it. Needless to say, I altered things as soon as I could, becoming Juno, which I believe to be infinitely better. What is your name, by the way?'

'Annabel.'

'Oh, dear. That is almost as bad as Dowsabel.'

Annabel didn't think so at all, but such an opinion was clearly not what was required. 'What do you suggest?'

'Something classical and titillating. Let me see now . . . Ah, yes, you shall be Tanith, who was the Phoenician goddess of love.'

Tanith? Annabel didn't like it particularly, but supposed Juno must know what she was talking about. She finished her wine again. Really, this was becoming quite easy, she thought. She no longer felt in the least bit nervous; in fact she was sure she would carry everything off quite effortlessly.

Juno smiled at her. 'Well, I think you are ready to go downstairs to see what price you can command.'

'Price?' Annabel repeated, not seeing the

fate that suddenly loomed so large before her, and no longer in a state to particularly care anyway.

'It will be fun, my dear, and I know you will enjoy it immensely when you go to the highest bidder.'

Annabel giggled. *Fun?* Oh, she always liked fun . . .

32

There came a sudden knock at the door, and Richard called out softly. 'Are you in there, Juno?'

Tregerran? Juno turned sharply. Why had *he* come up here? she thought.

Richard spoke again. 'Aren't you going to welcome me in?'

'Er, one moment, if you please!' Juno looked down at Annabel in exasperation. Of all the times for him to choose. She caught Annabel's hand and hauled her to her feet. 'In here, my dear, and don't you make a sound or it will be the worse for you,' she warned as she ushered her decidedly unsteady new charge toward the dressing-room.

Annabel trotted obediently in, then leaned against the long rail of dazzlingly improper gowns. She smiled foolishly at Juno, and sank to the floor, waving her fingers. 'It . . . it was nice to meet you again,' she murmured, then closed her eyes and went to sleep.

Juno stared at her in astonishment. The creature had no head, no head at all! One glass of the wine would clearly have been sufficient! Closing the door upon Tanith, Goddess of Love, Juno hurried to the outer door. 'Why, what a very agreeable surprise,' she said in her most seductive voice, because Mavor or not, she had always desired Richard.

He smiled into her eyes, then allowed his gaze to move appreciatively over her. 'Why, Juno, how very tempting you are tonight,' he murmured, reaching out to draw a fingertip across her breasts.

Her breath caught. 'And how very daring you are, sir, to call up here when Mavor might arrive at any moment.' She stood aside for him to enter, then glanced out toward the staircase, where her personal maid always waited. 'Kitty? The moment Lord Mavor arrives, I wish to be warned, is that clear?' she hissed.

'Yes, madam.'

Juno closed the door and turned to face Richard. 'To what do I owe this delightful honor, sir?' she asked, resuming her husky voice again.

'Well, I fear I am a rather base opportunist, Juno. You see, Mavor won't be coming here tonight,' he replied, wondering which of the other doors was that of the bedroom.

'Not coming? That's nonsense, of course he is.'

'He is still in Brighton, having been persuaded by the Prince of Wales to spend another night at the Pavilion.'

Juno stared at him. 'There must be some mistake . . .'

'No mistake.'

'But Mavor knows how much trouble I have gone to tonight — '

'Clearly it has made no difference,' Richard pointed out. He wasn't telling her anything that was not the truth.

'How *dare* he treat me this way! He hasn't even had the grace to let me know! I could have postponed things until tomorrow . . .' She paused to draw a furious breath. Never had she been more the hot-tempered redhead. She shook with rage, and her usually pale cheeks were on fire with anger and humiliation.

Richard would have felt sorry for her had he not known the things of which she was capable. He went closer. 'Mavor clearly doesn't appreciate you, Juno. I, on the other hand, see your qualities only too well. So I am here to offer myself instead. It may not be my birthday, but we can think of something to celebrate, can't we?' He held out his hand and smiled the sort of smile that made women, Juno Wyatt included, quite weak at the knees.

Her anger checked as if by magic, for this was what she had longed for until she had cast in her lot with Mavor. 'If this is some jest, sir . . . ' she whispered.

'Do you wish me to go?'

'No.' She went to him and entwined her arms around his neck. 'You have always known how I feel about you,' she whispered, pressing her voluptuous curves to him.

'I have been a fool,' he breathed, and bent his head to kiss her.

She moaned with pleasure, her lips parting weakly as she moved against him. She knew her art, how to excite, to tempt, to storm even the most determined defenses, and slowly Richard's arms moved around her.

In the dressing-room, Annabel suddenly awoke again. Her head was spinning, and she felt as if she weren't really there. Or anywhere else, for that matter. Slowly, she managed to pull herself to her feet and stood swaying. There were two doors, and light shone beneath them both. A frown puckered her forehead as she wondered where she was. Then a vague memory managed to edge its way into her befuddlement. This was Juno's dressing-room! But which door was that of the bedroom? She put a finger to her lips as she deliberated the immensely difficult problem. Then another silly smile spread over her face, and she tottered toward the nearest door and opened it.

Juno's bedroom was revealed, and on the mantel stood the four Indian candlesticks, the elephant, tiger, monkey, and crocodile. Which one contained the documents? She tried to guess. Oh, another terribly hard problem! She made her unsteady way to the fireplace and frowned at the candlesticks. She rather liked the tiger. Yes, she would look at that one first. Taking it, she wrestled it apart, and was delighted to be correct the first time, for the documents were there, neatly rolled up and tied with a red ribbon, as they had been when Toby left Perton House. Grasping the prize in her hand, she forgot that she was supposed to appear at the window, and wove instead toward the door into the parlor.

At that precise moment Hester and Mordecai commenced their planned disturbance, the specified half an hour being up and it seeming to them that something might have gone wrong. Poor Claudius was helpless to prevent them from pushing noisily into the house, shouting and banging for all they were worth.

Juno pulled swiftly away from Richard's embrace, her eyes flying alertly toward the outer door of the rooms. But Richard's glance was drawn in the other direction entirely as

Annabel appeared, brandishing the documents in triumph, and giving him a very silly smile. Stunned, he could only stare at her, for she was the very last person he had expected to see. Or wished to see right now.

Juno hurried from the rooms without realizing that Annabel had awakened, for all she could think of was putting a stop to the unseemly fracas in progress in the hall. The moment she had gone, Richard took a step toward Annabel.

'What in God's name are you doing here?' he gasped, startled by the gown she was only just wearing.

She giggled, and waved the documents. 'I'm king,' she said.

'I beg your pardon?'

'Hide and seek. I've found them, so I'm king.'

'To hell with hide and seek! What madness has possessed you to come here?' he cried, realizing only too well how close she had come to an auctioned fate.

She gazed at him, then wagged a finger. 'I saw you with Juno. That was naughty.'

'Not as naughty as the scanty rag you have seen fit to drape upon yourself,' he retorted, wishing the gown didn't allow him to see quite so much of her, delicious though she was.

'You mustn't speak to me like that, for I am Toothless, Goddess of Love.'

'You're *what?*'

She frowned as she tried to remember. 'The Fnee, Fneenee, Fneeneenee Goddess, Goodness of, Gladness of . . . Oh, of *Somethinoruther.*'

'Just how much of Juno's damned brew have you had?' he demanded.

'Two? Free? Four? Li'l teeny g-glasses. Hic.' She giggled again as the hiccups started.

★　★　★

Downstairs there was now utter mayhem. Hester and Juno were arguing at the top of their considerable lungs, and everyone else was urging them on in the hope of a proper fight. Mordecai slipped past them all and hurried upstairs, where he loomed quite suddenly in the doorway.

'Sir Richard?' Then he gasped on seeing the state Annabel was in.

Richard whipped around. '*Mordecai?* Is the entire complement of the lodge here?'

'No, sir, but I think we had better go before the constables arrive.'

Annabel beamed and waved. 'Hello, Mordecai!' she called.

Richard gave her a vexed look and reached

out for the documents, but she held them away infuriatingly. 'Finders keepers,' she said.

He put an arm around her waist and pulled her closer in order to try to take them again, but still she held them away. 'Pay a forfeit,' she whispered.

'A forfeit?'

Suddenly, she linked her arms around his neck and kissed him passionately, after which she meekly surrendered the documents. He tucked them inside his coat, then caught her up and flung her over his shoulder like a sack of flour. 'Come on, Miss Mischief, let's get you safely out of here,' he said through gritted teeth.

'Put me down!'

'Be quiet.'

Mordecai preceded him down to the hall, where Hester was proving more than a match for Juno. The fishwives of Billingsgate would have had a very hard job indeed of outdoing her as she set about Juno with a tongue-lashing second to none. When she saw Mordecai, and then Richard with a wriggling vision in cerise tissue draped over his shoulder, she stared for a moment, then hurried to the front door. Annabel's legs kicked and she beat Richard's back with her fists, but this spirited display of resistance was somewhat ruined by the sort of squealing laughter that heralded a singular headache come the morning.

Mordecai and Richard pushed through the crush in the hall, and once outside were followed by what seemed to be everyone else in the house — bishops, major-generals, Members of Parliament, and all. King's Place was soon as great a crush as Juno's hall had been, as the occupants of the other houses came out to see what on earth was going on *chez* Wyatt.

Richard was going to make for Pall Mall and his own carriage, but Hester beckoned quickly. 'My chariot is just through the archway!'

Turning, he ran that way instead, and in a moment Annabel had been bundled into the chariot. Hester climbed in as well, the coachman was instructed to go to the lodge, and the vehicle set off apace along King Street.

Richard watched it disappear, then drew a long breath. 'What a night, Mordecai, what a night,' he observed cordially.

'Indeed so, sir.'

'I presume that mine was not the only attempt to recover the documents?'

'Er, no, sir.'

'Why on earth did you allow Miss Gresham to do such a thing?'

Mordecai was wounded. 'Sir Richard, have you ever attempted to dissuade two very determined ladies from doing something they have decided upon?'

'Well . . . '

'Believe me, sir, it is an impossibility. All I could do was be there to see that all was well.'

Richard straightened his neckcloth and tweaked the lace at his cuffs. 'Oh, I suppose you have a reasonable point.'

'I believe so, sir.' The Cornishman was still offended.

Richard gave him a wry smile. 'Don't be so touchy, Mordecai, for *I* am the one with the problem.'

'Problem, sir?' Mordecai looked inquiringly at him.

'I rather fear that Miss Gresham saw me with Juno in my arms. If she remembers come the morning, my elegant hide will be worthless in her eyes.'

'Oh, dear, sir.'

'Oh, dear, indeed,' Richard murmured. 'However, there is nothing I can do about it now. Let's go. My carriage is in Pall Mall.'

'Are we returning to the lodge, sir?' Mordecai asked, falling into step beside him as they made their way back into King's Place.

'No, to Sir Humphrey Smythe-Castle's

address in Mayfair. I'm going to place these damned documents in his hand right now, then that will be the end of it.'

'Yes, sir.'

King's Place was now a veritable bear garden of noise and disturbance. Nuns in various states of undress leaned from upper windows, some of them throwing water out over those below. Juno's rivals were luring her gentlemen away, the abbesses more than ready to tell her a home truth or two in the process, and the soprano chose that unfortunate moment to trill again. '*Oh, quiet is the night, and lonely . . .*' She got no further because someone opened a bottle of champagne, shook it violently, then turned it upon her. There were shouts that the fracas was all the doing of Bond Street Loungers, and as Richard and Mordecai walked calmly through it all toward Pall Mall, the officers of the watch ran past, waving their staves and whirring their rattles.

33

It was just after sunup in Brighton, and in the sumptuous surroundings of the Prince of Wales's Marine Pavilion, Roderick was greatly annoyed to be aroused. He hadn't gone to bed until four, and had expected to sleep on until noon. Instead, a dolt of a royal footman was shaking him awake at ten to inform him that a very urgent message had been brought from Marylebone.

Marylebone? Roderick sat up with a jolt. 'Well, give it to me, give it to me!' he breathed, reaching for his handsome black-and-silver-striped dressing gown.

'I do not have it, my lord. The messenger says he must give it directly to you.'

Something must be very wrong, Roderick thought in dismay as he swung his legs from the rather grand gilt bed and slid his feet into his Turkish slippers. 'Take me to him!' he commanded, and was still buttoning his dressing gown as he followed the footman through the royal seaside residence.

Hester's man, Corbett, was waiting at a lowly side entrance, the message clutched tightly in his hand. He saw a look of suspicion descend on Roderick's eyes on seeing someone he did not recognize. But the story was well prepared, and the groom explained that his cousin Coogan had twisted his ankle and asked him to come instead. Still suspicious, Roderick took the message and read the contents with increasing dismay.

Miss Hensleigh has been taken very ill and is like to die. You must come quickly, for I do not know what to do. Mercury.

Roderick's mind raced. What a dolt Coogan was to actually mention Catherine's name! If such a message had fallen into the wrong hands . . . Still, it had been delivered safely, and there was nothing for it but to show Brighton a sharp pair of heels and get to Marylebone without delay. Suspicion lingered, however, as always it must with a man of such devious and convoluted a nature. He fixed Corbett with a steady look. 'What do you know of this message?'

'Know, my lord? Why, nothing. Coogan told me to keep my nose clean if I knew what was good for me, and that's what I've done. I've no more idea of what that message said than I have of flying to the moon. I can't read anyway,' Corbett added.

Roderick nodded. 'Very well, you may go.'

The groom lingered, hoping for a tip, but Roderick waved him off. 'I do not doubt that Coogan paid you well enough, so do not think to cozen me for more. Be off with you.'

Corbett hurried away. It had been worth a try, but he wasn't that stupid. He knew what the likes of Lord Mavor could do.

Within half an hour Roderick had taken his leave of the Marine Pavilion and was driving up toward the Sussex Downs as if the entire complement of Brighton Barracks was charging after him. It was just over fifty miles of excellent road to London, and he hoped to be at the Peach Tree sometime in the afternoon. He prayed Coogan was wrong about Catherine's condition, for what use was a dead heiress?

★ ★ ★

Meanwhile at Tregerran Lodge, Annabel was asleep as Richard stole into her room after sunrise. He stood for a moment beside the bed, then reached down to put his hand tenderly to her cheek. 'Oh, Annabel, my dearest,' he whispered, wondering what he would see in her eyes when they opened. Would she remember what she had seen at King's Place? He prayed with all his heart that she would not.

She stirred and looked up at him. 'Richard?' she whispered, wondering why her head pounded like a drum, and her mouth tasted like something unmentionable from the bottom of the canary's cage.

'How are you feeling?' he asked, taking her hand.

'I feel dreadful. Have . . . have I been ill?' She was confused.

'Er, not ill exactly.'

She searched his eyes. 'What then?'

'I fear you imbibed a little too much of Juno's hell-brew.'

Annabel stared up at him. 'I did?'

'You don't remember?' His heart hesitated between beats.

'No. I . . . I recall driving to King Street with Hester, but that is all. Are the documents — ?'

'They are safe. After I saw you safely into Hester's chariot, I took them to Sir Humphrey.'

'Oh, I'm so relieved . . . ' She closed her eyes gladly. It was over, and her future was safe. Then she looked at him again. 'You saw me into the chariot? You were there, too?'

Hope began to stir within. Maybe Dame Fortune was going to smile upon him after all. 'Annabel, what do you recall about last night?' he ventured.

'The way we parted, when you left on some business you had overlooked.'

How much did he dare confess without the risk of prompting the very recollection he wanted her to forget forever? 'Annabel, I didn't want to confide in you because I was going to Juno's to try to regain the codicil, and I didn't want you to misunderstand.' Please let that suffice, he thought.

To his joy she smiled. 'Well, I didn't confide in you either, did I?'

'No, you didn't.'

'So perhaps we had better leave it at that. We both thought of more or less the same plan, but neither of us wanted to tell the other.'

'More or less.' He gazed into her eyes. 'I love you, Annabel.'

'And I love you,' she whispered, her hand reaching toward him across the coverlet.

His fingers closed tenderly over hers. Was now the time to propose? But even as he wondered, she spoke again.

'What was I doing when you found me?'

'You had just located the documents and were coming out of Juno's bedroom.' He saw again the exceedingly interesting cerise gown, and the delightfully foolish smile upon her lips.

'And that is all?'

'Yes, that is all.'

Her brow wrinkled. 'I wish I could remember more.'

Let that wish never be granted, he thought fervently.

At that moment there came the sound of barking from the lawns outside, and her head turned eagerly toward the window. 'Isn't that Percy?' she gasped.

'The very same.'

'So Boskingham released him when the hundred guineas was paid?'

Richard glanced back at her. 'Not quite. Sir Cainforth Winstanton sent a lengthy message here this morning to explain certain events last night. Boskingham and Fragrant Freddie are under lock and key, and will appear before magistrates later this morning. Oh, it is yet another long story, and I think you are too tired to hear it now.'

She smiled. 'I still feel quite awful.'

'Here, drink a little of this. It will help.' He went to the table by the bed, where a jug of peppermint cordial stood in readiness.

She struggled up in the bed, and gladly accepted the glass he poured for her. Soon her mouth tasted respectable again, and it even seemed that the peppermint assisted with her aching head.

'Better?'

'Yes, thank you.'

'Then I will leave you to rest again now, for I wish to be there when Mavor walks into

Hester's trap. Sir Cainforth Winstanton and his constables intend to lie in wait at Barling's house, and I mean to be with them.'

'Take care, for Roderick will not submit lightly.'

'I know. Is there anything else I can do for you before I leave?'

As he took the empty glass and placed it by the bedside, she noticed for the first time that he was no longer wearing his wedding ring. He saw her glance, and smiled. 'I should have taken it off the moment I knew how much I wanted to kiss you,' he said quietly.

Salt tears stung her eyes, but they were tears of happiness. 'Kiss me again now,' she whispered, lying back on the pillows and holding her arms out to him.

He gathered her to him. He could feel her warmth through her nightgown, her pliant body and the firmness of her breasts pressing against him. Oh, to lie down with her now, to make love to her, then fall asleep with her in his arms. He could think of nothing more sweet than to awaken and find her nestling against him, her hair spilling loose as it was now, her perfume invading his soul . . .

He pulled away so that he could look into her eyes.

'Your future is secure now, my darling. With the recovery of the codicil you are certain of Perton House, and therefore free to decide what you want of life. I would regard it as the greatest honor imaginable if you said you wanted me. Annabel, will you do me the great honor of becoming my bride?'

Her lips parted. 'Oh, Richard . . . ' Doubts of her worthiness abounded. 'But I am a nobody!'

'A nobody? I do not think so, for you are vitally important to me, Annabel.' He pushed a lock of hair back from her cheek. 'Say yes. It is a very small word, but right now it will seal my happiness.'

Tears welled from her eyes. 'Yes,' she whispered.

★ ★ ★

All was quiet at Barling's house. Outwardly everything was as it should be, even to Xanthe still being with the other horses, her blaze dyed again to conceal her markings. But inside the house it was a very different matter. Richard had joined Sir Cainforth, his constables, and Mr Justice Fairbrother, a venerable and scrupulously honest gentleman whose word in court would be taken as gospel. As they awaited Roderick's arrival from Brighton, their mounts and Mr Justice Fairbrother's barouche were concealed behind the tea gardens. Everything was going on as normal around the Peach Tree, even to some boating on the little lake. When Roderick came, he would not notice anything amiss.

At last there came the rattle of an approaching carriage. Richard looked discreetly out. 'It's Mavor,' he warned, and every man immediately dispersed to his elected hiding place. Barling, a bag of nerves if ever there was one, had been given several large glasses of brandy to put some backbone into him, but even so beads of perspiration shone on his forehead and he looked fit to faint as he anticipated the knock at the door.

Roderick's carriage lurched to a standstill, then footsteps sounded. Everyone started as he thundered on the door. 'Open up!'

Barling swallowed, and his tongue passed dryly over his lips. Richard nodded at him. 'Well, go on,' he whispered.

Trembling visibly, Barling went to unlock the door, then stepped back fearfully as Roderick strode in. 'What's going on? Is she still alive?'

'Sh-she, my lord?'

'Miss Hensleigh! Coogan sent for me. Damn it, man, are you a halfwit?' Without waiting for a reply, Roderick ran lightly upstairs toward the room where Catherine had been kept.

Sir Cainforth caught Richard's eye. They would have to hold back, for nothing Roderick had said as yet would incriminate him in court. Thus far, he might be able to successfully claim he had received an anonymous message that Miss Hensleigh was imprisoned in the house.

Once upstairs, Roderick was alarmed to find Catherine's room empty. She must be dead! he thought. He would have to get rid of Coogan and Barling, for they could point a finger at him. Spinning around, he hurried back to the top of the staircase. 'Barling? Where is she? What's happened?'

'I . . . I don't know, my lord . . . '

'You don't *know*?' Roderick came quickly down again and seized the unfortunate Barling by the throat. 'I will have answers, damn it! Have you allowed her to escape? I left her well guarded, so if you — ' He broke off in shock as Sir Cainforth stepped quietly into view, at last satisfied that everyone had heard the necessary words.

'Well, now Mavor, I rather fancy we have you by the tail.'

Too late, Roderick realized he had fallen into a trap, but he wasn't done yet. Suddenly, he produced a pistol, which he began to level at Sir Cainforth. However, another pistol pressed coldly to the back of his neck.

'I wouldn't, if I were you. Now then, drop your weapon and release Barling,' Richard said quietly.

Roderick obeyed, and the unfortunate Barling promptly fell to the floor in a faint.

Sir Cainforth stepped nearer to retrieve the pistol. 'I fear you have jail to look forward to now, Mavor.'

'You will never secure a conviction.'

'Oh, we will, for there are many ears in this house, my lord.' Sir Cainforth indicated the other men who had now appeared, including the inestimable Mr Justice Fairbrother.

Roderick swallowed on seeing the latter. 'I didn't admit anything!'

The elderly gentleman eyed him. 'You spoke of leaving Miss Hensleigh guarded and fearing she had been permitted to escape. On top of which, you received a message that gave her name yet mentioned no address. You hied yourself straight here, which you would only do if you knew this was where she would be. If I had my way, you would be hung, drawn, and quartered for what you have done, but I will be content enough to see you locked away.'

Sir Cainforth seized Roderick by the scruff and propelled him from the house.

★　★　★

Annabel and Richard were married on a glorious day in September, when the sun shone down from a dazzling blue sky. The *monde* of London gathered at fashionable St George's in Hanover Square for the occasion. All eyes were upon the bride in her dainty cream gown, as she gazed adoringly into her bridegroom's eyes and said her vows in so small a voice that hardly anyone could hear. Mr Gresham had to wipe away a tear or two, as did Hester, but Catherine sobbed unashamedly into Toby's handkerchief, quite upsetting poor Percy.

On their wedding night at Tregerran Lodge, Richard stood on the rooftop balcony that opened off the bedchamber they would share from then on. The night was cool and moonlit, a peacock called on the lawns, and the roses still bloomed against the walls. He heard a soft step behind him, and turned. Annabel stood there, her honey-colored hair loose about her shoulders, her figure visible through the thin silk of her nightgown. He went to her, swept her up into his arms, and carried her to the bed.

She learned of love that night. He showed her pleasure, tenderness, passion, and more, much more. They fell asleep toward dawn, and when he awoke at noon the next day, she was in his arms, her hair falling over the pillow, her perfume filling his soul. He was in paradise.

34

It was the morning of St Valentine's Day the following year, the breakfast table at Tregerran Lodge sported a dainty bowl of snowdrops, and outside there was bright but cold sunshine. Inside, however, it was cozy and warm, with flames dancing in the hearth. Something had caught Richard's eye in his newspaper, and he looked up quickly toward Annabel, who was seated across the breakfast table from him. She wore primrose, and it became her very well. There was a glow on her cheeks, and a twinkle in her eyes as she met his glance.

'What is it? What have you read?'

'It concerns Mavor.'

'Oh. Nothing good, I hope.' She replaced her tea-cup on its saucer.

'Certainly nothing good as far as he is concerned. He has followed Boskingham to the hereafter.'

She stared at him. 'Roderick is dead?'

'It would seem so. As you know, he was sentenced to transportation to Australia, although what that unfortunate colony did to deserve it, I really do not know. Anyway, he was being rowed out to the ship at Wapping when for some reason he tried to escape. He jumped into the Thames, became entangled in a mooring rope beneath the surface, and drowned before he could be hauled to safety.'

She felt nothing. Roderick had been despicable to the end. He had appeared in court, charged with abduction and imprisonment, and had only been persuaded not to mention Catherine's name by the promise of transportation instead of something far worse. Even then he had attempted to extort money for his continued silence. He was no loss, no loss at all, she thought. Nor was Boskingham, who had shuffled off his mortal coil within the walls of Newgate, having been caught stealing from another prisoner, who hit him on the head with a three-legged stool.

Richard smiled at her. 'I have some good news for you as well, although not from the newspaper.'

'Good news?'

'Toby and Catherine are coming to stay next week.'

Annabel's face brightened. 'Oh, that is good news! No doubt we will hear all about the new house they have found in Rutland. It is Rutland, isn't it?'

'That or Huntingdon. Or is it Cambridge? Oh, it doesn't matter, because if my guess is right, they will not be telling us about just the house.'

Annabel gazed at him, and then she gasped. 'You mean . . . '

'I think so. In her letter Catherine mentions feeling unwell in the mornings and wanting to eat oranges all the time. She says Toby has the devil's own task acquiring them now she has eaten all there were in the orangery.'

'Oranges are always a sign, are they not? Oh, I do hope you are right.' Annabel's mind began to busy itself. 'When they are here, we must invite Hester and Mordecai to dine. Then I will have all my accomplices together!'

'Hester will insist that we all go to the Peach Tree. You know how proud she is of it now that she has enlarged the tea gardens. And how she likes to play hostess with Mordecai on her arm,' Richard added with a smile, for the tavern was home to another happy marriage.

'I hope she does, for I adore boating on the lake.' Annabel glanced outside. 'Weather permitting, of course. I froze the last time.'

'You soon warmed up when I got you back here,' Richard said, giving her a lazy smile.

'So I did. You have a very warming way with you, Sir Richard.'

'Long may you continue to think so.'

Her glance was wickedly flirtatious. 'Oh, I

will, make no mistake of that. In fact, if you wish me to prove it again now, I will gladly return to the bedroom with you.' Fruit creams crossed her mind . . .

'Shame on you, Lady Tregerran.' He studied her. 'Actually, I would not hesitate to take you up on your shameless offer, but I have to ride into town shortly.'

'Business?'

'Yes.' Their eyes met, and he smiled. 'Not in King's Place, I assure you.'

'I sincerely trust not, sir.'

'Actually, I have tittle-tattle about certain denizens of St James's. Would you care to hear?'

'Of course.'

He reached for another slice of toast. 'As you know, Juno has been the butt of much amusement. She was a very great fool to make so much noise about marrying Mavor when she knew she was already married. Boskingham was very spiteful to name her in court as his wife and next of kin. However, the latest snippet about her is that her real name isn't Juno but — '

'Dowsabel,' Annabel broke in as the name came to her from nowhere.

Richard was taken aback. 'You already know?'

'Er, yes, it would seem I do.' Annabel was taken aback as well, for she had no idea where she had heard the name.

Richard continued. 'Some mischievous soul has seen fit to name his pet poodle Dowsabel, and now it seems set to become the rage. Last week Juno was driving in Hyde Park when she happened upon Lord Craven and his latest *amour*, a nymph of barely fifteen. The nymph had a new puppy in her arms, and Craven took immense delight in calling Dowsabel as Juno drove by. There was great mirth all around, I'm told, but Juno's face was like thunder.'

Annabel laughed, but then looked inquiringly at him. 'Who else have you heard gossip about?'

'Fragrant Freddie and Molly Simmonds, although not as a couple, I hasten to add. As you know, Freddie managed to slip through the law's fingers. No one knew where he had gone, but now it seems he has turned up in Bath, of all places.'

'Sedate, proper Bath?'

Richard chuckled. 'That's the place. I have it on good authority that he managed to find a post at another haberdashery, an honest business this time, although the same could not be said of the goings-on in Freddie's rooms above it. The very latest is that the Viscount of Violets has become abbot of a thriving monastery in Queen Square — how very appropriate — and is likely to remain safe from arrest because he is patronized by several judges, a magistrate, and the Bath master of ceremonies.'

'Really? I did not know there were such places.'

Richard smiled at her innocence. 'Oh, yes, my dear, I fear there are.'

'What of Molly?' she prompted.

'Word has it that she made her way to New York, where she was rescued from another house of ill fame by a dashing privateering sea captain from Boston. An acquaintance of mine has just returned from the latter port, where he heard that she had absconded with some of the good captain's ill-gotten gains. Said captain was in furious pursuit. Nothing changes, it seems.'

Annabel nodded, then set her napkin aside and got up to come around the table. She moved behind Richard's chair and bent to slip her arms around him. 'Now I have some news to tell you,' she whispered.

He leaned his head back and enclosed her fingers with his. 'And what news might that be?'

'I think you will like it.'

'Oh?'

'Yes. You see, Catherine is not the only one with a fancy for oranges,' she whispered.

Tears of joy came to his eyes as he leapt to his feet and gathered her into his arms.

We do hope that you have enjoyed reading this large print book.

Did you know that all of our titles are available for purchase?

We publish a wide range of high quality large print books including:
Romances, Mysteries, Classics
General Fiction
Non Fiction and Westerns

Special interest titles available in large print are:
The Little Oxford Dictionary
Music Book
Song Book
Hymn Book
Service Book

Also available from us courtesy of Oxford University Press:
Young Readers' Dictionary
(large print edition)
Young Readers' Thesaurus
(large print edition)

For further information or a free brochure, please contact us at:
Ulverscroft Large Print Books Ltd.,
The Green, Bradgate Road, Anstey,
Leicester, LE7 7FU, England.
Tel: (00 44) 0116 236 4325
Fax: (00 44) 0116 234 0205

RAKEHELL'S WIDOW

Sandra Wilson

Alabeth had married the notorious rake Robert Manvers, but her beloved husband had died in a duel encouraged by his supposed friend, Sir Piers Castleton. Returning to London to guard her sister Jillian from romantic temptations, she cannot prevent her from falling in love with the heartless Piers Castleton himself. Then, surprisingly, she meets the very mirror image of her late husband in Count Adam Zaleski, the lover that every high-born lady in London vies for. Clearly Alabeth must battle the man she hated to save her sister — and suppress the memory of the man she loved to save herself . . .

THE ABSENT WIFE

Sandra Wilson

A proper young lady must hide her love for a lord who has even more to hide. Miss Roslyn Meredith knew so little about Lord James Atherton. Why had this handsome, charming, aristocrat married the notorious Vanessa, society's most heartless and scheming beauty? Seemingly vanished off the face of the earth, what had happened to her? And now, why did Atherton invite Roslyn and her improvident father to his estate in Foxcombe? One question overshadowed all others. Could Roslyn trust this man who had no right to make her lose her heart to him — and could she trust herself?